$7.25

INTO THE VOID

AMANDA FRAME

To Annie,

Thanks for supporting me!

[signature]

For permissions contact:
AmandaLFrame@gmail.com

ISBN: 978-0-9998311-0-6

PROLOGUE

He observed her for years, hoping what he was doing wouldn't affect her. He knew it was dangerous and he risked drawing her into it. She was just a child. He didn't want the same thing to happen to her. He had to be careful.

~

I pulled my purple comforter over my head and squeezed my eyes shut. *I'm dreaming, this is a dream,* I told myself. I lowered the comforter down to the bridge of my nose, just enough to peek out from under it. The room looked the same as before I had shut my eyes, and I tried to convince myself I was having a nightmare. A dim glow from an unseen source lit my bedroom just enough for me to see the crumbling walls that had been whole and new just moments ago, the soft pink color drained and pale. The rug on the floor and toy chest that sat near my closet were gone, stained and peeling linoleum in their place.

I saw a shadow skitter by. The thing looked like a short human with too-long arms that dragged on the ground, and an elongated head with a jaw that stuck out far beyond its forehead. My breathing was fast and shallow, and sweat beaded on my forehead as terror stronger than anything I had ever felt filled my entire being.

I screamed.

My mom came bursting through the door after an eternity. Right before she flipped the light switch, I looked at her dimly lit face. Her cheeks and eyes were sunken in and her lips too thin, as if her skin were stretched over a skull. Her hair was wiry and patches were missing. The spindly arm of the shadow monster reached its twitchy fingers slowly toward her, gently gripping her arm. My scream tore through the room once more and I slapped my hands over my eyes, trying to block out the nightmare before me.

"Anna!" my mom shouted. I kept screaming and wriggled upright, pressing myself into my headboard, hands still over my eyes. "Anna!" She pulled my hands down and I saw light through my eyelids.

I opened my eyes and stopped screaming, still panting and out of breath. My mom looked normal. The room looked normal. She wrapped me in a hug and held me while I sobbed and shook. I grabbed fistfuls of her blue silky night gown and pressed my head into her chest. When I had calmed down, she gently dislodged my fingers from her gown and pulled away so she could look me in the eyes. Her face was blurred and watery through my tears.

My dad rushed into the room, hair frazzled and eyes wild. “What the hell is happening?!” He looked scared. My dad never looked scared.

“Another night terror,” my mom replied. “It’s never been this bad.” She smoothed my light brown hair back and wiped the tears off my freckled cheeks, her worried eyes scanning my face as though she could determine what was wrong with me if she just looked hard enough.

“This is ridiculous,” my dad said, “she’s twelve years old, for Christ’s sake! We’re taking her to a specialist.” I had gone to my doctor a few months ago when this started and he said I was having “night terrors,” whatever that meant, and that they would probably go away within a few months.

My mom nodded in agreement and looked at the clock. 2:23 am. There was only about three and a half hours before my parents had to wake up for work and I had to get up for school. There was no chance I would be sleeping anymore tonight and no chance I would turn my light off ever again. My breath quickened again as I remembered the shadow-man’s grip on my mom’s arm. I feared shutting my eyes, thinking he might be there when I opened them. I jerked away and squeaked when I felt a light touch on my shoulder, but it was just my mom’s hand, trying to comfort me.

She sighed. “Okay, I’ll make an appointment for some time this week and…”

"No!" my dad interrupted. "She's going today! This is getting out of control."

"Okay, okay, Steven, relax. I'll get someone to cover my shift at the hospital and hopefully that neurologist the pediatrician recommended…what's her name? Hopefully she has an appointment available."

"Dr. Sharver, I think. I'm coming with you."

"Don't you have that big meeting today?" my mom asked.

"It doesn't matter, Margaret, she's my kid too, and I want to know what the fu…heck is going on." My dad never missed a day of work, not even when he had the flu.

"You should go to work, Dad." My voice sounded hoarse and it burned to talk. Probably from the screaming.

"It's fine, sweetie. I can reschedule my meeting." He gave me the best smile he could manage, given his bloodshot, tired eyes. "Try to go back to sleep…"

"No!" I shouted, startling both my parents. "Please don't leave me alone…" I managed to croak feebly, stifling a desperate sob.

"It's okay, Anna, you can sleep with us," my mom said gently. The three of us trudged down the hall to my parents' bedroom, me dragging my blanket behind me. I squeezed between them in their queen-sized bed. My eyes wouldn't stay open, no matter how hard I tried, and eventually exhaustion drowned me in a restless sleep filled with monsters and darkness.

~

At 10:30 am my parents and I sat in the uncomfortable chairs of the waiting room of *Dr. Caroline Sharver, Board Certified Neurologist with Specialty in Sleep Disorders*, according the plaque hanging on the wall. According to my dad, my pediatrician had "called in a few favors" to get me an emergency appointment.

I wriggled in my chair, uncomfortable and nervous. Would she tell me I was crazy? Would they lock me away somewhere and I would never see my parents again? Would the monsters and cracking walls haunt me for the rest of my life? My parents had assured me none of that would happen, but I wasn't convinced.

"Anna Flores?" I jumped at the sound of my name. A pudgy nurse in ill-fitting pink scrubs waved us over. She led us through the door that hopefully contained all the answers to my problems. I stared at the roll of fat hanging over the nurse's pants as she took my blood pressure. I jumped at the sudden tightening of the blood pressure cuff.

"Oh, I'm sorry, sweetie, did that squeeze a little too hard?" she asked, giving me an apologetic look and standing up. She assured us the doctor would be in shortly and left the room.

I grabbed the *Highlights* magazine from the rack next to the door and glanced at the hidden pictures page. Some kid had already circled all the objects. Frowning, I shoved it back into the rack. My mom stared off into space while my dad was zoned in on his phone, probably checking his company emails and silently freaking out about what he was missing at work.

The doctor walked in the room and startled all three of us.

"Good morning, Mr. and Mrs. Flores. And you must be Anna," she said, looking at me. I didn't respond. She gave me a little smile and sat in the black rolling stool near the opposite wall. She rolled over towards us, the wheels squeaking, making me cringe. "I'm Dr. Sharver." She paused, as if waiting for me to say something, which I didn't. "So what's going on with you?" she asked.

"Her pediatrician says she's having night terrors, but we wanted a second opinion. She also gets bad headaches sometimes," my mom answered for me. She launched into my story. I started screaming in the middle of the night about three months ago, telling my parents that things in my room were disappearing and that I knew monsters were going to get me. Eventually I stopped telling them what I was seeing and hearing, but I was still screaming in the middle of the night. It was happening a few times a month and taking a toll on all of us.

What I didn't tell my parents was that this had happened several other times. While I was awake.

"Does this ever happen during the day?" Dr. Sharver asked, as though reading my mind.

"N...no," I stuttered. It was the first thing I had said since she came into the room. I felt like I shouldn't tell her the truth, but I didn't really know why.

"And how do you feel when these episodes happen?" she asked.

"Scared."

"Can you be more specific?"

"Um…it feels, um…real." I spit this out without really thinking about what I was going to say. The doctor raised her eyebrows just the tiniest bit and wrote something down on her pad of paper. Maybe this wasn't something that happened during night terrors? "Or…or maybe not. I don't know," I retracted, getting nervous.

My dad sat up straighter and his forehead creased. My mom's lips parted as though she wanted to say something but couldn't decide what. I shrank back in my chair, afraid that now everyone thought I was crazy. Staring at my feet, I tried not to cry.

"Okay," said Dr. Sharver, addressing my parents, "I'm going to get an MRI and put her on two medications, Diazepam and Risperidone."

"And what are those, exactly?" my dad asked.

"Diazepam can be used for anxiety and sleep disorders and may help with the headaches. Risperidone is…an antipsychotic," she answered.

"An *antipsychotic?*" my dad shouted, "You think my daughter is crazy?" I looked from my dad to the doctor, terrified. *Oh my God, I* am *crazy.* I clenched my fists so tightly my nails dug into my palms.

"No, no. Not at all. Hopefully this is just temporary," she said.

"Hopefully?" my mom asked.

"Yes," replied the doctor. "It's important that we control this until she grows out of it. Was she born premature?"

"Yes," my mom replied, "why?"

"Sometimes night terrors are a sign of an under-developed nervous system, which can happen in children who are born premature. It's usually just a phase that will go away on its own. It isn't as uncommon as you think. We will gradually take her off the medication in about two months and see what happens."

"What if they come back?" my dad asked.

"Then we might need to consider that this might be something else. Her symptoms are quite severe for night terrors. But we can discuss that further when and if the time comes. Here are her prescriptions." She tore two sheets off her little pad of paper and handed them to my mom. "And the MRI facility will call you when they have approval from the insurance company. I'll see you guys back in two months. Call me if there are any further issues." Dr. Sharver smiled and shook my parents' hands.

We walked in silence to the car. My parents spoke in hushed voices on the ride home while I zoned out in the back seat. I stared out the window. At a red light, I saw our old neighbor happily cutting his grass with a push-mower. I felt as though I would never be happy again.

CHAPTER 1
ALBERT

On June second, 2007, Albert John Marshall was dead for seven minutes.

It was the weekend of his eightieth birthday and he was going to see his only daughter, Maureen, for the first time in more than six months. His granddaughter Allison was coming too, and bringing her four-year-old daughter. The only three living family members he had would all be under the same roof for the first time in three years.

He had been looking forward to their visit ever since Maureen told him they were coming. It was the first birthday since his wife died that he was actually excited about.

Mr. Marshall had spent the day cooking, something he hadn't done in a long while. He moved in the slow motion of old age, every stir of the pot taking twice as long, every cup of sugar twice as heavy. But he didn't mind. His family was coming. It was worth it.

The smell of lasagna wafted into the living room.

Bubbling cheese and tomato sauce tickled his nose while he sat in front of the TV, watching the news as he waited for the three generations of women who somehow all looked just like his wife. His heart ached every time he saw them.

The clock said 4:16. Maureen had told him they would be there at 4:00. He was starting to worry that they wouldn't come. Maybe the emotional tension between him and the rest of his family was too much and they had changed their mind. Sure, he had made mistakes, but he had been trying to atone for them for the last several years. It wouldn't make up for the decades he had spent as an absent father, but he would try anyway.

He desperately wanted to see his great-granddaughter. It would likely be the last time he ever would. He was old and only getting older, and Allison lived far away. The apprehension was making his chest feel tight.

It was hot in the house, and Mr. Marshall worried about comfort of his family should they decide to stay. He felt sweat bead on his temples and a lone drop slide down his cheek. His breathing became ragged.

4:31. *They aren't coming*. He gripped his chest and winced. Grabbing the remote, he turned up the volume to drown the pounding of his pulse in his ears and the anxiety in his heart. It was his birthday. They'd be there soon.

He checked his watch again. Tears welled in his eyes and pain shot up his neck and down his arm. *They aren't coming.*

Mr. Marshall stood up, his knobby joints cracking. Something was wrong. He reached for his cane and missed, and felt a sharp, hot pain in his hip as his body hit the floor. He cried out, but it only took a moment for the pain in his chest to overshadow the stabbing burn in his leg.

The front door opened.

"Dad?" a familiar voice called. "Sorry we're late, traffic was…Dad!"

Mr. Marshall felt the vibration of running footsteps under his cheek. He heard the high-pitched wail of a small child. What he would give to be able to turn and see her face.

"Call an ambulance!"

"I am!" came the panicked response from Allison. Her voice was so similar to his late wife's that for a moment he thought it was her. But she was gone, and he would soon be with her.

Mr. Marshall could only listen. He could pick out the unfamiliar noises that were only here because his life was fading. Sirens, squeaking wheels, men's voices, plastic and Velcro.

"Is he breathing?" I could hear the desperation in Maureen's voice.

"Step back, ma'am. If we can get him to the hospital, he will be…"

"He's not breathing!" Allison cried, cutting off the man's reassurance. The screams of the toddler in the background got louder.

Mr. Marshall wasn't breathing, but he was happy. *They came.*

They loaded him into the ambulance and got him to the hospital in time to restart his heart.

But seven minutes is a long a time to be dead.

CHAPTER 2
ANNA

"Anna! Anna!" I heard my name shouted from down the hallway. It was Becca. I finished the text I was typing to my mom about how cross-country practice would probably run late today so I wouldn't be home for dinner.

"Relax," I said to Becca, sticking my phone in my pocket and tucking my hair behind my ears. "What the hell is wrong with you?"

"I forgot to do my pre-calc homework. Can I copy yours?" She looked at me with the most pathetically hopeful look in her eyes.

I rolled my eyes but I smiled. "Ugh, fine."

"Oh my God, I owe you!" She scrambled in her pink backpack for the double-sided worksheet handed out yesterday by Mrs. Miller, our evil pre-calculus teacher who gave you an automatic zero on your assignment if you handed it in so much as five minutes late.

"We're in crisis mode here, Anna! Killer Miller is going to eat me alive if I don't hand this in; I already missed last week's quiz and she won't let me make it up." Her dramatic desperation was just the tiniest bit funny.

Becca sat on the floor, furiously scribbling down answers, using her chemistry textbook as a desk. I stood up, leaning against my locker, on the lookout for anyone who might report her for copying. It was ridiculously obvious; she had my homework on the floor next to her and kept glancing back and forth, her red curls bobbing with the movement.

A teacher was about to walk by so I kicked the locker next to me with my heel causing her to jump. She grabbed all the papers and tucked them into her chemistry book. She peered up at me beneath eyebrows that were so light you could hardly see them. She had a resigned look on her face. "The bell is about to ring anyway. This will have to be good enough. Whatever."

"I hope you changed my answers enough so that it's not obvious." We fell into step beside each other, on our way to Miller's class. My phone vibrated in my pocket, probably just my mom texting me back to be careful driving home, blah blah blah.

"Seriously Anna? I know how to cheat effectively." She gave me an incredulous look. We stepped through the doorway of the classroom just as the bell rang, and split apart to go sit on opposite sides of the room. Mrs. Miller had a habit of separating people she knew were friends so that they "wouldn't become a distraction from the importance of mathematics."

After the slowest, most boring hour of my life, the

bell rang. I sighed with relief, as did about half of the class.

"Oh my God, that was *torturous*," Becca said dramatically as I met up with her in the hallway. I laughed and hitched my backpack higher up onto my shoulders. We only had one other class together today, art, which was next. It was just an elective we needed to get enough credits for the semester; the class was pretty much a joke.

"Hey ladies." It was Aaron Norberg. He was annoying sometimes. He was on my cross country team, so I saw a lot of him. Unfortunately, Becca went all melty and doe-eyed whenever he was around. He was good-looking, I guess. His dark hair always looked intentionally messy, like a Calvin Klien model who just rolled out of bed.

"Hey Aaron," Becca said, batting her overly-mascaraed eyelashes at him.

"Are you coming to practice tonight, Anna? I know you said you might not be able to stay late," Aaron said.

"I can make it." Actually, I hadn't checked that text from my mom yet. "I just think it's ridiculous that coach is making us stay another hour. Like, I know we did pretty horrible at the last meet, but…"

"Okay, enough cross country babble," Becca interrupted, waving her hand in my face. "Are you going to Jess's party on Saturday, Aaron?" The urge to smack that doe-eyed look off her face was strong.

"Um, I don't know yet, probably," Aaron replied

distractedly, looking at his phone. "I'll see you later Anna." He took a right down the hallway and Becca started to follow, seemingly on auto-pilot. I grabbed her elbow and steered her in the opposite direction.

"Art class is this way, dumbass."

"You're such a buzzkill sometimes, you know?" She allowed me to drag her away, pouting. She sulked in silence all the way to class.

The whiteboard in the art room said "free paint" in big letters. Mr. Hornby sat leaning back in his chair, reading some trashy magazine, the epitome of "I don't give a shit". I smiled. "Free paint" basically meant *do whatever the hell you want, because I know this class is a joke and none of you give a crap anyway.*

"Free paint, hell yeah!" Becca loved art.

We grabbed some random colors from the huge, wooden, paint-stained table in the center of the room and set up two easels next to each other. I squirted a glob of black paint onto a pallet rather unenthusiastically.

"Why do you want to go to Jess's party anyway?" I asked Becca. "She's barely your friend, and kind of a bitch." I streaked some black paint across my canvas, looking at Becca.

"You're kind of a bitch sometimes, too," she responded cheerfully, giving me an evil grin.

"Okay, yeah, but she's like, perma-bitch."

"Ha! I like that," Becca laughed. "I want to go because everyone's going to be there, obviously. One day I hope to reach a social status slightly above drama club loser." She tilted her head to the side to carefully examine what I thought was the start of a painting of a bowl of fruit. Meanwhile, I was still throwing globs of black at my canvas and looking at Becca.

"We're seniors. I'm pretty sure we aren't gonna have enough time to move very far up the popularity chain. Why do you even care?" I asked, setting my brush down on my pallet as I remembered to check the text from my mom. *Ok, sweetie, drive safe.* I smiled. My mom was the best sometimes.

Becca still hadn't responded. Another text followed a second later. *You forgot to take Mr. Marshall's trash out again.* I rolled my eyes and regretted agreeing to do that for him every week. It wasn't my fault he was like thousand years old. I snapped myself back to our conversation. "Becca, why…"

"What *is* that?" Becca interrupted.

"What's what?" I looked up from my phone and followed her gaze to my canvas. It was a black shape, resembling a short man with arms that were way too long and hung past his feet. Its head seemed to be in profile, long and pointed with a line coming down at an angle like a jaw hanging open.

I yelped and pushed the easel away, jumping up from my chair and tripping over Becca's backpack to land flat on my ass. My head hit the wooden table behind us.

"Oh God, are you okay?" Becca whisper-yelled. She rushed to my side and squatted down next to me.

"I…I think so." I was panting and it felt like my

heart was going to rip out of my chest. I felt so stupid.

"What the hell happened?" Becca asked, touching my shoulder gently. It made me jump. My embarrassed glance scanned the room.

"I…uh…" The entire class was on their feet, staring at me. Including Mr. Hornby, who didn't get up for anything less than a fire drill. I felt heat rush to my face. My hands were sticky. I looked down and saw black paint dripping down my fingers. My eyes went wide and all I could think about was getting those slimy tendrils off of me. I wiped my hands on my shirt, forgetting that the whole class was staring at me.

"Anna, stop. I'll get you some paper towels." Becca grabbed my wrists and held on until I stopped struggling. She could be freakishly strong. I looked up at her and studied her face, imagining what it might look like if her cheeks and eyes sank into her skull.

What the hell is wrong with me? I shook my head to clear the confusion. Becca was standing over me and holding our backpacks with one arm. She grabbed my elbow with the other and pulled me to my feet. She led me out the door without saying a word to Mr. Hornby.

Becca led me down the hallway and into the girls' bathroom. I stood in silence next to the sink, staring at my hands.

"For God's sake, wash your hands!" Becca said as she crouched down to check under the doors of the stalls. The bathroom was empty except for us. She stood upright and looked at me with her mouth parted slightly and eyebrows pinched together. "Uh, hello? Clean yourself up!" She gave me a little shove towards the sink.

I watched blackness swirl down the drain, carried away by the icy water. There was a glob of paint by my ear. I tried to get it out with a wet paper towel but only managed to streak it through my hair. Grimacing, I pulled my hair back into a ponytail, hiding the mess as best as I could.

My ruined t-shirt went into the trash and Becca handed me her hoodie to put on over my tank top. I caught her staring at me in the mirror. "What?" I asked.

"What do you mean, what? What the hell was that? You just freaked the hell out for no reason." Her face softened. "Are you okay? Was that like a…panic attack or something?"

I didn't really know how to explain. I was embarrassed enough as it was. "Um…the painting…just kind of reminded me of something. Something that happened to me when I was a kid."

"Okay. So why did you paint it?"

"I wasn't paying attention, I thought I was just...I wasn't trying to paint anything specific, it just kind of…came out."

"Like subconsciously or something?"

"I guess."

"It's like, what's it called? A Freud Slip?"

"I think you mean Freudian Slip. And I don't know if that applies in this situation. I don't really wanna talk about it."

Becca put up her hands in a defensive gesture. "Okay, okay. I wasn't trying to…get into your business or whatever. But I am your best friend, y'know. If you want to talk about it, I'd hope it would be to me. And you've never told me much about your life before I moved here."

"I said I don't really want to talk about it right now," I retorted. Becca looked hurt. I leaned against the wall exhaustedly and sighed. "Sorry, Bec. I'm just frazzled right now. We can talk about it some other time?"

"Okay," she said with a tight smile, "I'm always here for you, you know."

"I know." I smiled back, but it was forced. I picked my backpack up off the tile and shrugged it on. "I think I'm just going to go home, I'll stop at the nurse and tell her I have a headache or something."

"What about cross country? You told Aaron you'd be there."

"Whatever. Our team sucks anyway. Missing one practice won't kill me. I'll just run a few miles when I get home or something." Becca gave me a sceptical look and turned to the mirror to run her fingers through her fiery red curls.

"See you tomorrow, Becca. Don't forget to do the pre-calc homework."

"Okay, Mom," she replied with a roll of her eyes and a smile, then more seriously, "Call me later, okay? I just want to make sure you're all right."

"I'll be okay, I promise," I said with the best fake

smile I could muster. "See ya." I rushed out of the bathroom before she could ask me anything else. I heard the door slam shut behind me and cringed at the echo down the empty hallway. The silence was filled with the clomping of my boots as I trudged past the nurse's office and toward the front door of the school. Looking around to make sure no one saw me, I darted through the double doors and closed them quietly behind me.

~

I just wanted to be somewhere else. As I walked through the parking lot, looking for my car, I debated where to go. Home was an option. My dad would probably be at work until at least 7 pm. He was spending less and less time at home and more time at the office. I knew it bothered my mom, but he was on his way toward a big promotion, which meant more money, and a higher chance they could afford to send me to somewhere better than the local community college. My mom was working second shift at the hospital, so she wouldn't be home till about 11 pm. Even though I would get about—I looked at my phone, it wasn't even 10:30—eight hours to myself if I went home, I had a strong desire not to be there.

I threw my backpack in the backseat and climbed into my car. The steering wheel was warm and soothing against my forehead. The mall, I decided. I pulled down the visor and looked at myself in the mirror. Black paint flaked off my hair. "Whatever," I said out loud, too exhausted and confused to give a crap.

I turned the key in the ignition, and my car made a "rrrr rrrr" sound a few times before starting. It had been doing this lately, and knowing nothing about cars, I was convinced it was going to blow up any day now.

I pulled out of the parking lot and headed toward the mall. It felt like I was hitting every red light. I drummed my fingers on the steering wheel impatiently while I scanned the radio for something good. Crappy song, crappy song, weather, crappy song, traffic report. Traffic report at 10:30 in the morning? Didn't those just come on during rush hour? I listened.

"Route 408 westbound is moving along nicely, eastbound doesn't look too bad either," said a woman's voice on the radio. "Interstate 4 north between exits 84 and 87 is stop and go due to two left lane closures caused by a disabled vehicle. Southbound is also…" The announcer's voice cut off abruptly as I slapped the power button. Damn it. I-4 north led straight to the mall. This trip was meant to kill time anyway; so what if it took me twice as long to get there? I flicked on my turn signal and got on the on-ramp.

I zoned out and continued driving the route I had taken so many times, usually with Becca, to sit at the food court and eat ice cream while talking about the latest boy drama. Boy drama. Why the hell did Becca have to like Aaron? He could be such a jerk and seemed to have no interest in her whatsoever. He did talk to me a lot, though. I tried to convince myself it was because we were on the cross country team together and not because he had a crush on me.

I rolled my eyes at my own thoughts and passed exit 34 on the highway, just before the slight hill. As I topped the hill, the cars ahead of me were slowing down abruptly, tires screeching a couple lanes to my right.

"Oh shit!" The smell of burning rubber hit my nose as I slammed on my breaks. My car skidded forward, stopping mere inches from the one in front of me. My white-knuckled grip loosened from the steering wheel. My head fell back against the headrest and I let out a sigh of relief. My parents would have killed me if I rear-ended someone. The traffic report had warned me, I should have been paying more…*slam!*

My head whipped forward and slammed down onto the steering wheel as my front bumper rammed into the car in front of me. Black spots danced in front of my eyes. I blinked a few times and tried to figure out what had happened. Oh God, someone rear-ended *me.* I tried to turn around to see the car that hit me but my neck ached. I took my seatbelt off and turned my body around just in time to see another car coming over the hill, barreling toward the one that had just hit me. My eyes went wide and my brain froze. *Oh no.*

In slow motion, the second car slammed into the one behind me. I flew forward, head and shoulder crashing against the windshield before I realized what was happening. I was dimly aware that I had taken off my seatbelt to look behind me. Warm liquid ran down my face and I tasted metal. Slowly pushing myself off the dashboard, I lowered down into the driver's seat. Dizziness and a throbbing headache almost blocked out the sharp pain in my side and shoulder. I groaned.

Banging on my window cut through the ringing in my ears. Muffled voices were outside. I held my head in my hands and tried to block it all out.

"Hey! Are you okay?" There was knocking on my window again. I cautiously raised my head out of my hands. My palms came away bloody. Someone was trying to open the driver's side door. A balding man with a concerned look on his face was looking at me through the window as I stared back, trying to process what he was doing.

"Are you all right?" He pulled on the door again but it wouldn't budge. "Roll down your window!"

I groaned and cranked the window open slowly. The glass was spiderwebbed with tiny cracks. It only opened about half way before I heard the squeal of glass on metal. "That's as far as it goes," I mumbled, trying to keep the slur out of my voice.

"Okay, just hang on a minute," he said, as if I could go anywhere. He motioned to another guy standing nearby. At least five cars had been in the accident, maybe six. Traffic was completely stopped. Horns blared and people were shouting. I saw the blinking of blue and red lights reflecting off of nearby cars. Police had shown up. *That was fast.* Maybe I had lost track of time.

I heard rattling and turned back to the driver's side

window. Two men were now pulling at my door. It finally opened with a screech and a loud pop. The balding guy fell over and the other stumbled backward. My brain was getting hazy…what was happening? The balding man got to his feet and came over to me. "Do you have kelp?"

"What?" I asked, confused.

"Do you need help?" he repeated. "Are you hurt?"

"Um…I don't know." My voice sounded fuzzy and distant. I looked down at my bloody palms and back up at him. People were milling about everywhere, someone was helping a man who was limping, and there was a guy sitting on the side of the road with a balled-up t-shirt pressed against his head.

"Well, uh, your head is bleeding. Do you think you can get out of the car?"

"Um, okay." I gingerly turned toward the door and grabbed the frame with my right arm. A white hot pain shot up into my shoulder and I cried out. Sparks floated in my vision and everything started going gray…

"Stay with me, girl!" the man shouted at me, startling me back to reality. He helped me gently out of the car. As soon as I stood up, a wave of nausea washed over me and I vomited onto the pavement. I stumbled forward but he caught me by the sleeve of Becca's sweatshirt. *Why am I wearing Becca's sweatshirt? I should give it back to her.* I tried to take off the sweatshirt but my right arm didn't seem to want to cooperate.

"How about you sit down with me over here." He

took my by the left elbow and lead me towards the shoulder of the road.

"I should really get home," I said slowly, "I think…my keys…my keys are in my backpack." I began walking back toward my car but it wasn't where I had left it. In its place was a smashed up pile of metal. *Where's my car?* My knees buckled and I decided that lying down might help me remember where I parked…

CHAPTER 3
ANNA

When my head finally cleared, I was inside a white room that smelled of bleach and something metallic. My eyelids felt like sandpaper, and my head throbbed like it was trapped in a vice. I groaned and sat up slowly. The cloth gown I was wearing confirmed I was in a hospital. The thin white sheet and blanket didn't keep the cold from seeping into my aching body. I could feel that I was wearing nothing under the gown except my underwear and felt my cheeks get hot with embarrassment.

Machines beeped around me and an IV tube snaked from my arm. I grimaced at the thought of the needle that I vaguely remembered piercing my flesh. My mom sat in a chair to the right of my bed. She was asleep, head hanging forward with a magazine neglected on her lap. The bed squeaked as I propped myself up a little higher. My mom's head snapped up, eyes wide and bloodshot. I was confused for a moment, then I remembered.

Car accident. I had hit my head… a few times. My

shoulder… as soon as I remembered my shoulder slamming against my windshield I noticed the pain in my right arm. It was in a sling. I reached up to touch my head and stopped halfway there at the sound of my mom's voice.

"Anna! Oh my God, sweetie, how do you feel? You've been out of it for a while. Do you remember talking to me? Do you know where you are? Do you know what happened? Are you okay?"

The questions hurt my brain. I took a deep breath and felt a sharp pain on my right side. I squeezed my eyes shut and held my breath to stop from crying out.

"Um, yeah." My mom stared at me with concern written all over her face, waiting for me to continue. "I was in a car accident."

"Oh baby, you remember!" She jumped up and pulled me into a hug, which made me hurt all over. My mom saw the pain in my squinted eyes and let me go quickly. "Sorry," she said, "I'm just so relieved you're all right!"

"I don't feel all right," I grumbled. "What happened?"

"You have a concussion, whiplash, two broken ribs on your right side, and you have a small fracture in your humerus…that's your arm." The fuzzy memory of an x-ray machine swam into my brain. I knew what a humerus was, but I didn't say anything. Tucking my hair behind my ears, I felt that it was matted down with blood. I looked at my fingers. The sticky, half-dried blood reminded me weirdly of raspberry jam, the kind my grandma would make every year. I sat staring at my hand, thinking about how I never realized raspberries were the color of drying blood.

"Anna?" My mom's head was cocked to the side, eyes wide with concern, trying to catch my gaze. I looked up.

"Where's Dad?" I asked, looking around slowly, very aware of how stiff my neck was.

"He's on his way," she answered, looking exhausted. Her brown hair was a tangled mess. It probably looked almost as bad as mine did, minus the dried blood.

A middle-aged man in pale green scrubs and a white lab coat walked into the room. A lanyard around his neck held an ID badge that labeled him as Dr. Joesph Cavanaugh.

"Hello Miss Flores, I'm Dr. Cavanaugh." As I had noticed. And "Miss Flores"? Who says that? I was seventeen.

"Uh, hi," I said uncomfortably. I was aware again I was wearing next to nothing under the hospital gown. My clothes were in a clear plastic bag under my mom's chair. I pulled the blanket up to my chest with my good arm.

"So, we've decided to keep you overnight for observation. Your concussion is pretty serious, but luckily your CT scan shows no bleeding in your brain." My eyes went wide, my sandpaper lids scraping over them. Bleeding in my brain? He said it so casually. Like a waiter telling me the specials on the menu. "We'll repeat the scan tomorrow morning to double-check, and then we can release you."

"Okay," I said automatically. My head felt foggy and I morbidly imagined it was because my skull was filling with blood and pushing on my brain. "What time is it?" I asked weakly.

The doctor checked his watch. "4:30. I'll be back in a little later to check on you." He left.

So, if I remembered correctly, I'd left school around, ten? Eleven? Something like that. So it had been several hours since the accident. Becca should be out of school by now. Did she know what happened? I told her I would text to let her know I was okay after my mini panic attack, or whatever it had been, at school. Did my mom know about that? Was she wondering why I had been driving away from school when I was supposed to be in class? I decided not to bring it up unless she did.

Well, she did. "Why weren't you at school?" my mom asked. She tried to hide her anger underneath a soothing voice, but I could tell she was mad. She was doing that thing where she pressed her lips together.

"I was having a bad day, I felt like I needed to get away for a while. I was planning to go back to make fourth period." That was a lie. I hadn't planned on going back, but she couldn't prove otherwise.

"All right, I guess it's water under the bridge at this point. We're just happy you're alive." We? Where was Dad?

"Can I check my phone? I promised Bec I would text

her when I…was on my way back for fourth period." My mom rummaged through the plastic bag under her seat. I could see the collar of Becca's sweatshirt was bloody. She pulled my phone out of the pocket of my jeans and handed it to me.

I had three texts from Becca. 12:02, *Whats up? I hope u r feeling better. Text me.* 1:36, *Text me, I want to know ur ok.* 3:07, *What the hell Anna? u never take this long to get back to me! call me!*

I had three missed calls. Two from Becca, one from Aaron. Probably wondering why I missed practice. Just as I was about to dial Becca's number before she had a stroke, my phone rang in my hand, the ringtone startling me. I jumped, so did my mom. It was Becca. I waited a second to answer, trying to think of what to say to her.

"Hello?"

"Anna! What the hell? I called you like six times!"

"Only twice."

"Whatever, twice, then. I texted you a bunch of times, too! Why didn't you get back to me? First you were all bitchy when you left and now, what? You aren't talking to me or something?"

"No, no, that's not it. I…I was in a car accident. I'm at the hospital. Uh, Greenlake, I think." My mom nodded, her chin resting on her hands, elbows propped on my bed.

"Oh my God! Are you okay?" I could hear the worry in her voice. She gets this shrill tone whenever she's worried.

"I guess, sort of."

"Okay, I'm coming." She hung up without saying goodbye. I rolled my eyes. I hated being the center of attention. And now I was going to have to go back to school with a sling and probably a messed-up face. Oh, crap, I hadn't considered what my face might look like.

"Can I get up?" I asked. "I have to pee." I didn't really have to pee that bad. I just wanted to look in the mirror. My mom helped me to my feet. I was shaky. Luckily there was a bathroom attached to my room so I didn't have to walk out in just a hospital gown with the anti-slip socks you see old people wearing. My mom escorted me to the bathroom by my left elbow.

"Do you need me to help you?"

"Mom! I think I can pee by myself, thanks."

She threw up her arms defensively and sat back in her chair.

I opened the bathroom door. I was dizzy and kind of afraid of falling over, but I wasn't going to let my mom watch me pee. The bathroom had those rails for handicapped people, so I used them to help me shuffle over to the mirror. The bathroom was dimly lit but I could make out my face well enough to groan aloud. The bridge of my nose and under my eyes was bruised. From slamming my head on the steering wheel, maybe? My hair was crusted with dried blood and there was a bandage on the right side of my forehead. I lifted it carefully and leaned in toward the mirror. I had a gash about two inches long that looked like a backslash extending into my hairline. I could make out ten stitches.

Damn it. That was going to be a nasty scar. Very Harry Potter-esque. How would I look with bangs?

"Are you okay in there?" my mom called.

"Fine!" I pressed the bandage back on delicately, wincing. The handicapped bars allowed me to maneuver over to the toilet. I did my business and hobbled out of the bathroom. Just as I was coming out, my dad barged in.

"What happened? Oh my God, you look awful!" Gee, thanks.

"Steven! That's not what she needs to hear right now!"

He wrapped me in a painful hug. I tried not to cry out. He helped me back to bed and sat down on the edge. He was wearing a shirt and tie; he must have just left work. Becca came storming in a moment later. She had obviously been nearby when she called me.

"Oh Anna! You look like crap!" She threw her pink backpack on the floor with a thud and rushed over to the bed, leaving me to endure another painful hug.

"Okay, everyone stop hugging me. Broken ribs, remember?" She gave me an apologetic look and opened her mouth to say something, but my mom cut in before she had a chance.

"Rebecca, how did you get in here?"

"Oh, I uh, said I was her sister."

"Wow, security is pretty lax around here," I said. Becca and I looked nothing alike. My mom gave her an incredulous look.

Exhaustedly, I told the three of them about the accident, or at least my recollection of it. Almost rear-ending someone after traffic came to a halt suddenly, then someone rear-ending *me*. Then getting hit again, I think because someone crashed into the car that had hit me. Getting helped out of my car by two guys who had to practically rip my driver's side door off…shit, my car!

"My car! How is it?" I could most definitely *not* afford another car. Every penny from my summer job last year went into buying it.

My mom gave me a sympathetic look. "I didn't see it myself, but the doctor told me that the paramedics said it was completely totaled." I groaned and hung my head forward, causing a twinge in my neck. Totaled. The exact word I had been dreading.

The paramedics. I vaguely remember being taken away in an ambulance. "Was anyone badly hurt?" My chest felt tight. I knew the accident wasn't my fault, but I would feel awful if someone had been badly injured, or *died*.

"A few other people are in the hospital, but I think everyone is stable," my dad answered.

"How do you know?" I asked skeptically, afraid he was just trying to put my mind at ease.

"It's on the news already," he answered. "I heard it on the radio on the way over here." Fantastic.

"Yeah, me too," Becca said, tears in her eyes. "They made it sound really bad. Like *really* bad. Seven cars were involved, multiple people in the hospital. No one was killed." She hiccupped a bit on the word "killed," trying to hold back her tears.

"Oh, Bec, don't cry. I'm okay." I tried to sound convincing. I *was* okay…ish.

The four of us sat in an awkward silence. "Rebecca, you should probably go home; your parents will worry." That was my mom's not-so-subtle way of telling her to leave. Becca wrung her hands and gave me one last concerned look.

"All right," she said, "call me later, 'kay?"

"I will," I assured her. She squeezed my hand and walked out, grabbing her backpack off the floor, and gave my parents a tiny wave.

I stayed overnight in the hospital. My mom slept in the chair next to my bed even though I told her she could go home. My dad went back to work. I didn't fall asleep till the early morning. My head hurt and I couldn't find a comfortable position because of my arm. Breathing was painful due to the broken ribs. Eventually, I fell into a restless, uncomfortable sleep.

In the morning, I got another CT scan of my brain and the doctor said I had a concussion, but there still wasn't any sign of bleeding so I was free to go home. He said to follow up with my primary care doctor in a week to get new x-rays of all my broken parts.

Yesterday had felt so surreal. Too many weird things happening in the same day. I guess "weird" wasn't the right word for a panic attack, concussion, and broken bones.

I flopped down on the couch, forgetting about my injuries for a moment, and felt a burning pain radiate through my chest and up my shoulder. I sucked air through my teeth and squeezed my eyes shut.

For a moment, I had the strange sensation that there was no longer a couch underneath me, like I was sitting on air. The room around me was hazy when I opened my eyes, textures and colors faded and details missing.

"What…?" I whispered, but it faded before I was sure I had actually seen it at all. I shook my head, deciding to take a nap and sleep off the odd feeling. Pain can cause strange things.

CHAPTER 4
ANNA

He hadn't seen her in a few weeks. He was worried. He could feel that something had happened. Just hopefully not what he had been fearing for the last six years. Please, not yet. Not ever.

~

I didn't go back to school until the following Monday. I was still in a sling and my black eyes were fading to a greenish-yellow. Of course, the news about me being in the accident on 1-4 had spread through the school like wildfire. I hadn't ever been high on the social radar, but now the whole school knew I had been in "the accident." I could hear whispers about me in the hallways and the cafeteria. Rumors that I'd caused the accident, or that I almost died, or even that I *killed* someone, floated around the school. I ignored it all the best I could.

I was more concerned that I still had a headache and

occasionally my vision would…dull. I couldn't think of a better word for it. Like the world around me would lose its vibrancy and detail. It was the same thing that had happened to me the morning I got home from the hospital. I wasn't sure why I was afraid to tell anyone. I mean, I should tell the doctor, right?

My worry was distracting, and I wasn't looking where I was going. Someone slammed into my shoulder. Pain shot down my arm and I clenched my teeth to keep from crying out. I stumbled and dropped by backpack.

"Crap, my bad!" A guy bent down to help me pick up my stuff.

"It's fine," I mumbled, standing awkwardly while he gathered my stuff off the floor. It was Brian Wilkes, Becca's cousin, a guy who would have never talked to me in any other situation. In fact, if I hadn't been so pathetic looking, with my black eyes and broken arm, he probably wouldn't even have stopped to offer "my bad". Who says that anymore, anyway?

Brian was on the football team, stereotypical jock, and was supposedly going to University of Central Florida on a scholarship to be a linebacker or something. I avoided eye contact and my cheeks flushed as he handed me my backpack. "Um, thanks," I said sheepishly.

"Yeah, sure. Uh, sorry again. About the accident, too."

Trying to ignore the sharp pain that still radiated from shoulder to elbow, I decided to try to hide my embarrassment by making confident eye contact. I regretted it immediately. Brian's face withered before my eyes and the other students faded from existence. The floor beneath Brian's feet peeled and browned, the lockers rusted and doors fell off hinges.

I froze, unable to tear my eyes away from Brian's emaciated body, his face pockmarked and blue eyes cloudy and red-rimmed. My breathing quickened and I stared at Brian with wild eyes. As suddenly as it had come, the world returned to focus.

It was gone. The hallway looked normal. Dented, blue metal lockers lined the hall and the floor was white tile, speckled with black flecks. A few students jogged past, trying to beat the bell to class. I stared at Brian, trying to calm my breathing. *It wasn't real. I imagined it. My head hurts and it's messing with me.*

Brian started to shuffle his feet uncomfortably. "Well, see ya," he said awkwardly, and headed down the hall to class. Some of his buddies fell into step beside him. Brian shrugged and glanced over his shoulder at me, then turned back quickly when he saw me still staring at him.

I walked quickly to class, Economics, slipping in right after the late bell. Normally, Mrs. Langley would scold anyone who was late, but she let me slide, my pathetic face coming in handy. I dropped my backpack on the floor next to the last empty desk in the room. It landed with a thud. I sank into the seat of the desk, bowing my head and trying not to make eye contact with anyone, since half the class was staring at me. *It wasn't real. I imagined it. Wasn't real.*

I heard nothing Mrs. Langley said the entire class, took no notes, didn't even open my textbook. I just stared at my hands in my lap and tried to forget the image of Brian's skeletal doppelganger. *Okay. I had a concussion. That can probably make me hallucinate or something.* Convincing myself wasn't easy, but eventually I was partially consoled by my self-diagnosis.

The rest of the day dragged. I walked through the halls methodically, in zombie mode. I was startled when Becca fell into stride with me.

"Ready to go?" she asked. I had hardly registered that school was over. Becca had agreed to drive me to and from school until I got another car. I had told her I could just take the bus, but she said that was lame and insisted on driving me. She only lived a few streets away, so it wasn't inconvenient for her.

I pulled a candy wrapper out from under my butt and threw it on the floor of the car, hoping I hadn't gotten chocolate on my pants.

"Uh, yeah, sorry about all the shit in here, I've been meaning to clean it," Becca said sheepishly. I didn't say anything. "Brian asked me to ask if you were okay. He said he bumped into you today?" she said as she pulled out of the parking lot.

"Oh, yeah, I'm fine. I little achy, I guess. I thought you didn't talk to him much."

"I don't, but he's a nice guy and seemed genuinely concerned, and I think probably felt awkward talking to you."

"Oh. Yeah, I guess." Everyone was being weird around me. Apparently even guys I never talked to. I tried to keep thoughts of Brian away, not wanting to picture what had happened in the hallway. *It wasn't real.*

I stared at my feet for the rest of the ride and was startled when Becca pulled into my driveway. My ribs burned when I pushed open the car door.

"See you tomorrow," Becca said in a concerned tone.

"See ya," I called back, already halfway to my front door. I dropped my backpack on the ground and fished out my keys. The door creaked when it opened.

"Hello?" I called as I shut the door behind me. Neither one of my parents were home, but I hadn't expected them to be. I went straight to the fridge and grabbed a soda. I always loved the sound of a soda can opening. The snap of the tab and the whoosh as the air escapes. I walked into the living room with my soda and flopped on the couch, its soft cushions relieving some of my tension. The TV couldn't hold my attention like I was hoping it would. I just wanted to drown in some crappy sitcom reruns, but I couldn't seem to shake the bizarre day I'd had.

Frustrated, I shut off the TV and delved into a magazine, the first one within reach. Eventually I fell asleep, having dreams about walking through a desert filled with my classmates, all of them looking like skin stretched over bones. They begged me to help them, so they wouldn't end up like this. But I didn't know how, so

I walked among them while they screamed in anguish.

I was startled awake by the front door opening and rubbed my eyes with the heels of my hands, trying to erase the nightmare. My phone said the time was 6:34. It was probably my dad. Mom was working second shift again, so she wouldn't be home till after 11pm.

"Anna? You home?" my dad called. The front door clicked shut and I cleared my throat before answering,

"Yeah, in the living room."

"I brought home some pizza. Come eat." It smelled delicious. *Please be pepperoni and onion.*

I grabbed another soda from the fridge and savored the two seconds of *snap, whoosh*. My dad pulled out a few paper plates and we sat down at the table together. He opened the box. Sausage. Meh.

Conversation was awkward. I didn't get much alone time with my dad; he was always working. He was a pretty popular attorney. His law firm had a few billboards plastering the highway. He asked me questions about my day. I gave one word answers and picked at the sausage on my pizza.

My dad's phone buzzed in his pocket and I could tell he was just itching to check it. "It's fine, Dad. I know work is important." He gave me a grateful smile and checked his phone. His smile faded as he squinted at the phone, responding to an email or text with deft fingers. I just watched, waiting for him to finish.

My head was starting to throb, maybe from the bright light directly overhead. I squinted my eyes and tried to blink the pain away. When I opened them, the room around me had dulled, like I was looking at a faded photograph. I glanced over at my dad and his mouth was still moving but no sound came out. He was ghostly and transparent, like an astral form that had left its body somewhere else.

It scared the shit out of me.

The world came back into focus and I sat frozen, mouth agape.

"Anna? Are you all right?" My dad looked concerned.

"Uh, yeah. It's just…" I debated telling him what had happened but decided against it, "It's just a headache." I released the table from my death grip and stood up. "I'm just going to lie down."

"Okay, just remember you have your follow-up appointment tomorrow at 3:30. Your mom will be here when you get home from school to take you."

I gave a noncommittal grunt and went to my room. I shut the door and sat on my bed, brushing some dirty clothes onto the floor. What the hell was happening to me? Was this all related to my concussion? I wanted to find out, to ask someone, but I was so afraid someone would think I was crazy. Not sure why I was afraid of that, I had a head injury, maybe this was normal. Should I tell my doctor tomorrow?

Google might know. I opened my laptop and hit to power button to wake up the screen. I kicked my shoes off and sat with my back against my headboard.

I typed "concussion symptoms" into the Google search bar. I'd probably finish reading and be convinced I had a brain tumor or something. Crap, maybe I *did*.

According to WebMD, "A concussion is a type of traumatic brain injury that is caused by a blow to the head or body, a fall, or another injury that jars or shakes the brain inside the skull. Although there may be cuts or bruises on the head or face, there may be no other visible signs of a brain injury."

Okay…I scanned the page for symptoms. "Not thinking clearly, feeling slowed down, not being able to concentrate…" I mumbled out loud. "Headache, fuzzy or blurred vision, dizziness…" Nothing about hallucinating or any of the other weird things that happened to me today, except the headache.

I slammed the laptop shut, frustrated and too scared to Google hallucinations. What was this? I wanted to tell someone, *needed* to tell someone. I needed to confide in someone, to cry or scream or punch something. *I'm not crazy. I'm* not *crazy.* Then why did it feel like I was?

CHAPTER 5
JOHN

Clozapine. The doctor said side effects include hypotention, nausea, fatigue, ringing in the ears, and a bunch of other stuff I didn't know the meaning of and couldn't remember anyway. My dad was silent in the driver's seat. The only sound was my mother's soft exhale as she blew cigarette smoke out the window. My hands sat limply in my lap, eyes unfocused, wishing I was at home with David and Shannon, probably playing video games and eating junk food. At nineteen and twenty-one, my brother and sister could basically do whatever they wanted. Not me, though. I was…different.

I remembered the first time it happened very clearly. It was four years ago, David's fifteenth birthday. He had gotten Super Mario Bros 2 and had been playing nonstop for an hour already, sliding it into the Nintendo console about five minutes after he ripped open the shiny blue wrapping paper dotted with little yellow balloons.

The game had just come out a few months before and

my brother squealed like a little girl as soon as he saw the box. David didn't even notice the pleased looks on our parents' faces, he was too busy trying to tear open the box with nothing but his fingernails. I ran after him as he darted into the living room, knowing I wouldn't get the chance to play until after he had enough, which would probably be hours later.

As I had sat on the couch next to Shannon, watching David sitting cross-legged on the floor, eyes glued to the TV set, I tapped my foot impatiently. I had asked him when I could have a turn and he didn't even hear me, the jingle of one-up mushrooms much more worthy of listening to. I was just his annoying little twelve-year-old brother and he ignored me most of the time.

The smell of chocolate had wafted from the kitchen, temporarily distracting me from the television. I heard the oven door squeak open and the scrape of glass on metal as Mom pulled out the cake. A sudden yelp from my mom was followed an instant later by a high-pitched clatter as the casserole dish shattered. It had slipped out of her hands hit the corner of the metal breakfast table.

That's when it had happened.

The room flickered. The rich smell of chocolate and the voices of my family faded like a wisp of smoke on a windy day. The floral wallpaper faded and peeled off the walls like sunburned skin. The screen of the TV was cracked and dull. The air felt heavy, pressing on my skin. I could still hear the piercing echo of shattering glass. As it slowly faded, so did the bizarre parallel of my living room. Mario was gradually becoming visible on the television, the fractals on the glass merging back together. I could hear my dad's voice, tinny at first, until the deep timbre of his speech tickled my ears. David faded back into existence, a pale shadow solidifying into a real human being.

Once reality had bled back into my surroundings, I realized every muscle in my body was tensed to the point of pain, fists clenched around the corduroy of the couch, my breathing shallow and rapid. Shannon's green eyes, so blessedly bright and real, had stared at my face, eyebrows slightly furrowed in concern. I didn't recall what happened after that or for the next week, or maybe month. I didn't remember because it didn't matter. But I did remember the next time it happened, and the countless times after that.

I leaned back onto the headrest of the car and blinked back the tears that threatened to slide down my cheeks.

CHAPTER 6
ANNA

I spent the whole car ride to the doctor's office debating on whether to tell him about my hallucinations. Why wouldn't I? It was a symptom, right? It should be addressed. But I had this nagging feeling that I should keep it to myself.

We walked into the office of my primary care doctor, Dr. William McCormick. I sat down in the waiting room while my mom checked in with the receptionist. I tapped my foot against the ugly green carpet and wondered how to ask the doctor about my hallucinations without seeming like a whack-job. *So I was just hoping that you can reassure me that I'm not crazy because I saw a guy turn into a walking skeleton while my school decayed around me.* Yeah, not good.

"Anna Flores?" I looked up at the sound of my name. My mom looked up too. I hadn't even noticed she had sat down next to me. A woman in blue scrubs had called my name from over near the receptionist's desk.

"We are going to start you off with some x-rays," Blue Scrubs said. I got up and my mom started to follow. "Mrs. Flores, do you mind staying out here while we take the x-rays?"

"Of course." My mom sat back down.

They took a bunch of x-rays of my arm and my ribs and then the technician walked me into an exam room. "I'll go get your mom."

"Wait! Can I talk to the doctor alone?" I asked hesitantly.

She chewed on her lip and looked at my chart. "Well, you are almost eighteen so that should be fine. He'll be in soon," she said, stepping out and shutting the door.

I looked around for something to occupy myself with. Fingering through the magazine rack, there was a *Highlights* magazine, the one for kids. It gave me weird déjà vu. I was playing Sudoku on my phone when the doctor came in.

"Hello, Anna," he said jovially. "So it looks like your arm and ribs are healing very nicely. The fractures were pretty minor to begin with, so I think we can go ahead and get rid of your sling. But you still need to take it easy, no P.E. or heavy lifting." He looked at me from under his bushy white eyebrows expectantly, but I wasn't sure what kind of response he was expecting.

"…That's good," I said, wringing my hands. "So are you going to check my concussion, too?"

"Of course," he answered, rolling he stool over to

me. He shined a light in my eyes and had me touch my finger to my nose with my eyes closed a few times.

"Your pupils are dilating fine, no loss of coordination," he said, rolling away slightly, "Any headaches?"

"Yeah, sometimes."

"Those should be gone by now, but it's not too unusual for them to stick around a while," he said, scribbling something in a notebook. "Looks like you are doing well."

"So that's it?" I asked, "You don't like… do a scan or something?"

"No, that's it, you're doing great," he said with a smile.

"Yeah, but you said having headaches for this long isn't normal, so maybe there's…other stuff. That's not normal, I mean," I said, biting my lip.

"It's not very common to have headaches this long, but it's still normal," he said, trying to be reassuring. "Are you having any other symptoms?"

"Well, it's just that, I mean… are there any other symptoms that maybe aren't common but still normal? Like, um—" I paused, trying to put some words together "—hallucinating, or…or something," I asked, trying to sound just curious, not worried. But it didn't seem like he was buying it.

"Are you hallucinating?" he asked slowly.

"Well, no," I responded quickly, "I mean, things sometimes…" Crap, I needed to get out of this. Asking was a mistake. I felt my insides twist with anxiety. What should I say? "Sometimes, things look…blurry." I cringed inwardly. That sounded so lame. And totally not believable.

"Sometimes bad headaches can cause blurry vision," he said, his bushy eyebrows furrowing. "I can give you some medication for…"

"Nope, that's okay." I stood up quickly, wanting to get the hell out of there. *Oh my God, it's not the concussion. I'm going crazy.* "So, I'm good to go? I'm fine, right?"

"Yes," he said, a bit taken aback. "Do you want me to talk to your mom?"

"No, no. I'll tell her everything you said. Thanks." I lifted my sling over my head, threw it on the exam table, grabbed my purse, and booked it the hell out of there.

I rushed out into the lobby, my mom leaned against the wall, squinting at her watch. "Anna! What took so long? Did you have to wait in line for the x-rays or something?"

"No, I saw the doctor already, he told me everything is fine and healing," I said, trying to seem nonchalant.

"You talked to him without me?" she asked, clearly annoyed.

"They said because I'm almost eighteen, I can talk to him alone."

"You are *almost* eighteen. Almost. You're still a minor." She narrowed her eyes at me.

"Yeah, but everything is fine, so not a big deal

right?"

She sighed, clearly tired. Hopefully too tired to care very much.

"Okay, let's just get out of here," she said. I couldn't agree more.

CHAPTER 7
ANNA

On the way home from the doctor, I decided I was going to have to figure this thing out myself. But how? I thought about talking to Becca. She would believe me, but I couldn't see how she could possibly help. Maybe I needed to stop being such a coward and figure out what these hallucinations were. Or just wait it out. Maybe the few times it happened were just isolated incidents.

A blank page of spiral notebook lay patiently on my desk. I tapped my pen against the side of my face and stared at the empty paper. I wasn't even sure what I wanted to write down. Should I keep a record of these…visions? I guessed that would be a correct term. The tip of my pen rested on the paper and wrote a brief description of each time something had happened. My surroundings turning dull and feeling…empty was weird but not nearly as concerning as Brian wasting away and my school aging a hundred years before my eyes.

An exasperated groan escaped my lips and I hung my

head in my hands. I didn't know how writing it down would help and if one of my parents stumbled across it, they would for sure think I had gone insane. And maybe they'd be right. I should probably just march back into Dr. McCormick's office, tell him I was crazy, and ask him to lock me away with all the other nut cases.

There was one more terrifying possibility.

Maybe it was real.

~

It was Sunday. Sleep had been difficult, plagued by nightmares. Thinking about Brian too much was certainly why. I just couldn't get his image out of my head.

I was still trying to come up with some kind of an idea on what to do, who to tell, if anyone. I was lying in bed, arms at my sides, staring at the ceiling. With a groan, I reached over to my nightstand and grabbed my phone to check the time. 7:04 am. I set it back down with a thud and tried to rub the sleep from my eyes. There was no use trying to go back to sleep.

A run would be soothing. My doctor had told me not to participate in P.E., cross country, or do any kind of contact sport, but a slow jog would probably be fine. My parents were both still asleep.

I rolled out of bed, threw on some running shorts and a tank top. It was April, and April in Florida was already hot. I stepped into the bathroom to brush my teeth and tie my hair back in a messy bun. A definite plus of being an only child was having my own bathroom. Palms resting against the cool porcelain of the sink, I leaned towards my reflection and squinted. It felt like I shouldn't look normal. With all the crazy surrounding me, it should somehow be visible.

It wasn't. I suddenly felt unbearably alone, and a knot of anxiety twisted my stomach. I sat on the edge of the tub and rested my face in my palms. I had to deal with this. Whatever was happening to me either needed to stop, or I needed to understand it. Maybe if I could figure out how to control it, I could figure out how to stop it. But right then, I just needed to run.

I tiptoed down the stairs and left a note on the kitchen table letting my parents know where I was going and slipped out the front door, shutting it quietly behind me. Then I started jogging, slowly at first. I turned right down Elm Street, not really having a destination in mind. I started running faster. Faster. *Faster.*

I sprinted down Elm Street, eating up distance with the soles of my shoes. My breathing was ragged and my ribs and right arm ached but I barely felt it. Desperation filled me and spurred me on.

I needed to get away. From what, I wasn't sure, but I could feel the need like a physical presence, breathing down my neck, raking scaly fingertips down my arms, vibrating through my body. Miles disappeared behind me, my legs pumping, face red, sweat stinging my eyes. The landscape whizzed by; I barely knew where I was. I was fleeing from something. From myself. No matter how fast I ran, I would never get away. It was like trying to run from my shadow. Impossible.

The blind panic faded and my legs began to slow. I stopped, hands on my knees, head hung forward, panting. I could feel beads of sweat rolling down my face like hot tears. After a few minutes of trying to catch my breath, I looked around. I didn't know where I was. I wandered around till I saw a street sign, Redmount Way. Holy crap, I was almost six miles from home. My phone told me it was 8:27. I wasn't sure exactly when I left the house but it was barely more than hour ago.

I began a slow walk back home, trying to clear my mind of all thought. My ribs hurt. My arm hurt. I had a headache and was probably dehydrated. After what felt like forever and a half, I found myself in front of Becca's house. I stopped with my arms by my sides and stared at the front door. I had promised Becca we would hang out this weekend and so far I had done nothing but space out for the last two days.

Sighing, I walked through the spongy grass to the door. The brass door knocker in the shape of a lion's head was tacky. I knocked a few times and waited. I saw the peephole go dark and then "Rebecca!" shouted by Mrs. Marsters. It sounded dull and watery from the other side of the door.

The door opened and Becca stood in front of me, eyebrows raised. She was still in her pajamas. "What are you doing here?" she asked quizzically. Then, "I mean, it's great you're here, it's just early and…unexpected."

Her perplexed frown dissolved into a smile. "Come in, weirdo," she said, taking in my sweaty, disheveled appearance with a single raised eyebrow. I walked past her into her kitchen and helped myself to a bottle of water. I paused before I turned the cap.

"Uh, can I have some water?" It was the first thing I had said.

"Yeah, of course. Clearly you just ran a marathon, or fled a pack of wolves. Are you okay?" I was starting to become all too familiar with the note of concern in her voice. She raked her fingers through her tangled red curls.

"Yeah, I just woke up early so I decided to go for a run. You know, not being able to run for the cross country team and all." I scratched the back of my head self-consciously. I probably looked like…well, like I had fled a pack of wolves, and I was pretty sure I didn't smell so great either. "I figured I would stop by on my way home. I guess I should have showered first," I said, pulling at the hem of my tank top and staring at the floor.

"I'm going to the grocery store, Rebecca. Do you need anything? Connor's coming with me," I heard Mrs. Marsters call from the foyer.

"Uh, no, Mom, I'm good. Or actually, some tortilla chips!" Becca called back. She turned to look at me with concerned eyes, and I felt guilt bubble into my chest. The front door slammed shut and I could feel it resonate through me like an earthquake.

My throat tightened and my eyes started to burn. *No,*

no, don't cry! I leaned back against the cabinets and started to sink down to the floor. The tile was cold under my bare legs. I buried my face in my hands and felt myself giving up, needing to get this huge weight off my chest. I cried, I sobbed. Salty tears pooled in my hands and I could feel Becca wrap me in a tight hug. My forehead rested on her shoulder and I could felt her soft curls brush my cheek. She held me. She didn't ask what was wrong, she didn't try to tell me everything was okay and I didn't need to cry. She just let me break down.

My arms hung limp by my sides, pulled tight against my body by Becca's embrace. Her t-shirt was damp with my tears and sweat, but she didn't let go. She didn't know what was wrong but she knew that right now I just needed her to hold me as I fell apart. It was at that moment that I decided to trust her. "Becca..." I hiccupped between sniffles. And I told her.

Everything.

~

After I was done vomiting the words I was afraid would tarnish me in her eyes, she just looked at me, her mouth slack and eyebrows drawn together. I couldn't quite place the emotion on her face. Confusion? Anger? Disbelief? I scratched my cheek and stared at the tile cooling my legs underneath me, not wanting to have to gauge her reaction. She didn't say anything.

"Okay, I really need you to say something right now,"

I stammered, the anticipation twisting my stomach into knots. *She thinks I'm crazy.*

"Are…are you sure that you weren't dreaming or anything?" Her voice wavered. I still couldn't meet her eyes.

"Yes, I'm positive."

"I don't think you're crazy," Becca said slowly, and the relief that flooded my head nearly drowned me. Her obsession with anything paranormal probably played into her acceptance of my story. She stood and reached for my hands. I numbly accepted her grasp and she led me to the couch. The sweat and tears dampening my clothes seeped into the fabric, but I didn't have the energy to care.

"Could you be seeing things? Like from the concussion? Or what's that thing soldiers get? Like when they come back from war?" She bombarded me with questions, most of which I didn't know the answers to.

"PTSD." The memory of a documentary on the war in Iraq surfaced from the recesses of my brain. "Post Traumatic Stress Disorder."

"Yeah, that."

"I doubt it." My eyes met hers, pleading her to believe me. "Bec, you don't understand. These visions or whatever feel as real as you and me sitting here right now. But it can't be, it can't. But it's like I can reach out and grab it, or step into it." I made a grasping motion with my hand, picturing Brian's gaunt face.

"Maybe you should." She whispered the words like she had trouble getting them out. Her eyes met mine, skepticism creasing them at the corners. Her fingers tapped on her chin. “Okay, I have an idea.”

CHAPTER 8
ANNA

I sat on my bed at home Tuesday morning after taking Mr. Marshall's trash out for him. I hugged my knees to my chest. It would be another half hour before Becca came to pick me up for school.

Her idea had been to make one of these visions or hallucinations or whatever it was happen again so we could verify that it was triggered by my headaches, which was what I was hoping for. I needed to prove to myself that I wasn't a coward and didn't believe that there was any way it was real, because that would make me crazy.

We were still in the Google research phase of how exactly to do this, but I figured since it had involved Brian, being around him would help the process along. On Monday I had discreetly followed him between classes so I could figure out what his schedule was.

The only time Brian was not surrounded by his posse was fifth period, which he had free. He had gone to a fairly secluded part of the library, which I thought was really weird. Brian, going to the library to study by himself instead of hanging out in the cafeteria with his friends? That was what most people did during free periods anyway. No one actually studied. But he hadn't been studying. He had been drawing strange diagrams, which I had realized were football plays. I hoped this was a regular activity for him, because it seemed like the only time he was alone.

I didn't have fifth period free but I planned on skipping class and going to sit a few tables away from him in the library on the off chance that I would get a headache and it would trigger an episode. This wasn't in the plan that Becca and I were concocting, or really any kind of plan at all, but I figured it couldn't hurt to just give it a shot.

The hope that he wouldn't notice me was pathetic. I wished that Becca was coming with me but I hadn't told her what I was doing and she had advised me to not do anything until we had a real plan mapped out. I felt guilty about going against her suggestion but I saw an opportunity so I was going to take it.

During first and second period, concentration eluded me. The notes I had taken didn't make sense, and I hadn't done the homework for either class. I didn't care even though I probably should have, but I just couldn't summon the energy. The bell signaling the end of fourth period made me jump. I took a deep breath and steeled myself to follow Brian to the library. I crept through the halls like a burglar, afraid of being caught. Deep down, I had been hoping that this would fall through.

Slouching over my chemistry textbook, I pretended to read. All the words and diagrams looked like gibberish. Nerves rattled my brain and my heart pounded. I peered at the back of Brian's head through the curtain of my hair. This was stupid. Nothing was going to happen. I sighed and decided to leave.

I pushed my chair back but my foot slipped. I slammed my pinkie toe hard against the leg of the metal table. Hot pain shot up my foot. I sucked air through clenched teeth and looked down to check for injury, but froze halfway bent over.

Something horrible started to happen.

I felt a heaviness in the air, an uncomfortable pressure in my bones. It sent electric tingles across my skin. Fear gripped me, and I held onto the arms of my chair, knuckles turning white and terror beating in my chest. The table in front of Brian was gone, along with the chair he'd been sitting it. It seemed as though he was sitting on nothing, floating in the center of the room. Empty bookshelves surrounded us, and I watched as rust ate gaping holes in the dull metal.

My breath rattled as I tried to push away the panic that was clawing its way up my throat. I focused on what I was seeing, trying to detach myself from the fear like just watching a scary movie, but it looked so real. Real enough that it felt I could step into this vision, or whatever it was, and become a part of it. *Maybe you should.* Becca's voice resonated in my head and gave me courage.

One step. Dust plumed up from the carpet, disturbed by my shoe. Two steps. The floor creaked under my feet. Each step was more difficult than the last, like mud was sucking my feet to the ground. Three steps. Closer.

Brian turned toward me and I froze mid-step, but he looked right through me with confused eyes, which were sunken and surrounded by dark circles. Could he see me? Could he see *this?* My eyes scanned the room and my heart thudded at the possibility.

My hands shook and a horrible dread seeped into my bones. A black, inky hand wrapped around the edge of the bookcase. The courage bled out of my veins. Eagle-like talons protruded from seven fingers that raked deep scratches into the metal. A foot snaked its way around the corner, its claws just as terrifying as the three-inch ones on the thing's hands.

The creature rounded the corner and I stared at its black form in disbelieving terror. My mouth went slack and I clenched my hands so tightly that my fingernails dug into my palms.

The thing was about four feet tall. Its claws scraped the floor, tearing up the dirty carpet as it stalked toward Brian. I stood frozen, not knowing what to do. Its legs were thin at the bottom and became muscular at the top, connecting to its impossibly skinny waist. The knobby knees bent the wrong way like a giant, creeping bird. I wanted to look away, but the terrified curiosity was overwhelming. The creature's shoulders were broad, and an elongated head sat on top of a short neck.

It turned toward me. The huge nostrils set deep within its face flared as it stretched its neck forward, like it could smell me. I took a step backward. Glowing yellow eyes narrowed at me and it cocked its head to the side, as if it were confused by my presence. I tightened my whole body, fully expecting it to jump at me and tear my throat out with its giant talons. But it didn't. It turned its face back toward Brian and dropped on all fours, walking closer and closer to him.

Brian began to look confused, peering around and blinking like he was trying to clear fog from his vision. The creature reached him and put its hand on Brian's, standing on two legs again. Brian rubbed his free hand over the other and it passed through the monster's paw. It was fascinating and terrifying at the same time.

Brian's skin started turning pale and the creature began to change, getting scalier like a black snake. Its body contorted, becoming more human-like and less deformed. Brian was wasting away, flesh and clothes draining color and skin loosening, drooping off his bones like a shirt on a hanger. His hair was becoming wiry and thin. I could see his eyes sinking further into his skull and his lips cracking.

I couldn't take it any longer. I felt a scream bouncing around my lungs, and I tried to hold it back, but a wail escaped my clenched teeth. Brian turned to look back at me, his skin turning to leather on his skull, mummifying.

The creature's head snapped up and it stalked toward

me. I backed up and put my hands out in a feeble attempt to shield myself. *No, no, no!* This wasn't happening. I needed to get away, back to reality. I squeezed my eyes shut focused all my energy on the library. The library. Bookshelves, nasty green carpet, metal tables and buzzing florescent lights.

I scurried backward, arms still outstretched and eyes glued shut, feeling like I pushed through a thick bubble. I fell flat on my back and opened my eyes, heart slamming against my ribcage.

I was in the library, full bookcases towering over me like comforting walls blocking out the nightmare. A huge sob of relief escaped me and I sank my fingers into the dirty carpet, reveling in its scratchy consistency. I looked up and Brian was turned around in his chair, squinting at me with suspicious eyes. He abruptly stood up, knocking his chair over, and rushed out of the library.

A faint shadow skittered after him.

CHAPTER 9
JOHN

I didn't tell my parents about the incident on my brother's birthday. I was too scared. But eventually they noticed something was wrong. How could they not? It happened again. And again. Publicly. I was the only one who could see it. Sometimes there were people there. Dim, ghostly people.

At the park once, a little girl on the jungle gym fell and screeched in pain. After the world fell apart this time, the little girl and her mother remained, their incorporeal forms mimicking their actions in the real world. Even through the hazy shroud that surrounded them, I could see the intense protectiveness and determination on the mother's face as she cradled her child's bleeding head, and the pain and wide-eyed terror in the little girl's eyes.

Sometimes I would go months without these episodes, and sometimes it would happen a few times a week. There was no predicting it, but there had to be a commonality. The fear that overcame me when it happened was paralyzing. And not being able to see what was around me in reality, I had trouble knowing how I should move or behave. Was my mother talking to me? Was someone about to walk right into me? There was too much confusion and emotion for me to fake normalcy.

Two years after the incident on my brother's birthday and I had begun to have a semblance of control over what was happening to me. I would force myself to calm down and remember what the world had looked like a moment ago. I would hold on to that memory so intensely that eventually I could force the world to come partly back into focus. I would see a mirage of the real world overlapping the washed-out, crumbling landscape around me. Sometimes I could even hear some of the people on the other side, their voices warped and metallic, like listening to someone through a soup can on the other side of a string.

I hung on for almost another two years. I was getting used to it. I was better at hiding it. For a while. Until something else happened. Something worse.

My dad and I were at the bank. We were standing behind the velvet rope, waiting for the next available teller to call us over. One of the customers was arguing with a teller. I could make out one side of the conversation. The teller was trying to hand him a stack of bills and some change, but the man was yelling that he had more money than that in his account. She was trying to assure him that he did not. He was becoming increasingly angry; I could see the veins bulging in his neck and his face turning bright red. Finally he lost it and smacked the teller's hand away. The bills floated lazily to the ground and the coins dinged loudly on the metal countertop, reverberating through the otherwise silent room.

My heart skipped as it happened again, but it felt different this time. A chilling breeze hit my face as a comforting warmth heated my back. The once sky-blue carpet faded and tore. The bright aluminum counters in front of the tellers were tarnished and dull. The air was thick, suffocating. All the details disappeared; pens, pamphlets, nameplates, and of course, the people. Except one. The angry customer.

Something was wrong. I could feel my hackles rise.

There was movement out of the corner of my eye and I immediately regretted looking. An impossibly thin, tall, humanoid creature moved towards the man. I could see the shadow of bones through its grey skin. Its prominent ribcage barreled out of a torso that was unnaturally long. Its face was elongated too, like someone had taken a human skull and stretched it like putty. Sharp cheekbones broke through the skin beneath sockets that held no eyes to speak of.

The thing floated above floor smoothly, its toes dragging on the carpet, its skeletal arms stretched forward, twitching slightly as though in anticipation.

It reached the man, who was oblivious to everything going on around him. Long, knobby fingers with too many knuckles reached delicately towards him, and wrapped around his arm. The man twitched and looked down, almost aware for a fraction of a second, before looking up again.

Muscles began to form underneath the thing's skin, its bony form becoming more solid, while at the same time sucking the man dry. He withered and aged as the creature became stronger. Its skin stretched and faint red webbing spread across its surface, like a drop of blood on a napkin.

I was wrong when I believed that the sight before me could get no more horrifying.

It looked at me.

I finally was able to scream.

CHAPTER 10
ANNA

I sat on floor of the library, stunned. What had just happened? I wiped my shaky palms, suddenly slick with sweat, on my jeans. I felt paralyzed, unable to get up. Nausea rushed into my belly and the taste of bile crept into my throat. I knew this had been real—there was no denying it anymore—but it was more terrifying than I had imagined. I didn't realize the deserted world I'd been seeing wasn't actually empty after all.

Becca. I needed to talk to Becca. How much time had gone by? Was the period over yet? My sense of time was completely out of whack. I pulled my phone out of my pocket, trying to slow my ragged breaths. The glow of the screen told me it was 1:32, a mere twelve minutes into fifth period.

I willed my legs to peel me off the floor and saw silver sparks float across my vision as the blood rushed back to my head. Grabbing my backpack, I stumbled through the bookcases and out of the library, numb. I had forgotten about the pain in my foot.

Talking to Becca right now was out of the question. I imagined swinging the door of her history class open with a bang and dragging her into the hallway, screaming that I needed someone to talk to or I was going to lose my freaking mind. That was not an option.

My boots clomped down the hallway, empty but for the occasional forgotten papers fluttering near the lockers. What should I do? Where should I go? I tucked my frazzled hair behind my ears and clenched my fists at my sides, willing myself not to break into a sprint to escape the memories of the library that were burned into my skull.

Hearing footsteps approaching from an intersecting hallway, I ducked into the girls' bathroom that was only a few yards away. The door swung shut with a clack and I cringed, hoping nobody had heard. I stood frozen for a few seconds until I was confident the footsteps had passed me.

I pressed my hands into the cool white cinderblocks. I supposed I could text Becca. It was likely she would respond; she was an excellent under-desk texter. I thumbed a message with clammy fingers. *Need to talk asap, meet u at your car after school.* Waiting for Becca at her car seemed like a reasonable idea, though I still had almost an hour to kill. Missing class was becoming a hobby.

I snuck out of the school like my life depended on not making any noise, vaguely wondering if my grades were going to suffer if I kept skipping school. Probably, but it was a distant concern. I made a beeline for Becca's car, seeing from a distance that the lock on the inside of the front door was popped up. I made a mental note to reprimand her for leaving her car unlocked later, but I was grateful for her absent-mindedness. Exhaustion had crept over me in my short walk from the library to the car. I slid into the front seat and wriggled my way into the back, lying face-up across the backseat. Staring at the ceiling, I tried to push all thoughts from my head, and eventually fell into a fitful sleep, waves of exhaustion overtaking me.

I jolted awake at the sound of the car door slamming. It had gotten crazy hot as the sun had moved the parking spot out of the shade. Becca climbed into the front seat. She turned to look at me, that all-too-familiar expression of concern written on her face. I sat up, my head pounding.

"Talk to me," she said expectantly. I took a few deep breaths, steeling myself for the possibility that she wasn't going to believe me. My mouth felt sticky, words frozen in the back of my throat. She waited patiently.

"I…" My words were cut off by a loud bang on the window. Both Becca and I yelped in surprise and my head whipped toward the sound. Brian's hands were pressed to the glass, the window fogging around his palms. His eyes were wild, staring at me with an intensity that could only be described as madness. His mouth opened and closed like a fish, as though forming words was beyond him. He set his lips in a hard line and peeled his hands from the window, walking quickly through the parking lot. We stared, baffled, Brian's sweaty handprints lingering on the glass.

Well now she has to believe me.

"What the hell was that?" Becca asked, hand clutched to her chest like she was preventing her heart from jumping out. I had a feeling that her confused expression was mirrored on my face.

"I…I don't know."

What if I had done something to him? What if this…alternate reality, or whatever, had affected him? The other times this had happened it was clear only I had seen it. Did I somehow make him aware of it as well? The image of his wild eyes seared my brain. Guilt seeped into my belly.

"Did you follow him to the library?" How does she always know? "I thought we agreed not to do that yet! What happened? He looked…shaken up," Becca said with a distant look in her eyes, clearly disturbed.

"Yeah, I followed him…" I trailed off, unsure how the hell to explain what had happened, if I even wanted to explain.

"Okay, you *have* to tell me. That was freaking weird. That wasn't a coincidence. How did he know where you were?"

I pressed my lips together in confusion. Had he been looking for me? Did he know it was me who had done this to him? How *did* he know where I was?

"I don't know," I said slowly.

"You need to stop saying you don't know and tell me what the hell is going on!"

She was right. I had dragged her into this mess; she deserved answers.

"I did it. It happened."

"Oh my God, really? Again?"

"Yeah. It's not the headaches; I didn't have one. Also I think he may have…" I paused, struggling to find the words. "…noticed something happening." My voice cracked at the end, crazed laughter threatening to choke me. This was ridiculous. All of the things that had happened since my car accident were so absurdly horrifying that it was almost amusing. And weirdly familiar.

"What does that even mean?" Becca asked, almost bursting with her thirst for explanation.

I struggled to find a way to put the experience into words. Brian's skeletal body being sucked dry by some…thing, leeching strength into itself. The haunted look in Brian's eyes when he saw me, right before he bolted from the library.

I took a deep breath. "Okay. So I followed him to the library," I began. She crawled into the backseat with me. "Everything was normal at first. I sat down near him for sec, then decided to leave, stubbed my freaking toe trying to stand up, by the way, like a freaking idiot." She glanced down at my foot, which was starting to bruise.

"Ouch," she said, raising her eyebrows, then

motioned for me to continue.

I tried to gather some words, but trying to explain to Becca what had happened felt like recalling some crazy dream I'd had, where I couldn't quite connect the bits and pieces together in a way that was coherent. After about a half hour of going back and forth, her asking me questions and me fumbling with the answers, she was finally satisfied with my story.

She sat facing me, hugging her knees to her chest as though she was cold, even though the AC wasn't working very well. The blood had drained from her face about ten minutes into our conversation and she was still as pale as a ghost, eyes wide in disbelief or maybe shock. My face started to get hot under her gaze. It seemed like her excitement at something possibly paranormal and fascinating happening in her life had dissolved.

"And this was real? You're *sure* this was real?" Her enthrallment and her concern for me were battling with each other.

"I know it. I *feel* it. It's just as real as you are sitting in front of me." I reached out to touch her to demonstrate her corporality. She tensed as if she was going to pull away, and I let my hand fall to the seat in front of me. It hurt.

"Okay. Okay." Her mouth twisted, as if she was struggling to find something to say. Instead, she crawled back into the driver's seat and pulled the car out of the parking lot. We drove in silence. My stomach was twisting, and I could feel fear radiating off Becca as though I could reach out and grab it.

I knew my best friend was scared of me.

CHAPTER 11
ANNA

He should have intervened sooner. He had gotten his chance and changed his mind at the last minute. Now it was too late. He had made a promise to himself and broken it out of cowardice, and now had to pick up the pieces. But maybe she would help him in return.

~

When I got out of Becca's car and trudged into school the next day, it no longer felt like a place of learning. Maybe it had never been a pleasant place, but it used to feel normal. Now it felt suffocating, like the hallways were closing in on me and the desks were too small.

Focusing on class was incredibly difficult. I was lost inside my head. Did I hurt Brian? I hadn't seen him yet today, even though I kept scanning the halls. As much as I wanted to avoid him, I also wanted to make sure he was all right.

After second period, I saw him standing in front of

his open locker, just staring into it. I almost didn't recognize him. His hair was disheveled and his face was pale. Brian's eyes, usually gleaming with mischief, were glassy and red-rimmed. I had never seen him look this shitty and I almost gasped out loud.

Someone slammed into my back as I stopped in the middle of the hallway, my eyes glued to Brian's profile.

I didn't know if it was possible for someone to lose ten pounds overnight, but it sure looked like he had. People kept slowing down as they walked by him, whispering to their friends and glancing nervously at Brian. Most people were trying to be discreet, but it was obvious that most people noticed his drastic change in appearance.

Everyone slowly filtered into classrooms until just a few stragglers remained behind, Brian and I included. Neither of us had moved. It was like Brian was totally oblivious. He dropped his eyes to the floor and let his locker swing closed. He turned toward me slowly, beginning to head towards class, trudging along distractedly. He finally noticed me and glanced up. When he saw my face, his eyes went wide and he stopped dead in his tracks. My heart raced and I felt like I should say something, but the words were stuck in my throat. I barely heard his hoarse whisper.

"What did you do to me?"

His words hit me like a hammer and I took a step back, clutching my chest and shaking my head. No, no, no. I didn't do this. I wasn't capable of breaking someone like this. Denial filled me from head to toe, and I wanted to scream at him that it wasn't true, it wasn't me. The guilt was overwhelming, but it was diluted by an inexplicable anger.

Before I could gather my thoughts, my skin prickled and electric goosebumps sprung up on my bare arms. Brian's gaze shot up so fast it seemed his neck would snap. I followed his line of sight and a strangled cry escaped me.

A dark form was crouched on the water-stained ceiling tiles. Even though it looked translucent enough to blow away like a cloud any second, I recognized it immediately, and even more terrifyingly, it seemed as though Brian did as well. It was definitely the shadow that had stalked after Brian out of the library yesterday. The thing sat on the ceiling like it had its own personal gravity. Blackness rippled out from it across the tiles.

The tapping of high heels echoed toward us as a teacher holding a stack of papers rounded a corner. She slowed her pace and squinted at us. I could see her out of the corner of my eye. Brian and I were still staring up at the ceiling wide-eyed, and she followed our gaze, confusion written on her face. It was clear she didn't see what we saw.

As soon as I flicked my eyes toward the teacher, an ear-splitting scream tore out of Brian's throat. The teacher jumped and I stumbled backward, my backpack sliding off my shoulder. I stared at Brian as he writhed on the floor, foggy darkness swirling around him. Terror distorted his face as he kicked and swatted at the incorporeal flesh enveloping him. His blows passed right through it. Soon Brian's limbs began moving more slowly; he was losing strength.

The teacher ran toward Brian and dropped to her knees, papers forgotten on the floor. I lurched forward and reached out to stop her, but it was too late. Her hand was already on him. But it didn't make any impact. It was like the shadow-thing didn't even notice.

"Call 911! I think he's having a seizure!" she yelled at me. But I was paralyzed with fear. "Now!" she snapped. I reached for my phone and dialed 911 with shaking fingers.

"911, what's your emergency? Hello? Hello?" I held the phone to my ear but couldn't talk. The teacher was suddenly next to me, prying it out of my hand.

"I'm at Cypress High and we have a student having a seizure, please send..."

The rest of her words we lost to me as a roaring sound filling my skull. I clutched my head, trying to block out the nightmare. Bile rose in my throat and I ran to the nearest bathroom and vomited what felt like all the meals I had ever eaten. Resting my head on the toilet, I sobbed for an eternity.

What had I done?

CHAPTER 12
ELIZABETH

The siren was nearly deafening. The glow of red and blue flashes played over my eyelids.

"Stay with me." The composed voice willed my eyes back open for a moment, and I peered into a gentle face. The creases of worry etched on his forehead didn't tarnish his calming smile. It was a practiced smile, used for many years to soothe bloodied bodies such as mine.

I closed my eyes again but remained aware, listening to the rolling pitch of the siren, seeking out the voice that grounded me.

Movement stopped for a brief moment, then I felt my body lurch forward and down, and the vibration of wheels over pavement. I opened my eyes when I heard the swing of doors and the onslaught of harried voices, too many to pull apart.

With a sudden awareness of the taste of blood in my mouth and agony in my head, I knew it was time to go. It was a peaceful revelation, an understanding that brought resolution and acceptance. Everyone's life in this world comes to an end, and this was mine.

I let go. The physical form that had sustained me for so many years breathed one final sigh of relief, the end of suffering. A bright light filled the space behind my eyelids then faded, leaving me standing, free of pain, looking down at my body.

With a detached curiosity I watched the people around me trying so hard to convince me to stay. How odd it was that strangers would put so much effort into saving the life of a person who was unknown to them, someone they had no feelings for, no love, no friendship, no hate.

"Clear!" I heard an electric buzz, then saw my body jolt, metal paddles touching my bare chest. I walked away. There was no need to witness this. I was already gone; the broken body on the table no longer belonged to me.

I strolled calmly out of the room and down the hallway. The people and noises around me dulled, the shining silver light returning and dimming my surroundings. I continued like this, only feeling a slight sadness for my loved ones who I knew would mourn me. Only twenty-eight years spent on this earth, but they were years well spent.

I thought of the children I would never have, the wedding I no longer had to plan, and the business I had created coming to an end. But it was okay, this was how it was supposed to be.

Suddenly, the calmness snapped away and I felt myself being drawn back down the hallway, back toward the room that contained the body I had no longer been connected to just moments before. This was wrong; this wasn't supposed to happen. It was my time to move on.

I stood next to my body once more, against my will, and saw a plastic hose down my throat, a machine making my chest rise and fall. Wires and tubes were attached in too many places, artificial devices that would keep a hopeless vessel in a semblance of life. It was unnatural, horrifying.

I caught movement in my peripheral vision and looked toward the swinging double doors. My mother and father were hugging, shoulders heaving in unheard sobs, witnessing the machines that were postponing their daughter's death.

A woman in a white lab coat gently blocked them from entering the room, shaking her head, directing them away. It took several people to wheel my body out of the room, one pushing the bed, four more guiding the machines that were attached. I followed somberly, entering a second room, this one free of blood on the floor, as though to make it seem like everything might be okay.

My parents came in and stood next to me, peering down at the bed. I reached towards them, but my hand passed through with an icy tingle.

Jordan rushed into the room, just moments behind. I wanted to kiss his soft lips, tell him that he would be all right, he would find someone else to spend his life with.

I watched the pain on their faces for a few minutes, blocking out their heartbreaking words. The woman in the white lab coat entered and all four of us turned to look, her expression dire.

"I'm so sorry, but she's not going to make it. We have her on life support now, but we are in the process of contacting organ recipients. I am very sorry for your loss."

Her words were matter-of-fact. Harsh and to the point, clearly said many times and to many families. But they only sparked anger, hot tears, and desperation.

"But if she's on life support, why do we have to take her off? She's alive!" my father pleaded.

"I'm very sorry Mr. Dixon, but there is no brain activity. Elizabeth's body is being artificially sustained. There is no hope of her reviving. It is very, very expensive to keep a patient on life support. It is not worth your pain or money to do so." I knew the truth in this.

"No. No!" my mom protested. "We have money! We aren't giving up! We can't, not yet. Not on my Liz." This terrified me. I felt a tether keeping me here, and this body was sustaining it. It was awful, pulling at my soul. I needed to move on; it was what was meant to be.

Jordan hadn't said anything. He was in shock. It was only three days ago he gave me the diamond that rested gently on my finger. He reached for that hand now, fiddling with the ring, feeling its significance.

Time went by. I watched my loved ones come and

go. I listened to the beeping of the machines. All the while the tether remained. Horrible and tight. Invisible.

With every passing moment, the world was fading. It was there, I could feel it. I could see it overlaying the empty room. It transparency scared me. I was losing touch with it. But my body remained, more opaque than everything else around me, but still out of reach and yet binding me there, to the physical world that was now emptying, my incorporeal form not capable of existing completely in such a corporeal place. Somehow I knew this to be true, as if this place had always been here, just out of sight, waiting for the ones like me, the ones who were meant to move on but couldn't. It was not natural to be in this empty place, and I knew it deep in my soul.

But I could feel a presence within that emptiness, one that *did* belong here, that survived here. And it could feel me too.

CHAPTER 13
JOHN

After the incident in the bank, my parents could no longer pretend that they hadn't noticed that something had been wrong for years. The silence stretched and the cigarette smoke burned my eyes as I read the prescription bottle. The list of side effects was beyond my comprehension.

"What's hypotension?" There was no response. "Dad?"

"Let your father drive, John," my mom said as she took yet another drag from her cigarette.

I guess it didn't matter. Nothing could be worse than what they said I had. Schizophrenia. It sounded like a dirty word. Oily, somehow. Like it would leave a residue in my mouth if said out loud.

Maybe that was why no one was talking.

When we got home from the doctor, my dad told me to read the directions on the paperwork for how often to take the medication. That's the last time it was discussed.

It was like my diagnosis was the family's dirty little secret and if we didn't talk about it maybe it would go away.

The meds made me nauseous and tired, but time went by and I didn't have any more episodes, so I had a little hope that maybe they were working.

Then about three weeks later, I felt a pressure in my ears. The noises around me dulled except for a faint high-pitched tone. I figured this was what ringing in the ears meant—another listed side-effect of the medication. It was annoying, but tolerable, just like the fatigue and nausea. Another three months went by and still no episodes.

"John, can you go get a container of tomato sauce in the freezer, please?" my mother asked me before dinner one day.

"Sure." I pushed my math homework to the side and trudged over to the basement door. I flipped on the lights and walked down the creaky wooden stairs to the expansive basement. As I stepped off the last stair to make my way to the chest freezer at the far end, my ears began to ring, but stronger than I'd ever felt so far. I grimaced and stuck my finger in my ear and wiggled it, trying to relieve the pressure. It didn't help. Not even two steps into the basement, my surroundings began to dim and the air started to feel heavy. I froze.

No, no, no. Not again, I thought. The paint cans on the wall shelving disappeared, and the wooden shelves rotted and fell apart. The washer and dryer were gone, the concrete beneath cracked and dulled.

I watched my basement age fifty years in ten seconds.

My hope that this nightmare of the last few years was over was crushed. The medication wasn't working. I thought back to the creature at the bank and my heart leapt into my throat. But there was nothing in the basement with me.

Then my fear evaporated and was replaced by anger. I was angry at myself, angry at my parents. Angry at the doctor. Everyone had let me down. Weren't parents supposed to protect you? Weren't doctors supposed to cure you? My parents ignored me and the doctor had failed me.

If this was indeed schizophrenia, then none of this was real, right? So fine, I would disprove the reality. I walked towards where the freezer should have been with my new bravery and anger fueling each step.

But after about fifteen feet, farther than I had ever gone into this void before, it began to feel like I was trying to walk underwater. I focused on one step at a time, forcing my way through the jellied air, determination etching my face. The air got so thick that the exertion forced beads of sweat to roll down my temples. I had made it another five feet when I suddenly felt a distinct snap, and stumbled forward. The atmosphere returned to the typical mild heaviness I always felt in this place.

As I stumbled, I also felt a drop in my stomach, like the feeling of falling in the middle of the night and then jerking awake, and a pain on the side of my head, but both faded in an instant.

Whoa! It caught me off guard. That was *not* what I had expected to happen. I didn't know what I *had* expected, but that sure wasn't it.

I turned back to the stairs, wondering if there was something physical I would be able to see, some kind of barrier I had broken through.

No.

There was no barrier.

What there was however, was…me.

Lying on the floor. A marionette whose strings had been cut. I backed away, not quite registering what I was seeing.

I stopped and hesitantly leaned forward but kept my feet rooted to the floor. My hands shook and I squeezed my eyes shut and opened them again, hoping I would find myself staring up at my bedroom ceiling, waking from a nightmare.

No. It was still me, my face pressed against the floor. Or an exact copy of me. I could see its hair, *my* hair, dark brown and in need of a haircut, and my thick eyelashes. All six feet of my seventeen-year-old body were sprawled on the ground, and a slight trickle of blood leaked slowly from a gash on my head, staining the concrete crimson.

Am I dead? I wondered with increasing panic. *Am I a ghost looking at my dead body? What the fuck is this?* I knew without a doubt now that everyone had been wrong. I knew in the core of my soul that this was real. It had all been real, *was* real. I had been glimpsing a world that seemed to be the old and broken reflection of our own, and now, somehow, I was *in* it. Maybe it *was* an afterlife.

What now? What should I do? Would someone come find me? Did my mom hear me hit the floor? Gathering some courage, I took a few steps towards the body. *My* body. I clutched my belly, feeling an odd pulling sensation deep inside me. As I stepped closer, the feeling got stronger.

Is this what happens when people have a near-death experience? Was I not quite dead, just about to be?

I took another step. And another, the pulling getting stronger. I crouched slowly and reached a trembling hand toward my body, eyes wide, heart pounding, and delicately touched my fingertips to my arm.

There was a roaring in my ears and everything went dark as I again felt like I was falling. After a fraction of a second, I felt fine. Normal.

Then, pain.

My head throbbed and burned. I felt a warm wetness filling my ear. Blood. My cheek was pressed against the cold basement floor. I groaned and reached a tentative hand towards my aching skull. The pain was almost a relief. *I am back. In my body.*

Had this all been my imagination? Did I fall down the stairs, hit my head, and hallucinate the whole thing? No. I was at least twenty feet from the stairs, the washer and dryer directly in my line of vision, albeit blurry and sideways. I had left my body and now was blessedly inside of it again. I felt hysterical laughter bubble at the back of my throat, the kind that comes with intense relief.

"John? Did you find the tomato sauce?" my mom yelled from the kitchen. When I didn't respond, I heard the door creak open from the top of the stairs. There was a pause.

"Oh my god! Oh my God! Rob! Rob, get over here now!"

I heard a set of heavy footsteps run towards the door that I recognized as my dad's. Both my parents dashed down the stairs and were by my side in seconds.

"John!" My dad's voice reverberated painfully in my brain. He crouched down and placed a hand on my arm, his expression too blurry to make out. I could see the shape of my mom's head peering over my dad's shoulder. As it slowly came into focus, I saw her face painted with terror.

"Is he alive? Is he okay? Rob, *is he okay?"*

"Yes, he's alive," my dad said with a sigh of relief. His voice got tense again, "but his head is bleeding." My mom gasped and clutched her hands to her mouth.

"Can you stand?" my dad asked.

"I…I think so," I croaked.

"What happened?" my mom asked from behind my dad's shoulder.

"I fell…down the stairs," I stuttered. My dad helped me to my feet slowly and I immediately vomited, the bile splattering on my dad's shoes.

"What's going on?" I heard Shannon call from the

kitchen.

"Just stay up there!" my dad shouted back. He glanced briefly at his shoes but didn't seem upset. "Let's get you upstairs."

CHAPTER 14
ANNA

That night over a tense dinner of mac-and-cheese, my mom told me it would be perfectly fine to skip school the next day. But I couldn't. I had to know what was going on, and I knew there was going to be a lot of rumors about what had happened. I felt guilty about skipping class and guilty that I cared about skipping class when there were so many other terrible things happening around me. The mix of guilt, curiosity, and dread turned my stomach to jelly.

Becca texted me the following morning saying she needed to take a mental health day and I should too, but I went to school anyway. A disturbing quiet followed me through the hallways, punctuated by curious glances that quickly darted away when I tried to make eye contact. Everyone already knew what had happened. The speed at which information traveled in a high school would put Google to shame.

I ran my fingertips over the cool blue metal of the

lockers as I walked down the hallway. I needed a break from the gossip. I was on my way to lunch and decided to chill outside instead. Clearing my head and trying to relax a bit sounded appealing.

Pushing open the double glass doors leading into the courtyard, I saw some other students sitting at the wooden picnic tables. I knew a few of them but I wasn't in the mood for small talk, so I sat down on the parched grass against the side of the building by myself. Thoughts of food didn't even enter my mind.

I pulled my knees up to my chest and picked at the grass by my feet. I needed to see Brian. I *needed* to know if he was okay. The guilt was eating me alive. It *was* my fault, as much as I was trying to deny it. Whatever I had done was responsible for what happened to him.

I would have to get ahold of him, but I didn't know how. I didn't have his phone number or his parents' number. I didn't want to ask Becca. I wasn't a good liar and I knew she would be able to tell something was up. Aaron probably had Brian's number.

I found Aaron after school stretching on the grass next to the track, waiting for all the other cross-country runners to show up. I felt awkward being there, like I was no longer a part of the team and was intruding, which I guess was partly true. He stood up when we saw me approach.

"Hey Anna!"

"Hey Aaron."

"How's it going? Are you coming to practice today?"

He looked me up and down briefly and his smile faded when he realized I was wearing street clothes. I felt my stomach twist with guilt when I saw his disappointed look.

"Uh, no unfortunately," I stammered awkwardly, ringing my hands. "The doctor hasn't changed his mind about letting me run." I tried to hide the heat creeping into my face. I actually hadn't asked him again since he told me to take it easy for a while. Cross-country was the furthest thing from my mind at this point. I wasn't the greatest liar.

"Oh. That sucks. We could really use you. We're sucking particularly hard lately," he said with an ironic chuckle.

"Yeah. Sorry about that. So I actually have a favor to ask you."

"Sure. Shoot."

"So…it's about Brian."

"Okay…" he said with furrowed eyebrows.

"Oh, it's nothing big. I just need his phone number or his parents' number, if you have it. I want to um… send him a card, you know, because I was there and all…" I let my voice trail off. I realized saying I needed to call them because I needed his address might be a mistake, in case somehow Aaron knew what it was. But I didn't want to say I was going to ask to see Brian. He probably didn't even know my name despite his cousin being my best friend.

"Oh, yeah, sure. I actually do have it. Before that

fundraiser in November to resurface the track, we all exchanged numbers."

The football team did laps on the track as part of their practice, so they had just as much incentive to resurface the track as the cross-country team did. I knew a few members of the team had exchanged numbers.

"Great! Thanks so much, Aaron."

"Yeah, no problem. So uh, you think maybe you want to come to the meet on Saturday? I mean, not to run or anything. You could cheer us on."

His last sentence was more of a question. I was actually flattered. As much as Aaron could be a douche sometimes, it was nice to know he wanted me around.

"That sounds cool. I can't make any promises, though; I've got a few exams next week I need to study for."

"Right. Of course." He blushed. "Well, I hope to see you there." I thumbed Brian's number into my phone as Aaron recited it to me, and thanked him again.

I shook my head slightly as I walked away. He never acted this way around me. He was always cocky and flirty, but had never acted shy or embarrassed before. It wasn't something I wanted to spend too much time pondering at the moment.

I pulled out my phone as I walked to the parking lot. I had forgotten I had no car and had missed the bus a while ago. I called my mom, who was thankfully off from work today, and told her I needed her to pick me up. She seemed annoyed but had no choice but to come get me.

I sat on the curb and waited. My mom arrived about twenty minutes later. She pulled up next to me and gave me a quick glance as I opened the door. Her hands gripped the steering wheel tightly and her jaw was clenched. I could tell she was mad and figured it was because she had to pick me up. She'd probably lecture me about being irresponsible. After a few minutes of silence, I had to say something.

"I'm sorry, Mom. I had to talk to Aaron about something. Please don't be mad."

"It's not that," she said curtly.

"Okay. What is it then?" God, what did I do now?

"Mr. Marshall called." Oh crap. I had forgotten his trash *again*.

"Mom, I'm…"

"I know you have had a lot going on recently but you need to go apologize to him. Tonight." I was about to roll my eyes but stopped myself. I didn't want to piss her off even more.

"Fine."

CHAPTER 15
ANNA

I shuffled over to Mr. Marshall's house, not looking forward to the exchange. I had far more important things to worry about, like what I was going to say to Brian and his family. *Hey Mrs. Wilkes. Just wanted to see how Brian was doing after he was attacked by some demon that I am responsible for unleashing into the school. How're things with you?*

I rang the doorbell and it played a little melody inside the house. I smoothed my hair back and tried to make my face look apologetic, but unfortunately I didn't care very much at the moment. The dude was like a thousand years old; he'd probably forget about it in a few days anyway.

The door creaked open just a few inches and Mr. Marshall peeked through the crack. He looked at me expectantly, and seemed sort of...nervous. After a few seconds of uncomfortable silence, I figured he was waiting for me to speak first.

"Uh, hi Mr. Marshall. I'm just here to apologize for not taking out your trash for the last couple weeks. I know I promised to fertilize your grass for you, too. I've just…I've had a lot on my mind lately. You know, school and stuff." I fiddled with the hem of my shirt and lowered my eyes. I realized I actually did feel bad.

As he opened the door fully, I noticed what looked like a strip of tiny bells rimming the top of his doorway; they chimed faintly as a gentle breeze blew into the house.

"Come on in." I didn't want to but felt obligated. He moved aside to let me by, but as I stepped hesitantly forward he raised his hand to halt me for a second. He tapped one of the bells so that a high-pitched trill echoed in my ears. Mr. Marshall leaned out the doorway and glanced around the front yard as the noise faded. I waited awkwardly, wondering what the hell he was doing, until he gave a satisfied nod and turned on a deft heel to lead me inside.

His house looked like it hadn't had a makeover since the '70s. He led me to the kitchen and pointed to a bar stool pushed underneath a fading yellow countertop.

"Sit." It wasn't a suggestion. "Lemonade?" he asked, pouring me a glass from a plastic pitcher without waiting for an answer.

"Uh, I guess? Sure. Thanks." My foot tapped restlessly on the dingy linoleum floor. I wasn't thirsty. He grabbed a second glass from the cabinet and began to fill it agonizingly slowly. I clenched my fists at my sides and tried not to start pulling my hair out. I just wanted to go home and figure out how to get in touch with Brian.

"How's school going? You said you had a lot on your mind," he said as he took the few steps he needed to cross the tiny kitchen and place the glass in front of me. Beads of condensation ran down his fingertips.

This was uncomfortable. I didn't think we had had a conversation of more than two sentences in the six-ish years we'd lived next to each other. He was old and had no family in the area that I knew of; maybe he was just lonely. I never saw him get any visitors.

I cleared my throat awkwardly and took a swallow of lemonade. The sweet, tangy liquid was surprisingly delicious, and I felt myself relax the tiniest bit.

"Well, you know, just normal school stuff. Homework, tests, social drama." I raised the icy glass to my lips and took another perfectly lemony sip. He stared at me with an expectant look and nodded, an expression encouraging me to continue.

After a moment, it felt okay to confide in him.

"I had to quit the cross-country team, which sucked, because I broke my arm and a few ribs in my car accident. Oh, I don't know if you know about that, Mr. Marshall."

"I do, and please call me John. I talk to your mother sometimes if we run into each other." I didn't know that.

"Okay. John. Yeah, it was pretty scary. I've never been in a car crash before. I mean, obviously I've seen banged up cars on the side of the road and stuff." I wrapped my hands around the cool glass, and downed half the lemonade. I was noticing Mr. Marshall had a comforting vibe about him. He refilled my glass from the plastic pitcher and I drank some more. I was starting to feel a bit numb but the words kept flowing.

"I keep getting these headaches, you know? The doctor said it's from the concussion…I had a concussion…but I Googled it and it's not supposed to last this long. I just feel like it wouldn't cause all this weird stuff."

"What weird stuff?" Mr. Marshall asked delicately. He was holding his glass of lemonade but hadn't drunk any. I wondered if I drank the rest of the pitcher if he would let me drink his too. I felt kind of loopy and tired. My words were beginning to slur. I rambled on for a few minutes and he nodded along.

"But it's theses scary hallucinations that bother me the most, you know? This monster or whatever. Or I think that's what…" Wait…what? What the hell was I saying? Why was I telling him this? My brain snapped to alertness, like it was all of a sudden catching up to itself. I stood up quickly, knocking the stool over in the process. I looked in horror at the almost empty glass of lemonade sitting on the counter in front of me, stumbling and dizzy.

"What…what? Did you…did you just…*drug* me?" I was so scared and angry at the same time, I didn't know whether to run screaming from the house or bash in his leathery old face with the toaster to the right of me. Fight or flight were warring with one another, and all I could do was freeze in place.

"Anna, calm down," he said gently, hands raised defensively.

"Calm down? *Calm down?* What did you *do* to me?" I backed away slowly. I could feel the blood drain from my face, my eyes wide.

"It's all right. I just had to be sure."

"Had to be sure of *what?*"

"That it was you. That it was you who let it out."

CHAPTER 16
ANNA

I froze. “Wha…what did you say?”

“I have answers, Anna.” When I didn’t move or speak, he continued, “Please. Don’t leave. Sit down.”

“I think I’ll stay here, thanks.” I crossed my still-wobbly arms over my chest and tried to plaster on the best glower I could manage, but confusion, fear, and some lingering fogginess were making my hands shake. “Did you drug me?”

He shrugged and looked apologetic. “Well, sort of.”

I scoffed. “How do you *sort of* drug someone?” I took another step back as my heart leapt.

“It isn’t a drug in the conventional sense.” He shook his head and scrubbed the heels of his hands over his eyes. He had seemed so sure of himself since the moment I walked in the door, and seeing frustration on his face was kind of unsettling. “We need to hurry this process along, we don’t have a lot of time. When did you let it out?”

"I don't know what you're talk—"

"Spare me. We both know what I am talking about."

My heart thudded painfully in my chest. I felt a flood of words on the tip of my tongue, and the dam was about to break. "I didn't mean to! I don't even know what happened!" I could feel guilt burning in my face and I silently pleaded with him to understand. "How do you know? What is all of this? I am crazy? Is it even real? Why is it happening?"

"The why is unclear, but…"

"But what?"

"I think it may be *partially* my fault." He cringed.

I was so confused. "Your fault? How? Can you make it stop?"

"I have been crossing over a lot lately and I think I sort of…" He paused as though trying to find the words. "Pulled it toward you? Made you more aware by thinning the Barrier frequently, I think. Obviously, you already had the potential for it to happen, though."

"But…wait. I'm understanding slightly less than nothing about what you just said." I tucked my hair behind my ears and sat back down on the bar stool, splaying my fingers out on the cool countertop, arm muscles tensed. Yes, he had just *drugged* me, but I needed to hear what he had to say, regardless of how nonsensical it sounded. *I should be sprinting out of this house right now and calling the cops. What am I doing?*

He leaned forward and placed his hands on top of mine. In spite of the crazy turn this evening was taking, his touch was comforting. His wrinkly hands were still damp from the condensation. He sighed.

"Anna. I need you to understand something. You. Are. Not. Crazy." He stared deep into my eyes, and I could see truth and wisdom in his. I felt an immense weight lifted off my shoulders, and somehow I knew I could believe everything he was telling me. I let out a tearless, short sob.

"Really?"

"Really." He smiled, but then it melted. "And I will absolutely help you but…I'm sorry, but…I need your help in return."

Again, confusion. My eyebrows knit together. "You? Need *my* help?"

"Yes. I'm afraid I might be dying."

CHAPTER 17
JOHN

They took me to the hospital the day I "fell down the stairs," where the emergency room doctor diagnosed me with a concussion. I was sent home and just told to rest, and then life went on.

The ringing in my ears continued, and when it was particularly strong, I would have another episode. I didn't make the mistake of walking so much as a foot when it happened, though. I had learned my lesson. I began to think of this place I would go as the Void, because it felt so unbearably empty, except for the occasional times I would see the ghostly people fade in and out. But the emptiness was welcome because it meant the emaciated monster from the bank that plagued my nightmares wasn't there.

I distracted myself as best I could. I put more effort into my schoolwork and joined the wrestling team, asked out the pretty girl named Courtney who was in homeroom with me. My life was good; I was happy, despite the occasional trips into the Void. I had accepted it. Months went by and the end of my senior year of high school was approaching.

My dad asked me to cut the grass on a hot day, the hottest so far this year, as the beginning of summer was creeping up. I was taking a break with a cool glass of lemonade, sitting on the front steps with sweat sticking my white t-shirt to my body.

I stared absently as I sipped from my glass.

I heard some muffled yelling and saw Mrs. Campbell storm out the front door of the house next to mine and sit on the front stoop, hanging her head in her hands. It looked like she was crying. I tried to keep staring forward while watching the drama from my peripheral vision, acting like I hadn't noticed. Her husband threw open the door a minute later, grabbed her arm and yanked her to her feet. I couldn't make out their argument through the rush of cars driving by. I strained my ears but it didn't help.

I snapped my gaze away from the confrontation when I saw Mr. Campbell glance my way and pretended I had been zoning out, staring at the street light on the corner two blocks away. It turned yellow just as a car sped past my house, doing at least twice the speed limit. The car slammed on its breaks just in time to stop at the red light. The squeal of the tires hurt my ears and I cringed.

I sighed resignedly as the car faded and the air pressed on my skin, the Void sucking away all the vibrancy around me. The cars were gone, trees died, houses crumbled. The fact that this no longer bothered me was disturbing.

But something was different. This didn't feel the same as it usually did and my heart skipped. Something caught the corner of my eye, and I turned back toward the Campbells' house and jumped to my feet.

Mr. and Mrs. Campbell were still there, misty white forms almost blending with the dirty stucco behind them.

It was the creature lurking behind her bushes in painstaking detail that made the bile rise in my throat. Hyperventilating, I stared at the monster, so reminiscent of a giant praying mantis. It crept on two insect-like legs and had huge reflective eyes, swirling colors like an oil slick on a pond. Hairy mandibles chomped with a wet clicking noise while gooey saliva fell in large globs on the ground.

It inched its way closer to Mrs. Campbell while I crept backward, trying to put as much distance between it and myself as possible, but I tripped over the front step, windmilling my arms to try to keep my balance. It didn't work. I stumbled into the shrubs, breaking some dry twigs in the process.

The insect creature turned toward me, drawn by the sound. *Oh shit oh shit oh shit.* I scrambled out of the bush as fast as I could. It began creeping toward me. It seemed to sense my panic and picked up speed.

I finally got upright and ran, darting for the street. Unfortunately there were no cars in this place to slow the creature down. In my adrenaline-fueled terror, I barely noticed that it was becoming more and more difficult to move my limbs. A moment later I was free. The feeling of running through water snapped away and I stumbled forward, the hindrance gone. I kept sprinting.

Sparing a second to look back, the mantis had lost interest and was skittering back toward Mrs. Campbell's ghostly figure.

When the thing reached her, it jabbed the pointed end of one of its arms, for it had several, into Mrs. Campbell's side. She jerked and paused for a fraction of a second, then went back to her silent yelling.

I slowed and crouched behind a tree in the yard across the street, watching, transfixed. A deep, almost black crimson began flowing down the creature's dark green shimmery flesh until its whole body was the color of dried blood. In under a minute the transformation was complete and it dislodged its arm from Mrs. Campbell as she faded into nothingness. It stalked away, having completely lost interested in me. I lost sight of it as it skittered behind the house.

My heart rate slowed and I wiped sweat off my brow.

Then, I noticed it.

My body. Lying in the middle of the road. *Fuck!* I jogged over to it, slowing my pace as I got closer. I could feel the pulling sensation getting stronger and it compelled me to reach out to it. It was so unbelievably creepy, staring at myself lying on the asphalt.

I reached slowly toward it, closing my eyes and taking a deep breath. *Okay, I can do this. I* have *to do this.*

Just as I was about to make contact with the body, it flew off the ground, rolled in midair, and landed about twenty feet away.

I was shocked, my fingers still poised over an arm that was no longer there. *What the hell?*

I ran toward it but slowed in horror before I made it all the way there. Its head was bashed open, bloody goo that could only be brain matter was splattered on the road. An arm was twisted behind its back, the elbow bent at an impossible angle. Legs were sprawled in opposite directions, one clearly dislocated at the hip with a shard of bone poking through one calf. A lone sandal had landed flat on the sole a few yards away, toe pointed toward the bloody mess, as though an invisible one-legged person stood there, observing the horror.

I don't know how long I stood there staring with my jaw dropped. A few seconds? Minutes? I couldn't look away. Then realization hit me.

I had been hit by a car. One that was on the other side. One I couldn't see.

And I was dead.

CHAPTER 18
ANNA

"You're dying? Like, from cancer or something?"

"No, not from cancer."

"Then what?" He lifted his hands off mine and the sudden lack of warmth was disappointing, even though the rest of me was sweltering. I could feel a bead of sweat roll down my temple.

"It's very hard to explain right now. First I want you to tell me what happened. Everything you can remember."

My shoulders tensed. I didn't want to do this. But somehow I knew he had answers and I could trust him. When he had told me I wasn't crazy and that this was real, I actually believed him.

"Okay," I rested my head in my hands for a second to try to unscramble the thoughts in my mind. My hands were damp with sweat when I looked up. "It started shortly after my car accident. It started with these weird…sensations? Or maybe visions, I guess. Things around me disappear and kind of look blurry. Or maybe not blurry, but dull? Gah, it's hard to describe. It sounds so stupid when I say it out loud." He nodded reassuringly.

"But then there was this other time with this guy at school. The guy, Brian, bumped into me in the hallway. You'd think he'd watch out and make sure *not* to bump into the girl who's wearing a sling, 'cause damn, it hurt. But anyway, all the students disappeared and everything except for him was kind of…washed out, and he looked…" I paused, trying to find a good description. "Like a skeleton. But with skin, and still wearing his clothes. But I could tell I was the only one seeing it."

John nodded. "And is that when you saw the…it?" He was obviously referring to the monster thing he claimed I let out. Guilt fluttered in my belly at the reminder.

"No. Not that time. It was the next time, a few days later. I was following him to try and see if it would happen again."

"What? You *wanted* to make it happen? Why the hell would you want that?"

I thought back and suddenly felt so stupid. "Honestly, I don't know. My friend Becca convinced me and I was so desperate to prove to myself I wasn't going nuts that it felt like a good idea. Obviously it wasn't." My face flushed in embarrassment.

"So. You intentionally tried to cross over and you told someone about it? I guess we have more damage control to do than I thought. How did you do it?" He made the motion of running his fingers through his hair, but they just slid over his mostly bald head.

"I have no idea. I didn't do it *intentionally.* I didn't do anything, unless you consider breaking my toe something. See?" I showed him my flip-flopped foot, and carefully removed my homemade splint made from a popsicle stick. My nail was totally black and the surrounding flesh was bruised and swollen.

"Ouch. It happened when you injured your foot?"

"Yeah. Is that relevant? What do you mean 'crossed over'? I am going somewhere else?"

"Yes. I call it the Void."

My stomach lurched. *I* am *going somewhere else?* No. There was still a good chance this guy was full of shit. "Why do you call it that?"

"It is devoid of many things." He gave me a slight grin.

I squinted and shook my head. "What does that even mean? What is it…" I jumped as my phone vibrated in my pocket. I pulled it out and checked the screen. A text from my mom. *How is it going? You've been there almost an hour.* Really? Wow. It's not just when you're having fun that time flies. "Sorry, give me just a sec." I texted back, *its fine we are having lemonade he is nice.* "My mom is wondering why I've been here so long. I bet she's wondering if you drugged me and cut me up into little pieces." I looked at him accusingly.

"Well, that was morbid. Sorry again, though." He shrugged apologetically.

"My mom watches a lot of TV, I'm not even kidding

that she's probably worried about that. I shouldn't stay much longer."

"When you get home, tell her you've offered to help me go through the boxes in my attic. That way she'll be okay with you coming over here often," he suggested.

"Often?"

"Well, yes. There's a lot more I need to explain to you, and I don't think we have much time."

I shivered despite the heat. "Before you die?"

"That, and before the leech does more damage than it already has."

CHAPTER 19
ANNA

I trudged, bewildered, across Mr. Marshall's—John's—lawn toward the front door of my house. He had refused to explain to me how he thought the Leech, as he had called it, had gotten "out," and what damage it was going to do. He said my mom would start to get suspicious and it would be a long conversation.

I opened the door with a shaky hand. This was a lot to take in. And even though it seemed absurd beyond belief that I was putting my trust in someone who had just drugged me, I felt a kind of connection to John and knew he could help me. Or, well, now it seemed more like I'd be helping him. He was dying? I felt a pang of sympathy. How in the hell was I supposed to do anything about that?

As I stepped into the blessedly air-conditioned foyer, I leaned against the door frame for a moment, closing my eyes and taking a deep, calming breath. Okay, I could do this. I could pretend like everything was normal, like I wasn't on the verge of a hysterical mental breakdown.

"Anna?"

I jumped at the sound of my own name. A perfect start to pretending my fragile understanding of reality wasn't just shattered into a million pieces.

My mom furrowed her eyebrows and tilted her head slightly like a concerned puppy. "How did it go?" she asked.

I cleared my throat. "Not bad," I said, trying to control my voice. Did I normally sound like a strangled Chihuahua? "I…uh, told him…or, well, he asked me, if I could help him go through his attic. As like, an apology, to make up for flaking on him so many times." I scratched the back of my head and then forced my arm back down by my side, aware that it was one of my tells when I was lying.

"Oh." My mom looked a bit confused. "Do you have time for that? What about homework and your college applications?"

I walked past her towards the kitchen, and pulled open the fridge, peering inside. I wasn't hungry; I just needed to do something. I pulled out a soda and popped the tab, taking a fizzy sip before answering. I had forgotten about the college applications and was trying to come up with a response. We had already agreed I would take a year off after graduation to make some money and figure out what the hell I wanted to do with my life. My stomach did a somersault at the thought of how clueless I was about my future.

"Homework is really dying down since it's the end of the year." That was sort of true. "And I'm not going back to cross-country so I'll have time after school. He's a nice man. I feel bad about slacking."

My mom gave a firm nod of approval. "Well good. I'm glad."

"Is Dad home?" I asked, changing the subject and taking another swig.

"No, it's only…" She pulled out her phone to check the time. "3:58. Maybe in an hour and a half or so."

"Mom…" I started.

"What is it, sweetie?" she asked.

"Can I have a hug?" I felt like a lost little girl.

"Aw, of course, honey." She sounded touched. "Everything okay?"

She wrapped me up in her arms and I mumbled into her shoulder, "Yeah. You know, just…everything." She squeezed a bit harder, thinking that she knew the cause of the stress I had been under. But she didn't know that half of it. And there was no chance in hell I was going to tell her.

CHAPTER 20
ANNA

I tried to walk at a normal pace down John's driveway toward his front door. My adrenaline was pumping, washing away my exhaustion.

I rapped my knuckles on the door, propping the screen open with my foot. He answered a moment later, his nearly bald, age-spotted head appearing from behind the door. He grinned, accentuating the wrinkles around his mouth and eyes.

"Come on in." He stepped aside and gestured for me to walk past.

"Hi. Thanks," I said, making my way inside. Walking through the living room, I noticed several bookshelves. One was filled with an entire encyclopedia set, along with some pretty hefty history books and several volumes on mythology. Toward the bottom, I saw what looked like a few textbooks. I could make out one with a yellow sticker that said "used" on it, obscuring the title "Algebra" on the spine. I wanted to explore his house and see what other random items he had tucked away.

I made my way to the same barstool I had sat in the day before and took a seat.

"I've gone over what we talked about yesterday and written down a ton of questions."

John sighed, "You really just get down to business, huh?"

"What? You said you had answers." I tapped my foot impatiently but gave him a wide grin.

"Okay, shoot."

"What exactly is the 'Void'?" I air quoted and he chuckled at the gesture.

"From what I have gathered, it is a mirror of our own plane, but more…washed-out. Dimmer. Some things can only exist in one plane or the other and some in both."

That definitely brought up more questions than it answered. He must have seen my perplexed expression because he continued, "I call it the Void because it's…empty. Lacking substance and details. It feels like a deserted movie set rather than real life."

"But it wasn't empty the last time I was there. It was boatloads of scary."

"Yes, because you were near someone getting leeched."

"I don't get it." I shook my head, confused. He sighed and took another pitcher of lemonade out of the fridge and grabbed two glasses from the cabinet.

"Oh, no way. Seriously?"

He looked puzzled for a moment, then laughed, "It's just lemonade this time." He sighed at my incredulous stare. "Fine." He downed half the glass. "See?"

"Okay. But I'm waiting to make sure you don't start confessing your deepest secrets. Like how you used to lead a double life and have a second family out there." His eyes fell to the floor and he looked sad for a moment. "I…I'm sorry, I was just kidding."

He gave me a small, sad smile. "It's okay. I just wish…never mind."

I glanced at the mantle above the gas fireplace, where pictures of his daughter and wife sat. They looked happy, normal.

I tried to smooth the awkwardness by getting back on track. "Why can I see it? Or go there, or whatever. Am I human?"

He laughed. "Of course you're human. What else would you be?"

I shrugged sheepishly.

"I'm not sure what makes us different, but I think the potential isn't that uncommon," he added.

"Really? Haven't you been dealing with this for a while? I mean, you've got to be…well, you're just…"

"So old?" He smiled, and I cringed inwardly and tucked my hair behind my ears. I was trying to put it more delicately. He backed away so I could see more of him, and flexed his scrawny, wrinkly arm like he was some sort of pathetic body builder. "This right here?" He pointed at his bicep with mock offense. "This physique clearly isn't more than forty years old!"

I laughed at the ridiculousness. John was pretty cool. I was kind of mad at myself for never getting to know him better. We clicked in a weird way, and I felt comfortable around him…once I got past the drugging incident, of course. He didn't seem the grandfatherly type. More like a cool uncle vibe. I thought of asking if he had any grandkids but then remembered how sad he got when I mentioned his family.

His expression became serious again as he continued, "I've been traveling back and forth between the Void and our plane for…" He paused as though doing the math. "Ten years, now. Fifteen years, if I am counting from the first time it happened by accident."

"Wow. Is that how you know so much about it?" I asked.

He chuckled again. "I don't know as much about it as you think I do. Most of the terms I use I came up with myself. And most of my knowledge is based on assumptions I had that proved to be true. There aren't really many people I can ask." He gestured towards the otherwise empty house.

"It's just us?" I asked, sitting up straight, a pang of anxiety shooting down spine.

"You're the only one I've run into. On this plane."

"So there are people on the other plane, too?"

John leaned on the counter and looked at me pointedly. "You are certainly asking a lot of questions."

"How else do you expect me to learn?"

He sighed, "I know, I just haven't spoken to anyone about this in a long time. I've never had to explain it from scratch before."

"Okay…" I chewed my lip, thinking for a moment. "How about I stop asking questions and you just talk?"

He paused, then nodded. "Let's go sit on the couch; you might want to get comfortable."

I followed him into the living room. I took a seat on the couch and he sat in the recliner, which was turned slightly in my direction, pointed at the TV in the corner. He closed his eyes for a moment, took a deep breath, and began.

"As far as I can tell, most people, if not all, occasionally appear in the Void. They don't know it. It's like they're in both places at once and can only see our plane. It's then that they are vulnerable." He paused again, clearly gathering his thoughts. It took everything I had not to fill the silence with a barrage of questions.

He began again, "I first saw a Leech when I was a kid. It was drawn to a guy who was briefly in the Void because he was very angry."

"Because he was angry? That's why people appear there?" I couldn't help interrupting.

"Sometimes. I've consistently observed that when people are in the Void, they are experiencing strong emotion. Usually negative, but sometimes positive. I have a theory that because the Void is so empty, it's like a vacuum. When someone is furious or scared or immensely happy, it is strong enough to leak through and get caught in the vacuum of the Void."

"How have you figured all this out?" I asked, mystified.

"I was trapped there for more than a year."

~

"*What?* A *year?*" I was shocked.

He chuckled sadly, "Yeah. It was quite…life-changing." He grinned and his eyes lost focus, as though indulging in an inside joke with himself.

"But how? How did you get stuck? How did you get back? What happened?" I was riveted, sitting on the edge of the couch, hands clenched in my lap.

"I think that's a story you might be overwhelmed with right now. Let's fill you in on the basics first."

"Okay." I tried to not sound disappointed. I was kind of ashamed and embarrassed to admit to myself that while all of this was for sure scary and bizarre, it was also sort of…exciting.

John opened his mouth to continue speaking but I burst out a question before he could start. "What about the root of all of this? What the hell *is* the Void? Why is it there? Why does it even exist?"

He shook his head slowly and I felt my heart sink. "Those are the questions I've been asking myself for fifteen years. I have no idea."

"I feel like there's got to be some kind of documentation. Someone has to have written about this. I mean, there are weirdoes who write down all sorts of crazy stuff they think has happened to them." I began to tick off on my fingers. "Alien abductions, vampires, ghosts, I read an entire novel about a guy who thought he had been to Hell. *Someone* has info on this. Hell, I bet someone has a *blog* about this. No one has a filter online nowadays."

John nodded. "The internet is a huge place. I've done research but haven't found anything concrete. I even went to a lecture series about Greek and Roman mythology hoping to get a hint. I'm sure there is something out there, but I stopped looking years ago. Feel free to take a crack at it." Damn right, I would.

"For sure. So what are these Leeches?" I asked anxiously, remembering the skittering shadow that followed Brian out of the library. A rock of guilt sat in the pit of my stomach and pressed my hands to belly, trying to ease the ache.

"It's my name for any creature that lives in the Void because they all survive the same way. They leech off of the emotions that seep through the barrier. It is their primary sustenance. It's the only explanation. Some are more timid and will avoid me as much as I avoid them. Others seem to seek out confrontation. Whether with humans like me, who are few and far between, or other Leeches. It wasn't an easy place to live for a year. I learned to…survive…pretty quickly."

"That sounds so awful." I shivered, imagining not knowing that there was a creature feasting on you that you couldn't see or touch.

"It was awful for me, sure. But as far as the people who they are leeching off of, they usually don't even know. They aren't killing anyone, and it's simply how they survive. It isn't their fault." I was taken aback for a moment. He saw my expression and continued, "don't get me wrong, it's terrifying, and Leeches are dangerous and can be violent and cruel, but they're simply trying to survive just like any other creature."

"But aren't they hurting people?" I asked.

"Well, yes and no. They drain a person's astral form, which then has to draw energy from their physical body. So a person who was leeched will often be tired and cranky, or if they were leeched badly, they might get seriously ill."

"So is that why Brian looked so horrible the day after I saw him get uh…leeched?"

"Unfortunately, no. From what you have described to me, it sounds like he didn't have any sudden emotional thing happening to him, so I'm thinking he was in the Void very dimly, maybe because of stress or anxiety. If I remember from my last days of high school, it's pretty stressful. There are some places Leeches like to hang out, places where there are a lot of astrals. Hospitals, schools at certain times of the year, any place that's really crowded, like a large city."

"Astrals?" I said quizzically. "As in astral projection? That thing where someone can supposedly leave their body when they sleep?"

"Not just when they sleep, but yes. It seemed like a fitting term," he replied, taking a slow sip of lemonade. It baffled me how calm he was. But like he said, he'd been dealing with this for more than a decade.

This still all seemed like a dream. Or a really riveting movie. The kind that draws you in so you almost forget it isn't real. Except this time there was no pause button. I was along for the ride whether I wanted to be or not. And I was pretty sure I didn't.

CHAPTER 21
JOHN

I backed away a few feet, still in shock. Then I snapped. I dropped to my knees, not even noticing the pain that shot up my thighs from landing hard on the road. Silent sobs wracked me, hands clapped over my mouth to trap the screams.

I sat back on my heels, still gawking at the mangled form on the ground. I leaned forward and gagged, but nothing came up. Then the body, my body, my *dead* body, faded from existence.

Tripping over my own feet, I got up and ran. How far I ran, I don't know, but I couldn't outrun the image of brain matter splattered on the road, staining the gray asphalt a sickly shade of dark pink. It was burned into my mind. I stumbled to a halt and leaned over the dead grass, gagging again.

I looked up shakily to see a house I didn't recognize. The light blue front door set in yellow stucco reminded me of my own. I needed to stop and rest. Or hide. Or have a mental breakdown.

As was typical of the Void, the colors around me were muted, and the grass looked brittle and dying. It wasn't hot outside either. The heavy air was a neutral room temperature. As I walked toward the house, I noticed the house lacked texture. Instead of the rough walls typical of homes in the hot climate of southern Florida, it created barely any sensation under my fingertips as I ran them over the wall next to the front door.

I rested my forehead on the wall for a moment, arms dangling limply by my sides, and took a deep shuddering breath. *Get it together.*

I opened the door and some of the frame crumbled and fell next to my feet. That was when I noticed I was still wearing both sandals, even though I swore I had seen one sitting near the mangled corpse miles behind me. I shuddered, once again seeing the image in my head.

I stepped inside, into a foyer with dirty cracked tiles and a crumbling wooden staircase to the right leading to a second floor. As I walked into the house I immediately realized my stupidity. There might be other monsters hiding out in here. Was the Void full of them, or were they rare? Maybe they took shelter in the empty houses, just like I was planning on doing. But what the hell else was I supposed to do? I couldn't stay out in the open. I would be vulnerable. I could climb up a tree, but how would I sleep? And that mantis thing was at least seven feet tall, and who knew if it could climb. I figured I had no choice.

I was a pretty muscular guy, having been on the wrestling team for a few months now. Well, I *used* to be on the wrestling team.

But now I'm dead.

I was strong and capable. Maybe I could find a weapon and if worse came to worst, I could fight one of these monsters off. What was the worst that could happen? Could I die again? And if I did, the nightmare would be over, and maybe that would be a relief. What was I, anyway? What part of me had survived in this place? My mind? My soul? It certainly wasn't my body, even though I felt like a physical being.

I pushed that thought aside for now and looked for a weapon. I tiptoed further into the house and came across a living room with a gaudy fake fireplace. There was a full set of decorative fireplace tools, which included a poker and a small shovel with a long handle. They were rusting and dusty but looked like they had potential to inflict damage. I grabbed both and crept back towards the stairs.

I decided to leave the front door unlocked—although it wouldn't be hard to break through anyway—to make a quick exit if necessary. I treaded delicately up each step, trembling, but straining my ears for the slightest noise, clutching the poker with a white-knuckled grip. The stairs creaked, but it was muffled as though they were covered in carpet.

There were three rooms and a bathroom upstairs, all

in poor condition. There was no water in the cracked toilet and the faucet didn't turn on. The largest bedroom had a bed with a stained mattress and some bare shelving. Another bedroom was painted a dull pink and had a bare twin bed frame. The last room contained only a desk.

I had learned through my several trips to the Void that there were rarely details or personal items anywhere. Every once in a while when I crossed over, I'd see an abandoned toy in a front yard or a personal ad tacked to a telephone pole.

*Crossed over…*I hadn't thought of it that way before.

I went back to what was presumably the master bedroom and sat on the bed, placing my newfound weapons beside me on the mattress. I hung my head and scrubbed my hands over my eyes, thinking.

Okay. I'm probably stuck here. I tried to think of any way this might not be true, but how could I not be? I had no body to return to. I choked back a sob.

I don't know how or where to find food and water. I wasn't hungry or thirsty, though, which was good news, even though I hadn't eaten since this morning and hadn't drunk anything since the lemonade, which was probably hours ago, and then ran God only knows how far.

How would I keep myself safe? Would these things hurt me if they had the chance? And what other dangers were here? I couldn't imagine that there were none.

I decided to just lay low for a while. Maybe try and sleep. I wasn't tired, though. I prayed for sleep to take me. Anything to escape reality for just a little while. I was afraid of being alone with my thoughts.

I noticed through the presumably west-facing window that the foggy, slightly green-tinted, dull sun was setting. It had been midmorning when this whole ordeal started…

since I died

…and I couldn't imagine that it was dusk already. Had that much time gone by? Or did time flow differently here? *What* is *here? What is this place?*

Where was I?

CHAPTER 22
ANNA

I stood in the middle of my room staring at the ten numbers on the screen, the giant green phone icon just waiting to be touched. I hovered my finger over it with a mix of dread and anticipation boiling in my gut. *Just do it.* Sighing, I hit the button and held the phone to my ear.

Ring. Ring. Ring. Ring.

I was about to hang up, half relieved, half worried that Brian wasn't answering.

"Hello?" a female voice answered. I was startled.

"…uh, sorry, wrong num…" I began.

"Are you looking for Brian?" she interrupted.

"Oh. Um, yes."

"This is his mother. Can I help you?" She sounded exhausted.

"Um maybe? My name is Anna Flores, I was with Brian when…"

"Oh yes, Anna. Hi. You're the one who called 911? It's good to hear from you," she said with a little more enthusiasm.

"It is? I mean, yeah. I uh…" God, I was so awkward. I had had a conversation planned out assuming that Brian would answer his phone.

"I was going to try to contact you to see if we could discuss what happened. The teacher who was there said you and Brian were alone in the hallway when she came across you two. No one I've spoken to so far can tell me much about what happened. I was hoping maybe you have some more details that can maybe help the doctors figure out what's going on."

I was not expecting this and had no idea what to say.

"Um, well they said he had a seizure, right?" I sat on my bed. My legs had turned to jelly. "The doctors? Like, as in more than one?" I asked.

I heard Mrs. Wilkes take a deep shaky breath, as though steeling herself for her next words.

"Yes. We've brought him to three different specialists. There's more going on than just seizures and we could really use as much information as possible…" she trailed off as though thinking, then began again, "Would you mind just coming over here, sweetheart? I'd really like to write everything down you can tell me."

"Oh. Uh, yeah. Of course." I was struggling to keep my voice steady, not let the guilt crack through. "When do you want me to come?"

"Well, I know it's getting a bit late now…how about tomorrow morning? I know it's Saturday but there's a boy stopping by around ten…Aaron, uh, Norman? I think that's his name. He's coming to drop off some things of Brian's that were left in the locker room."

"Aaron Norberg?" I asked. "Yeah, sure. I can come then." I felt a bit better knowing Aaron would be there and I wouldn't be alone with Brian.

"Thank you so much, Anna. We really appreciate it. I'll text you the address. I'm sure Brian will be happy to see you."

I was fairly certain he wouldn't be.

~

I sat in my mom's car in Brian's driveway. She had insisted on driving me but I had finally talked her out of it. I checked my phone for the tenth time. 10:06. Aaron's car was here. I assumed he was inside already.

With a sigh, I peeled myself off the driver's seat and pushed open the car door, setting one foot on the pavement. *You can do this.*

Each step felt like my feet were made of lead, but I finally made it to the front door. Before I could ring the bell, a woman opened the door and ushered me in.

"Oh, hi, Mrs. Wilkes," I stammered awkwardly.

"Anna, come in, come in." Her hair was frazzled and she had dark circles under her eyes. She looked drained. I felt awful all over again.

"Please sit." She led me over to the living room and pointed to the couch. I sat. She pulled up a folding chair and sat across from me, looking uncomfortable, a glass coffee table separating us with a pen and notepad waiting anxiously on top.

She took a deep breath and stared at me expectantly. I just looked back at her, not sure what I was supposed to do.

"Um, so…how's Brian?" She seemed to not even hear me even though she was looking right at me. Or through me.

"Do you think you can tell me a bit about what happened, sweetheart?" she asked, staring at her notepad with a fierce determination in her eyes. She was a mama bear refusing to give up on her cub.

"Yeah. Uh, yeah. He looked like he wasn't feeling very well, so I had stopped to ask if he was okay—" not true "—and then when I was about to walk up to him, that teacher came around the corner and saw the same thing I did. He just, like…had a seizure, I guess—" also a lie "—like…like they said." I shrugged. "I'm sorry. I wish there was something else I could do for him."

I was hoping to God there was; I needed to make this right. Fix what I screwed up. Whatever that was.

She sighed and slapped the notebook shut. "Yeah, we knew all that. Okay, sweetheart, thanks for coming." Her words were empty. I had crushed her hope.

"Is it okay if…can I go see Brian, maybe? Is he here?"

"Oh. Yes, of course. His room is that way." She gestured vaguely behind her.

"Um, thanks…" I walked away slowly, not knowing

if I should say goodbye or not. I was sure this was the only time Mrs. Wilkes had ever waved a girl through to her son's bedroom.

I walked down a carpeted hallway. All the lights were off except in one room and the door was cracked open. I rapped gently on the door frame. When there was no answer, I peeked through the crack. I could see the end of his bed. Brian was sitting there, blocked mostly from my view by Aaron's tall body. He was facing Brian and holding a big duffle bag. They were talking quietly. I couldn't make out the words, so I pushed the door open the tiniest bit.

"Hello?" I said tentatively.

Aaron turned around and gave me a small, surprised smile. I wasn't prepared for what I saw when he stepped to the side.

I barely recognized Brian. He was gaunt and disheveled, and there was an emptiness in his eyes. Something was missing.

And I was pretty sure I knew what had taken it.

"Hey Anna," Aaron said as he ushered me in.

"Hi Aaron," I said as I let the door swing open, "Hi Bri…" I froze mid-word. Dark movement caught my eye from the corner of the ceiling.

The thing. The monster. It was the shadowy form I had let out of the library that had attacked Brian in the hallway the day of his "seizure," except it wasn't a shadow anymore.

Its huge jaw opened slowly and it let out a low hiss

as it stared down at me with red eyes churning like molten lava. It cowered back into its corner, long limbs compressed so it looked like a grotesque giant spider waiting to strike.

Brian looked up and seemed to see me for the first time. His dead eyes met mine and now I saw something in them. Fury.

"*Get out!*" he screamed. He stood up, his bony frame towering over me. "Get out get out get *out!*"

I didn't argue. I ran. I caught Aaron's shocked expression as I fled, slamming the door on my way out. Running past Mrs. Wilkes, I made my way to the front door, heart pounding, thoughts racing.

I threw open the front door but paused on the threshold. A woman was standing in front of the window to the left of the door. We locked eyes. I stared at her in confusion.

She was…transparent. I could see through her.

She looked over her shoulder slowly, as though to check if I was actually looking at her, like when someone waves to a person right behind you and you think for a moment they're actually waving to you.

"What…" I began. I saw her mouth open as if shocked that I *did* see her. She peered behind me and faded to nothing. The last thing I saw was a terrified expression on her face.

I turned, simultaneously hoping and dreading to see whatever it was that she had been afraid of. The Leech was there, its claws wrapped around the doorframe, its body not quite corporeal but definitely real. It gave a low, warning hiss in my direction.

I fled and didn't look back.

CHAPTER 23
JOHN

Sleep did eventually find me but it was plagued by nightmares. I didn't feel any better, physically or mentally, when I awoke. I sat up slowly and swung my legs over the side of the mattress, temporarily confused when I noticed I was still holding the fireplace poker. Looking out the window, the sky was dark but the trees had a crimson glow, like the ghosts of photos developing in the red light of a darkroom.

I stood up and walked to the window, peering out through the dusky glass. I stared at the scenery below for several minutes, the skeletal branches of trees reaching for me, painted blood-red by an unknown light source. The landscape was so eerily still that I eventually felt as though I were looking at a photograph, or a still from a horror movie, and I placed my hand on the glass to ground myself.

Movement.

It was so unexpected and out of place that I let out a

startled gasp and crouched quickly below the windowsill. I watched my foggy handprint fade and hoped whatever had moved hadn't seen me.

My heart pounded as I gathered the courage to look up. I felt brittle wood crack under my fingertips as I gripped the edge of the sill, ever so slowly pulling myself up just high enough to peer out the window.

Regret knotted up in my belly immediately. There it was. The praying mantis thing. The bloody light illuminated its body enough for me to make it out. It was facing away from me and I could see spikes protruding down its back like a row of butcher knives.

I froze. *Shit shit shit!* Was it looking for me? It hadn't seemed interested in me yesterday when it was attacking Mrs. Campbell.

Was attacking even the right word? It didn't seem to be hurting her, more like…feeding off her, leeching something from her. It had seemed to grow stronger when it touched her.

Maybe I was its next meal. But then again, I was actually *here*, in this place with it, whereas Mrs. Campbell clearly hadn't been. So could—*would*—it hurt me? Attack me? Was it just curious? Whatever its plan, I didn't want to stick around to find out if I was on the menu.

I ducked back below the window. The mantis hadn't seen me yet. I debated whether to stay here or try to escape, but I didn't know where to go or if there was even a safer place to be.

I would try to secure the house. I did an awkward crouching walk over to the bed and tucked the fireplace poker under my arm, choosing to abandon the shovel for now. I scuttled out of the room and as soon as I was confident I would be out of the line of sight of the window, I stood back up. Cringing, I crept down the stairs, feeling my way blindly in the dark. Each tiny creak sounded like a freight train.

When I got to the front door I ran my fingers over it to find the peephole. I put my eye to it and peered out.

Staring back at me was a giant set of hairy, drooling mandibles.

I jumped back and almost yelled, biting my tongue at the last second. I was frozen with the poker held like a baseball bat, my eyes wide, chest pounding. I scanned the room for something to barricade the door, but it was too dark to see anything. I remembered I had seen an empty china cabinet a few yards down the hall during my initial inspection, but the mantis would no doubt hear me dragging it across the floor. I didn't even know if it knew I was here, and I certainly didn't want to draw its attention.

I didn't know what to do. I clearly couldn't just walk out the front door, and I was pretty sure if I tried to fight it, those mandibles would snap me in half like the wishbone from a Thanksgiving turkey.

Somehow and for some reason, it was tracking me, I decided. It was too much of a coincidence for it to be here. I could go back upstairs and just hope it didn't choose to check inside, but I would be so screwed if I got trapped up there.

Unless…the pink bedroom. I remembered its window faced the back yard; the creature wouldn't see me if I snuck out that way. Could I even get to the ground from a second-story window? And if and when I did, where would I go? I decided it didn't matter, as long as I could get a good distance away before it noticed I was no longer there.

I took painstakingly slow steps to the staircase, feeling my way to the edge with my foot, and proceeded to climb them as quietly as humanly possible, still hefting the poker. Even though I definitely wasn't safe, once I reached the pink bedroom, I breathed a sigh of relief. Luckily, I had scouted the house pretty thoroughly the day before and had an excellent visual memory, because the darkness was suffocating.

Feeling around for the window, I opened it ever so carefully and poked my head into the night air. I glanced below, praying to every god I had ever heard of for there to be something I could use to climb down.

A drain pipe. I could just make it out with the faint light. Thank God. Hopefully the mantis couldn't hear anything from the front of the house.

I stuck the handle of the poker in the waistband of the back of my shorts and slid the window open as wide as it could go. I envisioned the end of the poker stabbing me in the spine with one wrong move, but I figured that was a better way to die than become a giant insect's next meal.

Now how to do this? Okay, I could put my foot…

Cruuuuunch!

I froze, confused, then heard the sound again.

With a gasp of horror, I recognized the sound of splintering wood. The mantis was breaking its way through the door. There was no time for thought. I swung myself over the window ledge and half fell, half slid down the drain pipe. I landed with a stumble and sprinted harder than I ever had into the palm trees behind the house.

The unnatural crimson glow illuminated the trees just enough to prevent me from running head first into them. I tripped a few times over the uneven ground, but fueled by adrenaline and pure fear, I kept running.

I only slowed when I heard splashing. It took me a second to realize that I was the one making the noise. I had hit a stream, which seemed very out of place, if this indeed was a reflection of the world I used to belong to. I squinted in the dim light and thought it might be ten feet wide, with a fairly steep embankment on the other side, but it was hard to tell. I leaned over with my hands on my knees to try to catch my breath and gather my wits.

Where now? I didn't have a plan except put as much distance between me and the creature as possible. I could probably climb up the embankment on the other side with a little difficulty, but that would definitely leave a trail. I didn't know how the mantis had tracked me in the first place, maybe by smell or something, but doing this would make it easy.

I would walk in the stream. It would hide my tracks. I had pulled the poker out of my waistband a while back and had somehow managed to keep a grip on it while running. I used it as a walking stick now, making sure I didn't step in any holes or hit any large rocks in the water. It was only up to my knees so it wasn't too difficult. I absently wondered about alligators but then decided if they ate me, I would be all right with that.

It was slow-going and frustrating, but after only thirty minutes or so, the jaundiced sun began to rise, vanquishing the bloody glow. I could see better, but that also meant I could be seen. The embankment had shrunk, and I judged that I could probably get out of the stream just by taking a large step up, but decided to keep going a bit further, just to be safe.

The water was stagnant and cloudy so I couldn't tell if I was moving up- or downstream but I figured it didn't matter anyway. As I observed the way the water swirled around my legs when I took a step forward, I realized that I still was not thirsty. Or hungry.

I furrowed my eyebrows in confusion and was struck hard by the thought I had been avoiding. *I am dead.* I stifled a sob and kept trudging through the water. Once again I considered the possibility that maybe I was in hell. I had died and this was literal hell. What had I done to deserve such a fate?

My self-pity distracted me and I lurched forward. My right foot had stepped into a deep hole and caught me off guard. The poker slipped out of my grasp as I plunged awkwardly into the water. I gasped in surprise just as my face went under, and I not only managed to swallow a ton of the murky water, but inhaled some as well. I got my footing and stood back up, spluttering and coughing.

It took every ounce of strength inside me to not roar in frustration. I scanned the water for the poker but it was too cloudy to see the bottom. I walked around the general vicinity for a minute or two, trying to contain my anger, running my foot over the gravelly bottom, searching blindly for the poker. The toe of my sandal hit something hard and I realized two things: I had found the poker, and both my sandals were still on my feet, which was something close to a miracle.

I fished my weapon out of the water and stepped over the embankment, soaked and miserable. There were gentle rolling hills around me, and I was confused at first. Then I realized I had been walking through a manmade water hazard. I was on what would have been a golf course in the real world.

The real world? But this place was real too. Maybe I just hadn't fully accepted it yet, so in my thoughts I was referring to home as *the real world*. This place, this Void, this warped mirror of the world I knew was too hellish and bizarre to grasp the idea that it was real.

After walking for a while longer, I realized I felt odd. I was relaxing. In spite of these thoughts and my discomfort at being soaking wet, I just accepted my situation. But deep down I knew this feeling wasn't right.

It felt almost…drug-induced. Like the time I stole weed from my brother's room and smoked it with my buddies behind the McDonald's at midnight.

I smiled, lay down in the brittle grass and closed my eyes, trying to relive some of the happier moments from the life I would never live again.

CHAPTER 24
ANNA

I threw the door open without even knocking. "John! John are you here?"

He came around the corner, looking startled. "What are you doing here? It's Saturday." He finally noticed the terror painting my face. "Oh God, what happened?" He took my elbow and led me over to his worn-out couch. I sat.

"I…I went to see Brian. He…that *thing* was there." I started hyperventilating at the memory of its hiss, like nails on a chalkboard making my hackles rise.

"The Leech? Where? Take a breath, tell me what happened."

"I think it's attached to Brian. He looks awful, he looks like he's…wasting away. And he freaked out on me. I think it made him crazy or something. What do we do? *What the fuck do we do?*"

John wrapped me up in his arms. "It's okay. It's gonna be okay."

I pulled back. "Is it, though? Is it? Are you just saying that?"

"I don't think it's going to do much damage yet."

"Yet?"

"Brian is easy prey right now, and it probably doesn't even really understand what is going on."

I was confused. "What do you mean?"

He sighed. "Well, it doesn't live here. It probably got here by accident. It was just following Brian and happened to go through the gate you had opened."

I thought back to how it had cowered into the corner of Brian's room when I came in. Almost like it was scared of me.

"I had no idea what was going on when I got trapped in the Void. It's probably just as confused."

"So…we just have to figure out how to get it back in before it learns the ropes?"

John nodded. "That's my assumption."

I took a deep breath. We could figure this out. We still had time.

"There's one other thing…" I started slowly.

"Yes?"

"So when I was leaving Brian's house—well, fleeing is a better word, I guess—I saw a woman. But she wasn't really there. Or…I don't know. She looked like a ghost, but it was obvious she could see me and she knew I could see her. But I could look right through her. Brian's mom couldn't see her, I could tell for sure."

"Huh." John twisted his mouth and tilted his head.

"Just 'huh'?" I threw up my hands, frustrated. "This is like…a totally different thing, isn't it?"

"No, actually. I've come across these people before. They exist in both worlds simultaneously, but are aren't completely corporeal in either place. I don't know what one of them would be doing around Brian, but I can't imagine it's anything malicious."

This was crazy. From everything John had told me in our last five sessions together, he always implied that there weren't any people in the Void.

"Great," I exclaimed, scrubbing my hands over my exhausted eyes, "it's just one thing after another, isn't it?" But right now I had more important things to worry about. "Okay. What about Brian?" He hadn't addressed that yet. It seemed like he was avoiding it. "What's happening to him? Was it my fault?" I wrung my hands, terrified of the answer.

"Anna…" He paused and gave me a sympathetic look. "You didn't know what you were doing. You can't think of this as your fault."

"But it is, though, right? I mean, this happened to him because of what I did in the library."

"You didn't *do* anything. You were just the wrong person, in the wrong place, at the wrong time. From what you've told me, it seemed like the Leech had latched onto this kid. He was probably stalking him, liked the way he tasted or something."

I shuddered at the thought but wasn't going to be deterred, I had to know. "John. Just tell me. Did that thing get out because I was there? Did it attack Brian in our world and now he's seriously messed up?" I pretty much already knew the answer.

John sighed. "Yes."

I groaned and rested my elbows on the counter, head in my hands. I felt like I was going to vomit. This was all my fault, no matter how John tried to reassure me that it wasn't.

"But how?" I asked, mumbling into my hands. I looked up.

"How did it get out?"

"Yeah," I responded, "and can it live here? Can we send it back to the Void? Brian will be better after it's gone, right?"

"No," John said bluntly.

"No?" I asked slowly. "No to which question?"

"Brian isn't going to get better once the Leech is gone."

"How long will it take for him to get better?"

"Anna," John sighed and ran his hands over his bald head, "Brian is probably not going to be the same for the rest of his life. The Leech fed off of his physical form. He has nowhere to draw more energy from to heal his mind and body. He might improve a little as the years go by but..."

I jumped up. "No! No, you have to be wrong!" I started pacing, I could taste bile in my mouth and thought I was going to vomit, my body trying to physically expel the guilt that seeped into my gut. "You don't know everything, right? You've said that you don't know everything. I have to make him better. I have to! This is my fault!" I thought of Brian's family and friends, his football career, his entire life. Ruined. Because of me.

He was as good as dead. I killed him. I dropped back onto the couch, sobs wracking my body. I had never felt this way in my life. Guilt and despair suffocated my soul. I wanted to die. I wanted to trade my life for Brian's. I barely knew him, but I didn't care. I couldn't live with this.

I was crossing into the Void.

A tiny part of my mind that wasn't overwhelmed by emotion realized this. My grief was crossing me over. I felt John's arms around me but they were starting to feel different, stronger.

"Anna," he whispered gently, trying to calm me down, then more urgently, "Anna. This isn't safe. Take a deep breath. Try to relax." But his voice sounded weird. It was warping, each word sounding less and less like John. My head was resting on his chest, but the stiff linen of his gray button-down shirt began to feel different on my cheek. When I opened my eyes, the buttons were gone. His shirt was white.

I tried to look up at his face and ask him what was going on but I could feel that he was physically restraining me from doing so. I could only look down. I saw bare, muscular calves sticking out of jeans shorts.

Confusion cut through my grief and calmed me down. I took some deep breaths, and John's clothes faded back into a gray plaid button-down shirt and long pants.

My vision was blurry and watery with tears. Had I imagined that?

"What was…" I hiccupped, but he interrupted me, shoving a glass of water into my hands.

"Relax," he said, not meeting my eyes. "Drink."

I drank a few sips, took some shuddering breaths and started again, "John, how come you…"

He interrupted once more. "You started crossing over, Anna. It's not surprising, given how upset you were, but it's more dangerous when you're aware of it. Your consciousness crosses over with your astral as well, whereas with someone else it wouldn't. Given your recent experiences, I'd assume you are always going to be aware of it now. You need to be careful."

"But you were…"

He cut me off again. "Yes, I started crossing too. You drew me in with you. That's one way it can happen."

He wasn't going to let me ask, but I wasn't going to let it go. I was calming down enough to know what I needed to move on. For now.

"I will find a way," I choked. "I will find a way to fix him."

"And I will help you as best I can. But unfortunately you can't worry about him right now. We need to get the Leech back into the Void or it will find someone else to feed on. If you think you feel awful now, think of how you will feel when you have two people's blood on your hands."

His words shocked me, and he had meant for them to. He wanted me to focus. To forget about what had just happened.

I steeled myself and clenched my jaw in determination. “Okay. What do we do?”

“We kill it.”

CHAPTER 25
ANNA

Despite John's promises, he clearly didn't have all the answers. I refused to believe there was no way to help Brian. If we did kill it, like he claimed we could, things had to go back to normal. Didn't they?

I locked my bedroom door and got comfortable in my desk chair. I pulled up Google on my laptop and rested my fingers on the keyboard. What should I even search, though? I needed to learn more about the Void so I could figure out how to get Brian back.

Searching *parallel universe* seemed like a good start, even though it felt ridiculous. I combed through search results for about forty-five minutes. It was probably the first time ever I'd clicked past page two of Google. Mostly stuff about aliens and time travel and chaos theory.

"...the idea of parallel universes has boggled the minds of scientists, philosophers, bloggers, and average folk alike. Perhaps we're just a sliver of time away from an alternate existence, or perhaps regular people we pass on the street are beings from another universe that have already mastered the art of interdimensional travel."

Ah, this seemed like a good term. So I searched *interdimensional travel.* More bullshit. I combed through a forum about people claiming they'd traveled to alternate dimensions. A few people talked about getting abducted by aliens on a regular basis. One guy claimed he crossed into another dimension in his sleep where everyone spoke backwards and he was invisible. After lots of sighing and eye-rolling I held my cursor over the close box when I spotted an entry by user RgulrCat78 titled *Empty world? Anyone else??* I sat up a little straighter and clicked on the headline.

> "Sooooo, hoping someone has had a similar experience. Sometimes when I sleep I end up this like alternate dimension or whatever. It's pretty empty for the most part except one time I saw this huge scary ass monster looking thing, not human like at all. I got scared and kind of snapped back into my body and woke up. It used to be kind of cool to explore this place (even though I was pretty sure I was dreaming or crazy or something) because all the houses and stuff were empty and like old. But now I am terrified to go back because of this monster thing. How do I stop it?? I feel like if anyone is going to believe me it will be someone in this thread. HELP."

This caught my attention. It sounded sort of like what John described. Someone had replied.

"whats your email, I might know what you're talking about."

Comment Deleted

Damn it! I assumed the deleted comment was probably RgulrCat78's email. Then I noticed the date of the original post: 09/18/2013. I groaned. This was from over three years ago. The likelihood that RgulrCat78 still checked this thread was pretty low. Well, it was worth a try. I clicked *reply* underneath the original post and typed, "Did you get any info? I need some answers as well."

I hit enter and a box popped up telling me I needed to create an account to post in the forum. I scoffed. Of course. After filling out the stupid form with my email and a fake name, it finally let me reply. My comment posted as username anonymous19001. I didn't have much hope that this would reach Regular Cat, but whatever, it was worth a shot.

CHAPTER 26
JOHN

I traveled for three days. I spent the nights walking, and during daylight I holed up in buildings. I could feel in my gut that the mantis was still following me and I was coming to the reluctant conclusion that I was going to have to address the situation, to put it mildly, instead of just running from it. The biggest problem with that, though, even more so than how, was that I was fading fast. Every day I got a little weaker. It was like I was hungry but in my soul, like I needed sustenance but I didn't know what it was.

The sun was rising for the fourth time since I had arrived in this place, and I was searching for shelter. I spotted a sidewalk leading across from what would have probably been a lawn, but here was just dry, brittle grass sparsely populating a lot of sand and gravel. It looked like it may have once been a house but had been converted into a business since there was a parking lot around the back. It seemed as good a place as any. None of the doors were locked here, but I could lock them once I went in. I had yet to figure out the reason for the idiosyncrasies of this world.

I ducked inside, pushing open the glass door gently. Tiny cracks spiderwebbed out underneath my fingertips. I eased it closed, afraid it would shatter, and took in my surroundings.

Some of the shelves actually still had items on them, the likes of which led me to believe I was in an army navy store. I gathered the available merchandise and lined everything up on the floor.

There was a camo jacket, three backpacks, several blankets, a flashlight, and four pairs of boots. The store was actually kind of neat. Of course, all the things I found were in very poor condition: the fabric was frayed and torn, the soles of the boots were crumbling, and, to my dismay, the flashlight didn't work.

I rounded a corner to check out another room and froze.

Guns. Lots of guns.

I rushed toward the nearest one. My dad had taken me hunting a few times and showed me how to use a shotgun. Granted, these were nothing like a shotgun but after a minute or two of fiddling, I figured out how to check the chamber. My heart sank. Of course it was empty. What was I expecting? First of all, no store would keep a loaded gun hanging on the wall, and it wasn't surprising that this world wouldn't have helpful details like functional bullets.

But there were also knives. A bit rusty, but in usable shape. A couple were frighteningly large and still pretty sharp. Big step up from the fireplace poker. I moved them to a shelf in the main room, afraid they would fall off the wall and injure me.

This is it, I thought, *this is where I will stay*. Why not? Would I ever find somewhere better? I could be armed here. There were probably a few other useful things I hadn't discovered yet. I didn't know if these monsters could be killed, but if I had a chance, this was probably the best place to be. So I addressed one problem. I hadn't really realized it was a problem until this moment, not having a destination. I felt like I had accomplished something. A tingle of hope fluttered in my chest. Maybe I could find a way home after all.

But then there was the other issue. The one I dreaded thinking about. I was pretty sure I needed to kill the mantis. It was the only way I could stop running. And it had to be sooner rather than later because I was getting weaker by the day. Soon I wouldn't be able to defend myself. I would be a sitting duck.

My morbid thoughts crushed the sliver of hope I had had a moment before. Maybe I was done for anyway. That was kind of what this hunger felt like, wasting away. I could accept that I would die, if it was possible to die twice, but I was going to go down fighting.

Time to stop being prey and become the hunter.

CHAPTER 27
ANNA

More than a week had gone by and I hadn't gotten a response to my reply on the thread. I was losing faith that this would work. Waiting and hoping was making the days drag. The only thing keeping me from going crazy were my visits with John.

Every day he would tell me stories about the Void and explain a little bit more. We would talk for an hour or so after I got home from school, and more than once my mom had to text me to remind me to come home for dinner. My parents were so proud of me for helping the old man next door clean out his attic. I felt bad for keeping up the lie, but it wasn't like I could tell them the truth.

Every time I brought up Brian and the Leech, John kept telling me he was coming up with a plan but wouldn't give me any details. I was starting to think he was lying. He also still wouldn't tell me how he got stuck in the Void for a whole year, how he survived there, or why he thought he was going to die and needed my help. That last one was the main thing that bugged me. I deserved to know. I had asked him multiple times and it was always some promise of "soon", which seemed like a pretty bullshit time frame.

My relationship with Becca was suffering. She knew something was up that I wasn't telling her, and she was waiting. We had told each other everything since the fifth grade, and I was pretty sure she would believe me, but I was still looking for the words to explain this new aspect of my life without sounding insane.

It had been awkward between us and I hated it, so I invited her over after school to try to regain some normalcy. I grabbed a couple sodas from the fridge and handed one to Becca. I opened my can and plopped on the couch. As I reached for the remote, she grabbed it first and stood over me, staring.

"What?" I asked.

"Come on Anna! Out with it! You can't keep pretending everything's normal. This is so stupid." She sat down next to me and took my hand in both of hers, pleading with her eyes. "I'm your best friend. Don't you trust me?" Tears welled up in her eyes, making the deep blue sparkle like the ocean at dusk, and its waves crashed over me with overwhelming guilt.

"Okay," I sighed, and scrubbed the heel of my hand over my exhausted eyes.

"Okay?" she said, sitting up straighter.

"Yes. I'll tell you. But you have to promise to

believe me."

"Of course I promise!" She scoffed. After all, I had already admitted some of the crazy shit that had happened, and she had seen how messed up Brian had been after our encounter, so she had a bit of proof that at least *something* weird was happening.

"You know how I've been helping my next-door neighbor clean out his attic?"

"Yeah." She rolled her eyes. "That's total bullshit. You're finally going to tell me what's going on there?" Of course she knew. "You're not having some gold-digger affair, are you?"

"What? *Hell,* no! Seriously? *That's* your guess?"

"Well, I had to ask. You don't have a job and your parents are pretty stingy about giving you money, so…"

"Becca, stop!" Although she was right about the job thing. I should get on that.

"Okay, okay," she conceded, "go ahead." She clasped her hands in her lap and looked at me, eyebrows raised in mock patience. I sighed.

"John…my neighbor…knew some of what had been happening with me and sort of…talked me into telling him about the thing that happened with Brian." I rushed through the sentence, hoping it was a good intro. "The same kind of crazy, unbelievable shit that's been happening to me over the last few weeks started happening to him like fifteen years ago. He knows stuff."

"Whoa. No way. Are you sure he isn't messing with you?" she asked, wide-eyed.

"Positive. He described the same things without me saying anything first." I sat back on the couch, releasing a deep breath. I felt a little better already.

"So what kinds of things has he told you?" She was rapt, soaking it all in.

I told her a lot of what he told me. About the Void and what it was like. About the leeches and the echoes of people they fed on.

"So he…crosses over…a lot?" she asked, looking more doubtful by the moment. It was making me nervous.

"Well, yeah."

"Why? Why would he want to do that? It sounds awful." She shuddered.

"I…I don't know. He hasn't told me that yet." She looked at me skeptically. "He said he will soon, though!"

"I don't know Anna." She sat back on the couch and sighed. "What are the chances that this guy lives next door to you and just *happens* to have experienced the same stuff? How is that just a coincidence? This all sounds kind of…unbelievable. Like more than kind of."

"You said you'd believe me!" I pleaded. And I was pretty sure the living next door to me thing wasn't a coincidence.

"I know! I know. And I do," she said. But I didn't believe *her*. "It's just…are you sure he's telling you the truth? I mean, I know you think you saw what you saw, but maybe he's just taking advantage…"

"I *think*? Becca, I know what I saw!" I was angry

now. "I *know* it was real!"

"Okay, I'm sorry," she said calmly, softening her features, trying to convince me. "Just to be sure that he's telling the truth, though, could you ask him to prove it? To show you?"

"But would you believe me even then?" I felt my throat tighten and I clenched my jaw to keep the tears at bay.

"Yes. And I believe you now, I swear. But…just so you know. For sure." She paused, and my tears spilled.

"I don't know," I said, sniffling, and she gave me a hug. "I've been too scared to ask. I don't like that I'm dragging you into this." Which was also why I wasn't going to tell her about what happened when I went over to Brian's house. Not yet, anyway. "And he uh…he doesn't know—".

"Doesn't know you're telling me? Would he be mad?"

"I don't know. I mean, he's a pretty nice guy. Like really, you should meet him. He doesn't seem like a typical old guy. More like a cool uncle or something. He has a PlayStation!"

She laughed. "For real?"

"For real." I smiled. We'd played a couple times when things got too overwhelming for me.

"But Becca," I said, serious again, "I think I found something online that makes it seem like other people have been to this place too."

"What? No way!" Now she was curious. "Lemme

see!"

I pulled out my laptop and showed her the thread I found. She nodded slowly as she read the post from RgulrCat78 and my comment underneath.

"Okay," she said, "so have they emailed you?"

I looked at her incredulously. "Really? You think I wouldn't have mentioned that as like, the first thing?"

She scoffed. "Fine. Well, I bet Aaron can help."

"Aaron? Why? I am *not* sharing any of this with him." Especially since he'd already seen Brian freak out on me.

"No, no. You don't have to. You know he's thinking about majoring in computer science? He's really good. Just give him the username and tell him you're looking for more posts anywhere online from this Regular Cat person. It's a pretty unique username. I bet she uses it a lot."

"She? What makes you think it's a 'she'?" I asked. Becca shrugged. "Okay. I guess we can ask him. But we need an excuse for why we're looking."

"We could say that she posted something online about writing college applications and it seems really good so we wanted to see if she wrote anything else. I mentioned to him that I was having trouble with my application." She suggested.

"I don't know," I said doubtfully, "what if he asks to see it? And if he did find other stuff she posted, maybe it's all weird stuff like her comment there." I gestured vaguely to the laptop.

"Okay, well you suggest something then! Or we could just stick to the basics and Google it."

An idea hit me and its obviousness made me facepalm. "Her username. Like you said, it's pretty unique right?"

"Yeah. And?"

"Well, what if it's her email? I use my email as my username all the time, without the 'at gmail' part."

"Yes!" she exclaimed, "I do that too!" Her face fell. "But we don't know what server she uses."

"That's okay. We can just try a bunch. Gmail, Hotmail, all the popular ones. Just send a vague email saying we saw her post on that specific thread and she'd probably respond. Right?"

"Yeah, I bet you're right. Maybe even make it seem like we know her? She might be more likely to respond."

So we drafted an email.

RgulrCat78,

Hi there, haven't talked to you in a while! I saw your post titled *Empty world. Anyone else?* from 2013. I am hoping you can answer a few questions for me. I'd appreciate a response ASAP. Thanks.

Vague enough to not sound crazy if it wasn't the right person, but containing enough info that she should know what I talking about if it *was* the right person. Becca nodded.

"And now we wait?" she asked.

"Now we wait," I stated with a small smile. She said "we". She was in this with me. I knew it was selfish to be happy about that, and a pang of guilt ran through me. But I had missed her. Even though I had John, I still felt alone. Isolated. And she had wanted this, right? I tried to keep it from her and she wouldn't let me. So I tried to convince myself that I shouldn't feel guilty. But I did. This might be dangerous. It *was* dangerous. I had let out a monster.

We sat in silence for a while. I slammed the laptop closed and she jumped. "Sorry," I said, "I just can't think about this anymore right now. Can we talk about something else?"

So we did. We talked about boring school stuff and boys and college. I was definitely taking a year off. Becca had already been accepted into a community college to do her pre-reqs since she wasn't positive on what she wanted to do yet. We both needed to find jobs. Her for the summer, me something a little more permanent since I would be working at least a year. We browsed on our phones for a while, but we were both distracted. I kept looking for the little envelope icon to pop up on my alert bar.

I needed that email. And I needed to talk to John.

CHAPTER 28
JOHN

If only I had bullets. Based on my limited experience here, I was pretty sure that if I was able to cross back home from this spot, I would find the merchandise that I saw on the shelves right now, but in better condition, along with a fully stocked store. But why? What made the objects that had crossed over special? Was it just bad luck that there was no ammo at this store, but I could possibly find some somewhere else? Or was there something about bullets that prevented them from being mirrored in the Void at all?

I sat on the floor hugging my knees, discouraged and feeling sorry for myself. With a groan, I pushed myself up and inspected one of the pairs of combat boots that sat on a low shelf. They looked like a woman's size, but after inspecting the very faded and frayed tag on the tongue of the shoe, I was able to distinguish "mens size 6.5". Great. Who had feet that small?

I looked inside the tongue of the next pair of shoes

but couldn't make out the writing. Picking up the right boot of both pairs, I placed them sole to sole. Looked like the same size. So stupid. What are the chances of two pairs of the smallest sized boots crossing over, but no others? I cursed my normal-sized feet.

I checked out the jacket. It was on the last hook on the rack, as though in the real world it was behind all the others. XXL. Seriously? Was this place stocked for some kind of reverse clown? Tiny feet and a huge body?

The backpack was on the back of shelf labeled "tents" as though it had been put back in the wrong spot and forgotten about. I hefted it off the shelf and went through all the pockets. It was empty, but in decent condition. Placing it on the floor, I went over to the blanket. It was white camo, meant for snowy conditions. So not appropriate in Florida. I sighed. I wouldn't be able to use this outside. I might as well be waving a red flag.

There were some other items hanging around. Three parachutes and two ready-to-eat meal packets were labeled "liver and onions". I almost gagged. You'd have to be pretty desperate to eat that, luckily I still wasn't interested in eating.

There was something odd about the stock that had crossed over, but I couldn't quite put my finger on it. It seemed like everything here was either unpopular or in the wrong place, like it was something that wouldn't have been even looked at, let alone bought, in ages. Was that the commonality? Unwanted things? But no. I had seen beds, school desks, cash registers, even a few antique cars in garages. None of those things would be unwanted.

Not unwanted but…unmoved. Yes. Unmoved. I thought of all the things I seen.

Okay, beds. Check.

Desks, cash registers. Check.

Cars. No, cars get driven. I sighed, disappointed that my theory fell through.

But wait. I distinctly remembered all of them being *antique* cars since my dad was a fanatic. Some people had cars like that in garages for years. They were collectors' items, not for transportation.

I hadn't seen any clothes, buses, dishes in cabinets, chairs, or, of course, people. These were all things that moved around constantly or got used on a regular basis. It was like things that stayed in the same spot for a while kind of burned through, or get imprinted.

This made sense. I wasn't sure how useful this knowledge was, but I felt proud of myself for figuring it out, assuming I actually had. I stood up a little straighter. I was smart. Kind of. *I can do this. I can survive.*

But this wouldn't help me find bullets. It reinforced the fact that anything remotely useful wouldn't be available in the Void.

Unless…

I rushed to the room with the guns hanging on the wall and started throwing open the cabinets lining the floor.

Empty. Empty. A box that had some packets labeled "emergency purified drinking water". I rummaged through it, feverishly whipping the packets over my shoulder. Nothing. I groaned in frustration. *Keep looking.*

Another cabinet. Empty. The next one had another box, and my heart raced with anticipation. I ripped it open. More goddamn parachutes.

"Damn it, damn it, damn it!" I whipped the box back into the cabinet as hard as I could and went to slam the door when I heard a faint "clink" as though the box had hit something.

I calmed my breathing and carefully removed the box, setting it on the floor. I leaned into the cabinet, which was a good three feet deep, wishing I had a flashlight that actually worked.

I swept my fingers across the bottom back edge of the space and paused as I felt a small box way in the corner. I fished it out, fingers shaking. The cardboard was too faded to read the label. I carefully tore open the box and dumped it into my hand, holding my breath. *Please please please.*

Batteries.

My heart sank and rage boiled in my chest. I just couldn't catch a break. I leapt to my feet and hurled the handful of batteries at the wall. I roared profanities at the empty room and kicked the cabinet door until it splintered and hung off the rusty hinges.

There wasn't much left to take my anger out on so I stood red-faced and chest heaving in the center of the mostly empty room. I grabbed a gun and was about to throw it at the lone window on the far wall but froze right before I let go.

The mantis was across the street, facing away from me.

I stood completely still, just staring, mouth agape, as it stalked toward the ghostly image of a man standing outside a convenience store. The figure was solidifying as the creature got closer.

Suddenly it turned and I ducked but realized it wasn't looking at me. I stood up slowly and leaned to the left so I could see what it was focused on, forgetting to be scared for a moment in my curiosity.

Another monster.

~

Holy shit! I crouched down quickly but couldn't take my eyes off the thing. It was lizard-like, walking on all fours, slightly smaller than the mantis. Its belly skimmed the ground as it slunk forward, huge talons scratching the pavement. The mantis tensed, the knife-like scales on its back rising like hackles. Its mandibles spread open and I heard it shriek, a sound somewhere between nails on a chalkboard and the eerie baby-like scream of a fisher cat. I flinched at the noise and stifled the urge to clap my hands over my ears.

It was pretty clear an epic battle was about to ensue.

I was sure the mantis had it in the bag until the lizard opened its mouth and I saw three rows of deadly looking teeth, dripping a bright-blue liquid that steamed when it hit the ground. My pulse quickened as I imagined those teeth piercing my flesh, and I decided I'd much rather get eaten by the mantis's hairy drooling mandibles.

They lunged at each other and I watched in horrified fascination from the relative safety of the gun room. The lizard was quick. It reared up on its hind legs and sank its teeth into the insect's belly. The mantis shrieked again and snapped its jaws onto the side of the lizard's shoulder.

The battle picked up and it was hard to follow exactly what was happening, just a whirlwind of claws, teeth, and scales.

After what seemed like forever, the movement started to slow. There was black oily blood everywhere and both creatures were badly injured. The lizard stumbled back down to all fours. Big mistake.

In a final burst of strength, the mantis clamped its bloody mandibles down on the back of the lizard's neck, and with a twist, snapped it at an impossible angle. The lizard fell into a heap on the ground, black blood mixing with the florescent venom dripping from its mouth.

The mantis wobbled, clearly seriously injured, one hairy arm hanging limply at its side, a deep wound in its belly oozing blood. It limped toward the hazy figure who was presumably the cause of the battle, although I had forgotten about him in the chaos. It was then that a very frightening realization hit me.

This is it; this is my chance. The mantis was badly wounded. It was distracted. I would never get a better opportunity. I was getting weaker by the day. It was now or never. I didn't think it through any further.

I sprinted back into the main area of the store and searched frantically for the large hunting knife I had set down somewhere. *Where is it where is it where is it?*

Aha! I swiped the knife off a nearby shelf and rushed to the exit but paused with my hand on the door. I took a deep breath. *Do it. Don't think.*

I pushed the door open and stepped out, heart pounding in my chest. As it swung shut behind me, I felt very exposed, but the mantis either didn't notice or didn't care about me. It seemed to be assessing its injuries.

Pushing my fear into a dark corner of my mind, I sprinted at it with a yell. It turned toward me but I was on it before it could react. I jumped on its back and searing pain shot through me as the razor sharp scales protruding from the center of its spine pierced my flesh.

I didn't slow, couldn't afford to. I wrapped my left arm around its neck and heaved myself up, feeling its hot drool drip on my forearm.

It reared up and screeched, trying to shake me off. Its mandibles snapped at me, but it couldn't lean its head at the angle needed to get a grip on my arm. With another cry, I raised my right arm high and brought the knife down as hard as I could, stabbing the top of its slimy head.

Zombie movies had given me an unrealistic expectation about how easy it was to stab something in the head. The fourteen-inch blade stopped less than a quarter of the way in after I hit something hard.

The mantis shrieked again and bucked wildly. I saw its arm reach around towards me and I cried out as a sharp claw raked the flesh of my calf.

Fueled by adrenaline and terror, I wrapped my legs around the creature's thorax. Letting go of its neck, I gripped the knife with both hands and pulled it down into the creature's head with every ounce of strength in my body, feeling the deep burn of my ab muscles tearing with the effort of holding me in place. I felt the knife crack through bone and then slide into soft tissue with a sickening squelch.

The mantis gave one final shudder and fell to the ground.

CHAPTER 29
ANNA

"Fine."

"Fine? For real?" I asked, shocked.

"I suppose. You almost crossed over by accident last week so I might as well help you do it responsibly. I knew we would need to do it soon anyway, so I prepared."

I sat on John's couch, nearly bouncing with a nauseating mix of anticipation and dread. My talk with Becca yesterday had spurred me to press him for more information. I had made some good arguments, apparently. I was waiting until *after* our session to break the news that Becca knew about almost everything. I was pretty sure he wouldn't be too thrilled.

He stood. "Okay get up. Help me move the couch."

I furrowed my eyebrows, but helped him push the couch and coffee table against the far wall.

He left me standing awkwardly in the center of the now mostly cleared out area while he went into his bedroom. He came out pulling a fully inflated air mattress resting on its edge. I ran over to help. This was so weird.

"Okay. Drop it here," he said with a grunt. His arms shook a tiny bit after we set it down, and I was reminded that he was probably in his late eighties, maybe early nineties. He just seemed so cool that sometimes I forgot.

We stood next to the air mattress for a moment in silence, him with his hands on his hips. We were both unsure but for different reasons.

"Alright," he said with a sigh, "come on." I followed him into his bedroom where there was a square marked out on the floor with painter's tape. *What the hell is going on?*

He looked at me pointedly. "So. A few things. Entering the Void intentionally is different from when you get pulled in accidentally like you did when you got upset about Brian. I have to…*we* have to actually pull apart from our bodies. It's a weird and uncomfortable process, but I can help you through it."

I was not liking the sound of this and was definitely considering backing out, but he continued, "Next thing. We each have a trigger that allows us to enter the Void. I assume everyone who can do this has one. Mine is high-pitched noises. Took me a while to realize it." He reached to his night stand and grabbed a whistle. I had the urge to laugh at the ridiculousness of whatever this bizarre ritual was, but then he looked at me with sympathy.

"What?"

"I was hoping your trigger was the same as mine, but

from what you've told me, I think I've figured it out, and unfortunately it isn't."

"Okay, so what do you think it is?"

"Pain."

"*Pain?* Fantastic," I replied with a groan. "So what happens now?"

"Well, I figured I can either step on your foot—" he pointed at my very bruised, probably broken toe "—or slap you across the face. Unless you have a better idea."

I laughed out loud, but then saw his blank expression.

"Wait…you're serious? Hell no!" I scoffed.

"Don't you want to do this?" he asked in all seriousness. He put the whistle to his lips and blew. I cringed at the pitch.

"Well, of course I do!" I said, covering my ears.

"Okay then, here we go." He stomped down on my foot and I screamed. White-hot pain shot up my leg and I squeezed my eyes shut. Just as I was about to shout some pretty harsh obscenities, I opened my eyes and the words died in my mouth. The room was nearly empty and the carpet was tattered and gray. The mattress was gone and I watched the metal bedframe rust before my eyes. The air felt heavy, pressing on my skin.

"What the…" I looked over at John and he was…blurry. I blinked and shook my head, thinking for a moment that it was my eyes, but no, it was him. His image was jumpy like I couldn't focus.

"Why are you…" I started.

"Don't worry about that right now," he said, but his voice sounded weird too, possessed almost, two pitches overlapping.

"Do you see the tape on the floor over there? Head towards it, I'll be right behind you."

I was terrified, pain forgotten. I couldn't do anything other than follow his direction. Breathing heavily, I took some shaky steps forward. After several feet it started to get harder. I felt John's hand on my upper back, pushing me forward. Even with his help, it was difficult. I felt like I was walking through waist-deep mud. I started panting but urged myself on, my legs straining. Determination hit me. Clenching my jaw, I pressed on, still feeling John's presence behind me.

I was nearly out of steam by the time I reached the middle of the living room, barren except for the square outlined on the floor with tape. I lunged forward with one final burst of strength, my runner's legs carrying me just over the tape. I was caught off guard by the sudden release of tension, like someone had cut an invisible rubber band that had been holding me back. I stumbled forward, nearly falling on my face.

"What the…" I started as I turned to look at John, but my gaze locked onto a body lying face-down in the middle of the living room. It was wearing a black tank-top, jeans, and purple flip-flops. Straight brown hair hung over its face.

My face.

I gasped and leapt backwards, not comprehending

what I was seeing.

"John! What's hap—" But John wasn't there. There was a kid. Tall, dark hair, maybe just a little older than me.

"What the fuck!" I yelled, cowering back. "Where's John? Who are *you?*" I looked around frantically. "John! John! There's someone here!" I yelled for him, backing away slowly, even though he didn't seem threatening.

"Anna, it's me." Held up his hands in surrender, not attempting to approach.

"What are you talking about? What's going on?" I was so confused. My body was lying on the floor and a strange boy who claimed to know me had appeared in John's living room. *Where the hell is John?*

"It's me, it's John," he said delicately. I looked at him blankly, still not understanding. His bright white t-shirt clashed with the drab landscape around us.

I laughed nervously, on the edge of hysterics.

"No, really, Anna, it's me, I swear." He gestured vaguely to himself. "This is who I am, it's just that you haven't seen…the real me, I guess?" He shrugged and gave me a small smile.

I just stared at him, mouth open, trying to make words happen, but I couldn't find any that would make sense coming out of my mouth. There was something familiar about him, but I wasn't sure what. His crooked grin? His eyes? Just as John didn't seem as old as he was, the reason for which I could never put my finger on, this boy didn't seem as young as he looked.

I shook my head. "Prove it!"

"Okay. Well, I just stepped on your foot, which you were not happy about…sorry about that, by the way. We first spoke at length when you came over to apologize about not taking out my trash." He started to tick off on his fingers. "I drugged you with lemonade…again sorry, you told me I was the only old guy you knew who owned video games, when you were twelve you fell off your bike in front of my house and I went and got your mom for you. Is that enough?"

"But…but why…why do you look different? Why aren't you old? What the *hell* is happening right now?" He had the same mannerisms as John, the same inflection in his voice. But how could this be the same person?

"Well," he sighed, "it is a *very* long story."

CHAPTER 30
JOHN

I rolled awkwardly off the mantis's back and stared at the two dead monsters. My limbs shook and my skin was slick with sweat and blood. I was standing in a puddle of congealing non-human gore. I dropped the knife and dry-heaved over the pavement. Cutting through the overwhelming feelings of disgust and horror was tiny trickle of relief and amazement.

I did it. I killed it. I was free.

For now.

Seemingly out of nowhere, a deep need hit me. It was like smelling food when you're starving. I stood up a little straighter and furrowed my brow, perplexed.

I almost missed it. A faint, dark shadow was rising like an ominous cloud from the massive dead insect at my feet. Before I could think about what I was doing, I reached out to touch it, to see if it had substance.

A wave of electric pain shot up my arm.

Sadness, fear, anger, joy, resentment, rage, and a

thousand other emotions that I didn't know the name for raced through me at once.

I fell to my knees and gasped, overwhelmed with the sensation that I was about to rip apart, my body unable to contain such an onslaught of feeling.

I don't know how long I was on the ground with my head in my bloody hands, my mind unable to do anything except try to process the intensity of emotion. When I could finally move, the shadow was gone.

So was my hunger.

The deep, soul-crushing, non-physical hunger I had been suffering from for the last few days had vanished. Not only was it gone, I felt amazingly refreshed, like I had just slept for ten hours. But under all that I felt just a tiny bit…dirty. Tainted. Wrong.

Not wanting to process what the hell had just happened quite yet, I stepped away and kicked off my sandals. I stripped off my ruined clothes down to just my boxers, discarded them in a careless heap on the ground, and walked back toward the army navy store. It wasn't like anyone was around to see me mostly naked anyway. Even if there was, I was pretty sure the gore behind me would be far more notable.

I vaguely noticed that the sign out front named the store as Military Surplus Outlet, but the middle of the word military was faded so it looked like M Y Surplus Outlet. My surplus outlet. I was the only one here, so I supposed that was fitting.

Walking inside, I grabbed the white camo blanket

from the shelf and sat down on it on the floor, like I was at a bizarre, morbid picnic. I pulled my knees to my chest and rested my head down, but popped it back up immediately.

I was barely in pain. I jumped to my feet and twisted awkwardly so I could see the back of my calf. There was indeed evidence of a pretty significant wound, but it was more like a scar, still healing. Except where a fresh scar would normally be pink and raw, the skin was gray and shimmery like an oil slick. There was crusting blood around it and some black substance I preferred to not think about.

I tucked my chin to try to get a good look at my stomach. I realized how much I had taken mirrors for granted. There were five inch-long vertical wounds running in a line diagonally across my abdomen, about two inches apart, where the spines of the mantis had pierced me. They had also partially healed into this odd gray scar.

I touched one delicately. It hurt like a bad bruise, but nothing like the pain I had felt when it had happened and should be feeling now. Even though my sense of time was warped here, it couldn't have happened more than fifteen minutes ago.

I shook my head in confusion. I was filthy, bloody, and overwhelmed. I lay down on the blanket and begged sleep to come, but I wasn't tired. I felt physically energized, but my brain needed a break. I didn't want to think about anything right now, but I guess I had no choice.

I had a lot of new information to process. I knew, or was pretty sure, why certain things were in the Void and some weren't. This knowledge was bound to be useful. The mantis was dead. There were other creatures here who leech off the echoes of people who appear here briefly. I had assumed that already based on my limited experiences when I still had a real body and lived amongst other people. God, I was lonely. Already.

But the final thing. I no longer felt like I was wasting away. And that feeling had disappeared the moment I touched the shadow floating over the mantis. Even though I had just slaughtered a giant insect and had confirmed I was living among monsters, this fact bothered me more. Because whatever I had been starving for, whatever the thing was that my soul had craved, had risen from the body of a dead monster, and I had no way of knowing if or when I would need another meal.

CHAPTER 31
JOHN

I woke up the next morning and it took me a minute to figure out why something felt off.

I was wearing clothes, and I was clean.

What in the hell?

Had I gotten dressed and forgotten? No way. It took me forever to fall asleep. I would have remembered. I checked my calf and stomach. I still had the weird silvery scars, so yesterday definitely hadn't been some vivid nightmare. It was like I went to sleep and pressed a reset button.

Maybe that was exactly what happened. I scrubbed the sleep from my eyes and sighed. Just one more mystery to solve.

I went to the gun room and looked out the window. The bodies of the dead monsters were gone, a trail of dried blood leading behind the convenience store, as though they had been dragged. I shuddered. In my mind, something bigger and scarier had taken the opportunity for a free meal. I had concluded that the Leeches didn't need physical food, but maybe I had been wrong.

The bloody heap of clothes I'd left outside was gone too, although I supposed it was possible that it had been swept away with the carcasses. I was grateful to not be half-naked and dirty, of course, but this was just too weird. I stood up and examined the blanket. The white camo was smeared with blood. I shook my head, confused.

A few weeks ago, my buddy Andy had showed me a computer game he had just gotten. The player controls a marine who goes around killing monsters and if you get injured enough, you die. But then if you have another life, you re-spawn, good as new, and get to start again.

It felt eerily similar to that. Except instead of dying, I went to sleep and woke up fresh as a daisy. I pulled at the hem of my shirt, creeped out. But the more I thought about it, it started to make sense. It was hard to forget the image of my dead body. I'd been wearing the same clothes, same hair, same sandals. Like I was a projection of what I had been right before I crossed over.

This held true with the one other similar experience that I had. I had told my parents a head wound was from falling down the stairs, but it was really when my physical body had collapsed after I accidentally separated from it. But unlike this time, my body was alive and waiting for me when I was ready to get back into it.

I, me, it. I kept thinking of my physical body as a separate entity than myself. But I guess I had confirmation of that, since my body was dead and I was still here. Alive. Surviving.

There were still so many unanswered questions. I felt like a physical body. I bled and slept, but didn't have to drink or eat. Well, not food anyway. The thought of my fingers touching the foul cloud that rose from the dead mantis made me shudder.

So I was some*thing*. I wasn't a ghost or hologram. I remembered a history assignment where we had to write a paper on a mythological archetype. I picked dragons because I thought it was pretty cool. We were paired up with another student to edit our essays. The girl I was working with chose astral projection and out-of-body experiences. It's an idea that has spanned across many different cultures for thousands of years, which theoretically means there may be some reality to it. I had to read her paper. I discussed it a lot with her. I tried to convince myself now that it was because it was an interesting topic, which was true, but I knew in my heart it was because she was really attractive and I had wanted her to like me.

From what I could remember, a person's astral form has some substance, not quite a physical body, but also not quite your soul. Something in between. This seemed like a really accurate description of my current state of being. Your astral body reflects how you view yourself, so you might be dressed, and you might not. I remembered this part specifically because I had visualized her astral body without clothes.

I rolled my eyes and groaned at my past self. God, I was a moron sometimes. Maybe I was just visualizing myself with clothes on because that was what I had looked like when I crossed over, so now I was stuck with them.

Was my astral body what solely existed of the person I once was? Made sense. Well, as much sense as anything else around me. I came up with a few things I could do to test out this theory and maybe once I had some results, I could put a few more pieces together.

Another critically relevant fact I remembered from the assignment hit me. Your astral could be killed.

CHAPTER 32
JOHN

In the back of my mind, the thought that I would have to eventually kill another monster was tapping away. I needed to learn more and somehow get prepared for the possibility. But first things first. I did *not* feel safe. Even though the mantis was dead, there were other creatures lurking out of sight. Since I had resigned myself to staying here, I decided to fortify my current location. How and with what I wasn't sure yet.

According to my own theory, the objects that had echoes here had burned through because they were unmoved for a long time. So where would I find things like that? Attics, basements, museums, anywhere abandoned.

It was lucky for me that I'd lived in this area my entire life, because I obviously had no map. Back in the land of the living, I was annoyed by this fact and had vowed to attend a college at least a few hours' drive from my childhood home.

I strolled through my surplus outlet, taking note of the layout of the store. Mostly empty racks bolted to the floor, similar to a small department store. Shelving on the walls. Dingy, fading, dark green carpet. There was a glass entrance door that looked concerningly easy to shatter.

Wait, why *was* there a door? Doors open and close, they move all the time. Great, another flaw in my theory. I inspected the glass, running my fingertips over along the edges to check for cracks, other than the small ones I had created yesterday. It was cloudy and bubbled in places, but I could still see through it. It would need to be covered. Maybe boarded up at night. There were no other windows in the main room, which I was thankful for.

The gun room did have a window set into the pegboard wall. It was kind of hard to get to since it was above one of the deep cabinets that lined the floor. The cabinets were only about three feet tall, the tops acting as a long table around the whole room. I could climb on top easily. The room was about half the size of the main area, maybe fifteen by twenty feet. There was a storage room in the back of the store that was about the same size, with shelving all the way to the ceiling. I had yet to look through it. That was next on the agenda.

I stepped into the storage area, which I had figured would be the safest place to sleep since it was farthest from the entrance. I looked down when I felt tile crack under my feet. The shelving was in good shape; there were some boxes way up by the ceiling. I pulled down lightly on one of the shelves and a small cloud of dust plumed out from the drywall behind it. I waved my hand in front of my face and coughed. Definitely would not be climbing up there. I needed a ladder. Of course, there was not one to be found.

I crossed my arms over my chest and leaned against the doorframe, looking into the main area. My inspection had taken all of ten minutes. I sighed. I was hoping to put off exploring outside a bit longer. I considered waiting another day, but I was afraid I would get…hungry…again. I couldn't think of a better word for it and that terrified me.

~

I backed up toward the glass door, pushing it open with my hip, and dumped the last load of crap on the floor. I had explored attics and basements of a nearby residential area all day and I was exhausted.

Going through the echoes of people's forgotten lives had actually been kind of fun at first. I got to trash houses, albeit carefully and quietly, with abandon. Then it had gotten tedious. And then of course there were the multiple stress-laden trips back to the store to drop off my cache. By some God-given stroke of luck, I had found an antique-looking Radio Flyer wagon in the corner of the basement in the first house I searched. It had been immensely useful.

But every time I left a house, my heart rate skyrocketed as I panned my surroundings for Leeches. I had only encountered one, as soon as I was about to leave the third house I had ransacked. Peering through the window of the front door of the house, I saw a beetle-like creature the size of a bobcat. Far less scary than the couple I had encountered so far, but I'd still waited till it was long out of sight before trekking back home with my next wagon-load of junk.

I took a deep breath and scanned the objects in front of me. I made sure to only bring items in good shape, otherwise what was the point? A shovel; a decent stack of two by fours; two rolls of duct tape; a crank flashlight; a small rusty toolbox containing a screw driver, hammer, plyers, and nails but no screws. A fleece blanket, pillow still in its original packaging, an entire box of paper towel rolls, a bag of crayons, six pretty large tent stakes, another hunting knife, a bicycle, and a gallon jug of paint thinner. I didn't know what I would use that for but I knew it was flammable. I'd also broken down about twenty cardboard boxes and stacked them in a corner.

I grabbed one now and taped it to the far left wall of the main room where there was no shelving. I drew six tick marks on it with a red crayon and stepped back to stare at it. Six days. I had been here almost a week. In this place, this Void, this empty hellhole.

The emptiness wasn't just physical. There was a lonely hollow feeling that accompanied being here, like something inside me was missing.

Maybe I would find another person eventually. Someone else's astral. Maybe I wouldn't be alone forever. The series of events that led to me getting stuck here was so specific that I found it pretty unlikely that I would find another person. I had crossed over randomly like had happened many other times over the last few years, then I encountered a Leech, which caused me to flee, accidentally separating me from my physical form, and then of course I got hit by a car and presumably died. Definitely died. There was no way a human could survive that.

I shuddered and backed up against the wall next to my makeshift cardboard calendar, sinking down to the floor and hugging my knees. That image haunted me. I would never heal the burn it left in my brain.

I sat there for a while, picking at the pebbles stuck to the bottom of my sandals. With a groan, I got to my feet and went about taping cardboard over the front door and window of the gun room with the crank flashlight stuck in the back of my shorts. I had already tested it and thank God it had worked. The cardboard blocked out the meager light of the setting sun, and I was left in darkness. I clicked on the flashlight, grabbed my new blanket and pillow, and headed over to the supply room to sleep.

I was drained. It had been a long day. Tomorrow would be longer.

CHAPTER 33
ANNA

"A long story? Why don't you sum it up for me?" I asked, crossing my arms over my chest, still wary.

"Okay, well first, take a look back into the bedroom." He gestured with his thumb over his shoulder. I peered around the door frame, giving the new John a wide berth. It was John's body. Well, the one I knew, anyway. The bald eighty-something-year-old guy with age-spotted skin and old man clothes. He was floating above where the bed should be, looking peaceful but unconscious.

I looked back towards my body, lying face down in the middle of the living room, hair a mess, limbs askew. John saw my worried look and said, "Don't worry, you fell on the mattress."

I stared at him, eyebrows raised, waiting for more information. He sighed for like the hundredth time in the last few minutes. His eyes were tired, drained.

"Your body looks like you, mine doesn't."

"Obviously."

"Okay, let me rephrase that. That is your body," he said, pointing, then gestured toward the bedroom again, "that is not my body."

I was still confused. "So like, your body ages, but whatever this is—" I swept my hands in front of me "—doesn't?"

"Our astrals. But no. I mean it literally. That is not *my* body. I don't have one anymore. I borrowed that one."

"You *borrowed* it? How do you *borrow* a body? Do you plan on giving it back?" I asked, incredulous.

"Well…no," he replied slowly.

"Then that isn't borrowing!"

"Okay, fine. I took it. But the original owner wasn't ever going to use it again so…" he trailed off.

"So whose is it? And where is he?" This was sounding sketchier by the moment.

"His name was Albert John Marshall. He was pretty much dead. He didn't have an astral that was able to take it back, so I've been, uh, using it."

"*Pretty much* dead? What does that even mean?" There were so many questions that I didn't even know where to start. "Who *are* you, anyway?"

"I am…or was…John Piscatello."

"That's a name, doesn't really tell me much. You're like, what? Eighteen? Nineteen? Did you go to my school? Should I know you?"

"I didn't go to your school. I didn't get to finish high

school, unfortunately." He held his thumb and forefinger close together. "I was *this* close, though. Still disappointed about that one. But that was…" He twisted his lips, thinking. "Eleven years ago now."

I was shocked. "So why do you still look like a senior in high school? And where is *your* body?"

"St. Augustine's cemetery, row sixteen, plot two. I was almost nineteen when my body died and I got stuck in the Void. So I'd be…thirty now, I suppose. At least I still have my good looks." He smiled at his own morbid joke. I didn't. He didn't look so great. Bony, pale, bags under his eyes, and some weird scars on his visible skin.

"This is insane. Insane!" I scrubbed my hands roughly over my face, making sure I wasn't dreaming. "So why am I here? Why did you drag me into this?"

"I didn't *drag* you into this. Well, I am a little responsible, but it wasn't intentional. I've known you since you were a little kid. I knew that you were like me—you would accidentally slip into the Void. I actually sense it in a lot of people, but I doubt most are aware of it. That opens you up to some real danger." He took a deep breath, "Same reason you want to help Brian, you feel guilty. I feel guilty. You were always prone to this, but I'm pretty sure I made it possible because I thinned the barrier by crossing over so much. I was looking out for you, trying to make sure that what happened to me didn't happen to you!"

He was angry, but not at me. At himself. "I've just been trying to survive all of these years. I never wanted any of this. I was trapped in the Void, I saw a potential way out, so I took it. You don't know what it was like. The loneliness."

I felt bad for him. I truly did. But I was still afraid he had done something horrible to that poor man whose body he wore like a jacket.

"And now a Leech has escaped. I think I know how to fix it, but I want to be positive. There's a chance that my assumption about how to kill it might actually make the situation worse."

That was *not* news I wanted to hear. My own research hadn't turned up much so far, but maybe once John taught me more, I would be able to help further. But right now there was another huge question I was finally going to demand an answer to.

"You said you think you're dying. You just told me you're already dead. How are you dying? Are you, like, a ghost or something?"

"No, and what died wasn't *me.* I just don't think it's possible that I'm a ghost. If the Void was an afterlife, wouldn't there be a lot of people here, and how is it that you are here, and that people fade in and out? I still don't have a great understanding of *why* this place exists or what it is, but it's definitely some kind of twisted reflection of our world.

"My astral… this form—" he gestured to himself again "—is losing energy. What was sustaining me isn't working completely anymore. And I don't have the strength to separate entirely from the other John over there anymore. The already weak tether that I used to be able to stretch very easily has gotten weaker and more…brittle. I am afraid it's going to snap any day now. I slip in and out of the Void without intent and that used to never happen. It's getting more and more frequent."

"So how can I possibly help with that?" I was getting more tangled up in this by the moment and I was starting to feel dread in the pit of my stomach. The excitement had drained away quickly.

"I don't have the energy to carry out this plan by myself and I think I can borrow some from you," he replied with hesitation, probably not expecting the greatest reaction from me.

"But what's the plan? I'm not agreeing to something unless I know exactly what it is. This isn't the Terms and Conditions. I need to read it before checking the box."

He squeezed his eyes shut and paused, then the words tumbled out. "I need to break the bond with this body, find the Leech's physical form and kill it, and then find a new body to tether to. And I need to use some of the energy from your astral to do it."

"What? No! No *way*! What if I get stuck in the Void like you did? Help you find a *body?* Don't you mean *steal* a body? This is crazy! Find someone else!" I scoffed, but could feel panic bubbling in my gut.

"Anna, there is no—" he started.

"Yes there is! There have to be other people! We were next-door neighbors since I was a little girl and we both just *happen* to have this ability? It *has* to be common!"

"Well, I think you're right, I think it is common to have the potential for it. But like I said, I think I triggered it for you." He cringed. "But I just don't have the strength to find anyone else. I don't have enough time left and I don't even know how!" He composed himself again. "Okay. How about this. You help me break away from this body so I can find and kill the Leech. Then we will revisit the…last request."

I gave him a skeptical look.

"I'm just trying to survive. You can't blame me for that."

"If surviving means taking someone else's life, then yes. Yes I can," I replied.

"I *told* you! It's not…" He took an angry breath and regained composure. "I am *not* taking anyone's life. You don't understand."

"You're right. I don't. I don't understand how a person can survive without an… astral or soul or whatever, or how an astral can survive without a body."

"It's complicated."

We both paused, staring at each other, waiting for someone to make the next move. Should I do this? Should I help him? I wanted so much to fix Brian and get the Leech back into the Void, because it was my fault. It was obviously dangerous, though. But I couldn't live with this on my conscience. I sighed and threw up my hands in defeat.

"Fine! Show me around, I guess?"

"Come on." He smiled and beckoned me to the front door.

I clenched my fists and steeled myself for whatever was about to happen next because I was pretty sure I wasn't going to like it.

CHAPTER 34
JOHN

I spent the next couple days exploring more houses in a wider radius. I'd found a few other useful items and continued to get more comfortable about my ability to dodge Leeches. It was hard to know what to take back with me since I wasn't looking for anything specific. It was time to go somewhere I knew for sure I could bring in a good haul since I was starting to get weaker. Again.

I had remembered a middle school field trip to a small, local history museum. It was as good a place to start as any. Maybe I could stop at a hardware store on the way back if I saw one.

It took me about three hours to walk there, longer than I expected, which made me nervous. I was constantly on the lookout for the creatures that could easily kill me permanently, or Leech away my soul. I first spotted one about a quarter of the way through my walk. I hadn't gotten a good look at the Leech, but it seemed like it might have been a smaller, less scaly version of the lizard with the poison teeth.

I was sticking to walking close to buildings or houses when possible so I could duck inside or find cover if I saw any flash of movement. Since Florida was basically one giant strip mall, it wasn't too hard to do.

I found that there were more Leeches in areas that corresponded to busy parts of town, which made sense. More people to feed off. Since I had theorized years ago that these wraiths of people crossed into the Void when they were very angry, or scared, or were experiencing some other strong emotion, I determined that this was what the Leeches were feeding off. I was distracted by my contemplation and almost missed the creature stalking slowly around the corner of a store across the street.

I darted behind a clump of three dead-looking palm trees growing in the median between the sidewalk and main stretch of road near a fast food place. I realized what an idiot I had been to travel so far from my surplus outlet, with only a backpack, flashlight, and a knife in a sheath. This had been a stupid idea. I knew deep down that part of the reason I had set out on this journey was boredom, and I had been feeling cocky.

My heart raced and I took a deep shaky breath as I crouched down and peered slowly around my pathetic hiding place. The Leech resembled a wolf walking on its hind legs. Its coarse fur was the sickly greenish-black color of scum on a pond. It was so odd how different all these creatures were, and there seemed to be no rhyme or reason to it.

Luckily, it was traveling in the opposite direction, so I just waited until it grew tiny in the distance and turned down a bend in the road.

I was jumpy and stressed out for the remainder of my travel, but finally reached the museum. I always felt safer in buildings, although logically, there was no reason the Leeches were any less likely to be hiding inside than outdoors.

It was dim inside, and I pulled out my flashlight. I was trying to save the lightbulb on my crank flashlight so had brought the rusty one I had found in my surplus outlet. The batteries I found in the back of the cabinet in the gun room had worked, barely. The light was dim and flickering, so I resolved to complete my exploration as quickly as possible.

The foyer contained a desk and some rotting artwork hanging on the walls. Entering the main area, I swept my pathetic light across the room. Foggy glass cases contained some items in shockingly good condition. I examined each case carefully. A pedal-operated sewing machine from the 1920s, according to the plaque. A typewriter also from the 1920s and cuckoo clock with a sad-looking bird hanging from a dejected spring. This room seemed to be devoted to household items from the early 1900s. Boring.

I approached another case in the corner and smiled as I peered through the glass. A yo-yo, leather football, and a deck of classic Bicycle playing cards. I lifted the glass cover and it cracked under my fingertips. Unzipping my backpack, I delicately placed the objects inside, looking forward to bringing them back home (*home?*) and checking out their condition.

The next room was what I had been excited about and remembered from my field trip. Hunting equipment. A Marlin 39 rifle hung on the wall behind a railing meant to keep curious museum-goers from touching. There was one other rifle I didn't recognize hanging next to it. Sitting on a shelf inset into the wall under each gun, were their respective bullets, three of each behind a sheet of glass. My heart leapt and I hopped over the railing and delicately tapped on the glass panel below the Marlin 39. It shattered easily. I gently placed the bullets in a small, padded pocket of the backpack. The other panel fractured just as effortlessly. The first bullet I picked up crushed between my thumb and forefinger as if it were made of tin foil.

"Shit!" I growled, and was startled by the sound of my own voice. I realized I hadn't spoken since yesterday. Maybe even the day before. Loneliness pushed on me like an oppressive humidity.

The other bullets seemed far sturdier, and I set them delicately in the pocket with the other three.

The guns were too long to fit in my backpack, so I left the barrels sticking out the top and zipped around them to hold them in place. I hefted the pack carefully onto my back and explored the rest of the room, feeling damn good about my cache so far. A bow hung on the far wall along with an empty hook that I assumed would have held the arrow. As soon as I touched the bow, the string snapped. I squeezed my eyes shut and clenched my teeth, trying not to get too upset, and put it in my bag beside the guns anyway.

There was a display in the middle of the room, also in a glass case, of what looked like a fake bear foot. I didn't understand at first until I saw the metal contraption next to it. A bear trap. Oh, yes. This was a keeper for sure.

It was too big and clunky to put in my backpack, not to mention I was afraid it would damage the guns. I'd have to carry the damn thing. I removed the hazy glass case and was pleasantly surprised at the great condition of the trap. It was huge. When I went to pick it up, it was way heavier than expected. Must have weighed over sixty pounds. I groaned. Carrying it was not an option.

"God damn it!" The trap looked dangerous. In a good way. I needed it. I looked around, but there was nothing else useful in the museum. Some artwork on the walls, decaying tables, and some old artifacts I had no use for. I needed to find something to haul it with, but there was nothing here. I'd have to come back for it. I knew I should have brought the wagon.

I had walked about a third of the way back and ducked inside an open garage as I saw some movement up ahead. After waiting quite a while, I was about to leave when I spotted a glorious sight hanging on a few large hooks on the wall. A wheelbarrow.

I rushed over to it and hefted it off the wall with a grunt. I paused, considering my options. Head back to the store, or return to the museum to collect the bear trap and risk arriving home after dark. I'd risk it.

Getting the bear trap into the rusty wheelbarrow proved difficult, but I eventually managed without tipping it over. Finally, I headed back.

Even with the wheelbarrow, it was heavy and cumbersome and took a lot of effort to keep it from tipping. I started to panic halfway back to the store as the anemic sun started to set. I made it right before it was completely dark.

Exhausted, I dropped the backpack on the floor a little too heavily and cringed, hoping I hadn't broken anything. I decided to wait until morning to check. I trudged back to the supply room, flopped down on my makeshift bed, and fell asleep almost immediately.

Tomorrow would be a new day in this barren hellhole, and for once, I was looking forward to it.

CHAPTER 35
JOHN

I sat on the floor staring at my cache. I needed to fortify the store and figure out a way to kill Leeches if the need arose. I also needed an escape plan if one made it inside. I sighed. At eighteen years old, I thought I'd be planning out my college applications, not how to protect myself from death by monster.

I spent almost the entire day hacking the ends of the two-by-fours into sharp points. The hatchet I had found a few days ago came in handy. When I was finally about to go insane with monotony, I stopped and counted my pile. Twenty. Not bad.

I carted them outside and shoved them in the ground in a half circle around the door, about ten feet out, spaced about a foot and a half apart, angled slightly toward the road. My arms shook with the effort as I hammered them deeper. Admiring my work, I decided that I'd need another row eventually, and would have to go searching for more wood, but for right now, I figured it would at least slow something down for a minute or two, maybe long enough for me to escape by a different route if necessary.

But how to know when something was approaching? I thought of the cliché tin cans on a string. I had tent stakes that would work well to secure a tin-can alarm, but I had no cans and no rope. I would add that to my list of things to search for.

Could I dig a trench? I had a shovel and the ground was fairly soft, but it would take ages. Did it really matter, though? Last time I checked, my schedule was pretty open. I'd get to work on it in a day or two. There wasn't much daylight left.

The problem with all of my fortification planning was that I had no idea how intelligent these creatures were. I had been assuming they were animals, treating the situation like I needed to protect myself from a bear or lion. For all I knew, they were as smart as I was and would take one look at my tin can alarm, and just step right over it.

Sighing, I went back inside and opened the backpack. I gently removed the guns and set them on a shelf. The chances they would work were slim, so I was trying not to get my hopes up. Examining the bullets, I noticed one was dented. Definitely wouldn't work, but I set it on the shelf next to the guns anyway.

The bow with no string seemed useless but I wasn't going to discard anything just yet. I carefully removed the football, playing cards, and yo-yo. When I attempted to unravel the string from around the yo-yo, it frayed and broke. I groaned. Well, maybe I could find a replacement.

I quickly scrawled a bulleted list on my sheet of cardboard taped to the wall. Wood, cans, rope, yo-yo string.

The football was definitely useable, which was exciting at first, then depressing when I remembered I obviously had no one to play with. The box of the deck of cards fell apart, but the cards inside were useable.

I decided I had done enough today and played solitaire until my eyes grew heavy. I settled in for another restless night, hoping to get enough sleep to have another productive day tomorrow. And the next day. And the one after that. Presumably forever.

~

Misery was setting in as I spent the next few days searching houses, dodging Leeches, digging a trench, and playing solitaire before bed. Even though I was keeping busy, I was so *bored.* I knew I should be grateful to be bored; it meant nothing was currently trying to kill me.

Rocking in an old rocking chair in someone's attic, I was going through photo albums. The pictures were faded and torn but I could make out some of them. Birthday parties, weddings, graduations. Celebrations I would never again attend. I shut the album and ran my hand over the cover, taking a deep breath, as though to breathe in the memories and make them my own.

I grabbed another album off the stack on the floor. This one had some black-and-white baby pictures in it. The tears that pooled in the corners of my eyes surprised me. I had never even thought about whether I wanted kids; it had been too far in my future. But I was hit with the realization that I no longer had the option. No wife, no kids, no white picket fence. This was my life now. Sitting in a dusty attic going through other people's memories for fun.

A screech from outside made my heart skip.

Crouching so as not to hit my head on the low ceiling, I crept slowly to the tiny window set near the peak of the roof and peered out. Two Leeches stood there facing the house. I couldn't tell if they were looking at me but I ducked under the window anyway. This was odd; the only time I had even seen two this close together was when the mantis killed the lizard. I thought they were lone creatures. Both of these were small and vaguely beetle-like so I wondered if it had something to do with being similar.

I stood up the tiniest bit so I could see out the window. I didn't see any echoes of people nearby so either they were just chilling here for no reason or they were looking for me. Judging by their spindly insect limbs, I didn't think they would be able to get into the attic even if they got into the house, so I figured I could just wait it out.

It seemed like hours passed, and the two bugs just kept pacing back and forth in front of the house, screeching every now and then as if communicating. Now it was pretty clear it was me they were after. Why else would they just wait around? How did they know I was here? Could they smell me, sense me somehow? Did they see me go inside?

I fiddled for the switch of my flashlight to turn it off since it was getting dark and I didn't want them to see the light through the window. It slipped out of my shaky hands and landed with a thump on the pile of photo albums, glass breaking and a huge spark jumping to the open pages.

"Oh shit!" I leapt back as the stack caught flame almost instantly, the brittle pages making the perfect kindling. I frantically glanced around for something to smother the fire, but saw nothing. With growing panic, I noticed that I was surrounded by cardboard boxes and a mound of very old newspapers. I needed to bail or I was going up in flames along with the rest of the attic. I half fell down the ladder leading down to the second floor and tried to locate a route other than the front door from which to escape, since I assumed they were still waiting for me.

I peered out a bedroom window facing the street just in time to hear the shatter of glass and see a flash of light, the result of the small attic window exploding, and ducked with a yelp. The Leeches screeched and ran away in panic.

It made sense. I couldn't think of any other situation in which they would have experienced fire. There was no weather here that I had seen, so no lightning strikes. There were no humans to make campfires, or light a furnace. No active gas stations, cars, or anything else likely to cause an explosion.

Thank God. I ran down the stairs and out the front door, looking up to see flames shooting out of the window and the roof about to collapse. Holy shit, that was fast. I looked around in shock, not knowing what to do. I heard a vast amount of eerie screaming, squealing, and other frightened vocalizations that I couldn't even think of a name for. Some sounded far away, others much closer.

Mouth agape, scanning the area around me, I realized two very important things. Leeches were afraid of fire, and there were more of them nearby than I originally thought. A *lot* more.

CHAPTER 36
ANNA

John scanned the area, only halfway over the threshold. I peered over his shoulder, anxious to get this show on the road. There was nothing out there. No cars, no people. The plant life looked shriveled from dehydration, the grass brittle and dying. The pavement was cracked and riddled with potholes, as though abandoned for decades.

It wasn't hot anymore, which I found odd. Just a generic room temperature that gave the impression that you would be comfortable in any amount of clothing.

The physical feeling was oppressive, like the air was just slightly thicker, humid almost. Not the wet humidity that I normally associated with Florida's springtime, something different.

"Coast is clear. I'm going to show you a few important things. Come on." He headed down his front steps and shut the door. The sound seemed dulled, sort of like I was wearing earmuffs.

He walked with confidence down his driveway but I was scared to follow. "Wait," I whispered-yelled, "aren't you worried about Leeches?"

He turned around and took a few steps back toward me. "No, they're rarely in this area."

"Why not?" I asked. "This is a pretty busy neighborhood."

"Well, " he started slowly, "they're sort of…scared of me."

"*Scared* of you? Why?"

He paused. I knew this look, even on his new and younger face. He was debating whether or not to tell me the truth.

"I kill them. Efficiently and often."

"What? Why? *How?*" I asked, scared of the answer but also feeling a bit soothed that he could protect us if necessary.

"That one," he said, pointing to a house a little ways down the street, surreptitiously avoiding the question. "Let's start there."

I followed him with a huff, annoyed but definitely curious. We entered the house, which I remembered being fairly new. It had been built probably built about six months ago, with bright sky-blue siding and a beautiful oak front door. Here it was decrepit, gray siding rotting and cracked, holes in the roof through which I could see exposed beams. It was in the worst condition out of all the houses on the street.

"Why is that house in such bad shape? It's a

beautiful house in reality."

John turned to me and grabbed my shoulders, startling me. "Anna, you need to realize something. This—" he gestured around us, arms open wide "—*is* reality. It may not be the reality you are used to, but you *can* be injured, even killed. Someone will find your human body, dying and empty, never knowing why or how you died. An autopsy will show nothing, and you will leave your family grieving a loss they don't understand. *Never* come here by yourself, do you understand me? There are creatures here that are straight out of nightmares, and trust me, you *do not* want to encounter one."

"Okay…" I started, shocked at his sudden outburst. "It's not like I would…"

"Do you see this?" he interrupted, lifting up his pant leg. "This is the result of one of the closest calls I have ever had here. It was absolute sheer luck that I managed to escape the thing that did it, and the injury itself nearly killed me afterward anyway."

I looked at his leg, speechless. A raised gray scar dominated most of his thigh, about a foot long and two inches wide. It was *huge*.

"The same incident where I almost became a human kabob, I got trapped in a fire." He pulled the neck of his shirt over and I could see a large splotchy patch of silvery skin. "I almost burned to death alongside a Leech. It was the most painful thing I've ever experienced. I've gotten lucky more times than I can count. I am absolutely shocked I lasted for so long, considering what I had to do to survive."

"What did you have to do?" I asked quietly, fascinated and horrified by his accounts. Instead of answering, he broke eye contact and turned away.

"Come on," he said, and started walking briskly towards the decaying house, leaving me to jog to catch up.

"But why does it look like that? It's the newest house on the block." I said, falling in line next to him.

"That's exactly why. The newer and more used something is, the weaker it echoes."

"But…that makes no sense."

"Nope, but a lot of things here don't," he said matter-of-factly.

We entered the rundown house, which didn't even have a door, and crept carefully up the rickety stairs. The entire house was empty but I didn't bother asking what the hell we were doing here.

He led me to a room with an empty window frame facing the back of the house. In front of it sat a telescope.

"That looks new, though," I said confused. "How did it get here?"

"Oh, I brought it from somewhere else. It didn't echo through this house," he said. I was glad I was starting to pick up on his terminology, because some of the things he said would sound ridiculous otherwise. He peered through the telescope and adjusted it a few times until he was satisfied. He stepped back and ushered me over.

"Take a look."

I looked through the lens and saw two creatures near a sand trap in the golf course, spindly limbs and knobby joints moving in spurts and jolts as they stalked around. They walked on two legs and looked vaguely similar to mummies you might see in a museum. Emaciated, papery skin, exposed teeth. I let out a small gasp when I saw that the tops of their skulls were missing starting right below where their eyes would be. I could see black, pulsing brains exposed to the air.

Pulling back from the telescope, I looked up at John, wide-eyed and feeling the blood drain from my face. There was a very real possibility I was about to throw up.

"Those…those are Leeches?" I stammered, fighting the urge to vomit. "They look nothing like the one I saw."

"They're all different. Well, not *all* of them, but I've seen hundreds of them, so different that I can't make sense of it. Those down there pale in comparison to others I've seen."

"So…why…why are you showing me this?" I asked shakily.

"You need to know, Anna. You need to have a realistic idea of what you might encounter. Like you said, you want to know what you're getting into before you agree to help, and I respect that, so I'm showing you an example of what we might—what we *will*—come across. I'm going to keep you as safe as I can but I'm also going to show you some places to hide out if we get separated, and how to get back into your body on your own."

I was shaking, trying to keep my teeth from chattering. I needed to build up some courage and fast. This was more than I could mentally handle right now and I needed to get my shit together.

"So what's the plan? How are we going to get rid of Brian's Leech?" I asked hesitantly.

John turned to me and took a deep breath. It was so weird seeing him in this form. He looked so different, and yet very familiar at the same time. It was hard to wrap my mind around.

"I have a few ideas, all of which have flaws. The first couple are built on the assumption that the Leech's physical body is still alive and it is tethered to it. My first idea is that we kill its body in the Void, and hope that its astral, which is caught in the human plane, dies with it."

"But isn't that essentially what happened to you?" I asked. "And you didn't die."

"Yes," he sighed, "so if the same rules apply, then it won't die, but maybe it would be more vulnerable. Or maybe cutting its ties to the Void would give it free range in the human plane and we're in a worse situation than we were before."

"Okay, so I'm not really feeling that one. Any other ideas?" I was worried that if he started off with an idea this sketchy, then his others might not be any better.

"We lure it back to its body, then kill it when it's back in the Void if necessary. This unfortunately means getting Brian to cooperate with us."

I groaned. "He *hates* me. I don't think that's gonna

happen."

"It actually might not be that difficult. The Leech crossed over in your school's library, right?" I nodded. "So its body might still be there. If we get it close to its body, it will be drawn to it and might just go back on its own."

"Wow," I said cheerfully, "that doesn't sound bad at all."

"Not so fast. There's a lot of 'ifs' in that scenario." He leaned against the wall with a sigh and a small chunk of plaster cracked free, falling to the floor in a cloud of dust. He brushed it absently with his foot. He began ticking off on his fingers. "It will only work *if* Brian agrees to go there, *if* we get the Leech to follow him, *if* its body is still there, and *if* it willingly goes back to the Void and just leaves us alone. Its body might not even be alive anymore in which case, I'm approaching this from a totally wrong direction altogether. So much can go wrong. Your school is crawling with Leeches. Especially at the end of the school year since all the kids are stressed out about finals and college and whatnot."

Yeah, I should have been freaking out about that along with them. I'd barely studied for finals and they were next week. I hadn't found a job, either.

"Chances are its body isn't in the same place. It could have been dragged away by something else. It might not want to or even realize how to get back in its body."

"It seemed scared when I saw it last, though," I

remembered. It had been cowering defensively, hanging out in the corner of Brian's room, looking trapped. "It probably wants to go home."

"Maybe," said John, running his fingers through his dark hair. I recognized now why he did that all the time over his bald head in his physical body. "That's what I'm hoping for."

"Well, even if it doesn't willingly go back into its body, that doesn't seem like a very dangerous plan. We try it, if it doesn't work, oh well, right? We don't have to be in the Void when it crosses back over, and it doesn't seem like it can hurt us here in this world." I shrugged.

"It's hurting Brian, so it can hurt us, albeit probably slowly. I know the plan seems simple, but I have a feeling something's going to go horribly wrong. I feel like I'm missing a key piece of the puzzle but don't know what it looks like. It just feels too easy. I still don't even entirely understand the situation. The Leech obviously isn't completely in the human plane. No one but people with a connection to the Void can see it or interact with it. But it isn't completely in the Void either." He kicked the piece of plaster and it landed near my uninjured foot.

"I think you're just being paranoid," I said, trying to reassure both of us. "You've been dealing with this bullshit for too long and you expect the worst because of it." I kicked the drywall back at him and it hit him in the shin. He didn't notice.

"You got that right," he snorted. "Come on, let's head back, we can't have your parents wondering where you are only to break in and find you unconscious in the middle of my living room on a mattress. I have a feeling they wouldn't let you come over anymore.

I laughed. "Yeah that seems like an accurate assumption."

We made our way back to John's house. His brief explanation of how to get back into our bodies sounded surprisingly easy. When I got inside, I felt an uncomfortable pulling in my chest that only got stronger the closer I got to my form lying on the floor. All I had to do was touch it.

I knelt on the floor and paused with my fingertips inches from my skin, just realizing something.

"John, wait."

He came out from the bedroom, still in his younger form. "Yeah?"

"Why are our bodies here? I thought we left them back in the human plane."

"They aren't here. You just see its reflection. See?" He knelt down next to me and went to touch my arm. His fingers passed through even though I looked completely solid. He stood back up and I looked up at him.

"When we cross over, our astrals are still inside our physical form, so the position of our body in our world and the position of our astrals in the Void are the same. But you need to pull yourself out of your body to travel any deeper into the Void. That's why *that*—" he gestured to my drunkenly sprawled-out body on the floor "—happens. I've practiced enough to be able to leave my body much more easily, hence old Albert lying nicely on the bed over there," he said, pointing back toward the bedroom. I was reminded again that he was using a body not his own. "Hopefully I can teach you to do the same, because that air mattress is a pain in the ass."

"But that doesn't answer the question of why we can see them," I said, frustrated.

"I'm not totally sure, but I think it's because they're strongly tethered to us. I have a theory that when we're far away they fade, but I have no way of knowing." He nodded absently, deep in thought, then suddenly slapped himself in the forehead.

"I'm such an idiot! *Now* I do! Stay here!" He got up and jogged out the door.

"What are you doing?" I yelled after him.

"Go watch my body!" he yelled over his shoulder.

I went in the bedroom and sure enough, the image of his body was slowly fading, becoming more and more transparent the further away he got.

He came back, out of breath, and stopped with his hands on his hips. "Well?"

"Yeah, you started…fading."

"Okay, so then I think I'm right. I think we see a *reflection* of our body. Kind of like seeing your reflection in a pond. The closer you get, the clearer the image becomes."

"Ah. Okay, that makes sense. Well, I mean the analogy is good, but whatever this is—" I pointed to my body "—is just ridiculous."

"Yeah, okay, I know, nothing is logical here, but it's the best explanation I've got."

I gave him a skeptical look.

"Just get back in your body!" he said with a huff, and walked away. Definitely one of the weirdest instructions I'd gotten in my life.

I crouched down and reached out to the image of my arm. I felt a rush, like I was rocketing up from the bottom of a deep pool, the pressure releasing from my ears. I gripped the floor and waited for the spinning to stop. Feeling the squeaky plastic of the air mattress under my cheek, I opened my eyes one at a time and brushed my hair out of my face, sitting up slowly.

There was John, the old John, the one I knew, standing over me. Arms crossed, with a small grin painting his face.

"How are you doing?" he asked.

"Dizzy, a little nauseous. Everything is so…*loud.* And bright." I groaned and squinted my eyes. He threw back his head and laughed, catching me by surprise.

"Really? After less than an hour?" He chuckled again, shaking his head. I glared at him, my cheeks flushed even though I didn't know what I was supposed to be embarrassed about. He held out his bony hand and helped me to my feet.

"You should go home and get some rest. Focus on school for a while. I've thrown a lot at you all at once and you need a mental break." He hit the nail on the head with that one.

"You know, I used to follow your instructions because I thought you were like a hundred years old or something. The whole, like, respect your elders thing. Now that I know you aren't, you really can't boss me around anymore." I grinned at him and he shook his head with a laugh.

"Get outta here Anna, go study for finals. Let me worry about finalizing a plan."

I held up my hands in defeat. "Fine by me!" I walked shakily to the door, bracing myself on the doorframe for a moment before going outside. He was right, this day had been mind-boggling and I needed a break from the insanity.

"Bye John." I stepped over the threshold, marveling at the bright sky, birds chirping, beautiful palm trees swaying in the Florida breeze. People were walking dogs, cars were driving down the road, kids playing on front lawns.

I couldn't even imagine how lonely John must have felt in the Void for over a year, without so much as a squirrel to keep him company. Dulled senses and heavy air instilling an unescapable claustrophobia. It must have been awful. Not to mention living in constant fear.

I wondered what terrible things he must have done to survive.

CHAPTER 37
JOHN

I stared at my cardboard and tapped the marker on my chin. There were seventeen hash marks. I had been here over two weeks.

In that time I had stabbed a Leech in the head, whittled forty-seven spikes and dug a three-foot trench to fortify my new home, gathered several wagonloads of potentially useful stuff, and accidentally burned two houses to the ground. The attic fire had jumped to the house next door. I wasn't too upset though. What did it matter, really? It wasn't like anyone lived there.

I was getting progressively weaker, but not nearly at the rate I did when I first arrived. With a mixture of disgust and dread, I had come to the conclusion that I probably needed to kill another Leech to sustain myself, so these last few days had been spent planning.

I had guns that probably wouldn't work, but I hadn't wanted to waste a bullet to find out just in case they did. I was beginning to think I had no choice. I had a knife, though, and the ability to make fire, so that was good.

I had explored around my surplus store in about a five mile radius using a bike I had found, and discovered a couple of places that were crawling with Leeches: my old high school, and the courthouse. A lot of stressed-out people there, I guess.

I observed from afar, trying to learn their movements and see if they had a routine. They often had small skirmishes, some more brutal than others. There was one Leech in particular who had gotten in a pretty bad fight a few days ago near the high school. It looked like what I imagined a chupacabra would look like, a goat-humanoid hybrid a little taller and more muscular than myself. It had long horns protruding from its head, but didn't look very dangerous compared to other ones I had seen. It seemed to be at the bottom of the food chain.

It was injured, limping, and had to stop frequently. The remains of dried blood were still on its abdomen. It hung back, careful not to instigate another fight. It would hang around the outskirts of the school grounds every day, presumably looking for echoes of people that weren't being pursued by other Leeches, but hadn't found any yet. It always gave up after a few hours, took the same path away from the school, and headed back to the same strip mall to hole up there.

I was hunting him, and he was getting weaker.

It was morning and I had slept in a restaurant a few stores down from where the goat lived. I was waiting for it to leave and head to the high school, just as it had done every day for the past three days.

I crouched under a table that was bolted to the floor and watched out the window, legs cramping from being in that position for so long. Finally it left, looking weaker than ever. My heart beat faster when I realized that now was the time.

I went through my backpack again. Pliers, screwdriver, paint thinner, hunting knife, rifle with three bullets, a roll of newspaper, and a lighter that worked half the time.

I finally gathered the courage to head over to the goat's hideout. I darted inside and looked around to make sure I was still alone. I was. Taking a shaky breath, I examined the door and found the hydraulic spring that allowed the door to close slowly on its own. I took it apart and discarded the pieces in a nearby bush.

I opened the heavy door and let it go to test my work. It slammed shut and I cringed, looking around to make sure I hadn't drawn attention. There was still nothing in the area that I could see, so I went back to work.

I had brought over the bear trap in the wheelbarrow last night. I lugged it over and dropped it just inside the doorway with a grunt, stepping over it and shutting the door slowly behind me. This was the second scariest part of this plan. I had to set it up. I knew how to do it *in theory*, but had never done it. I was about fifty percent sure I was going to lose an arm.

Picking up the vice grips that had been displayed with the trap, I clamped one spring, then the other, and was pleasantly surprised when the jaws fell open. I backed away very carefully, terrified I would fall for some reason and end up stepping on the trip plate. I had nothing to anchor the trap to but hoped it would work anyway.

I rummaged through my backpack to find the paint thinner and drizzled a large ring that encompassed the bear trap and about ten feet of floor behind it. I poured a thin stream leading down into the back room which had an exit leading to an alleyway that connected to a parking lot behind the complex. It was my escape route if something went horribly wrong, which I assumed it would.

I gathered all my stuff and hid in the back room, waiting for the sound of the door. I loaded the gun and set the knife down on the shelf next to me. All I could do now was wait.

~

My heart was jumping out of my chest and I felt like I was going to pass out, sweat beading on my temples. The gun was within reach, ready to position to fire. I had a lighter in one hand, newspaper in the other. I had been here for hours and was considering giving up.

I heard the door creak open. I peered around the doorframe of the back room carefully, a clear view of the front door. The goat stood there, looking down at the trap quizzically, horns pointed my direction. It was propping the door open with its hoof, still only halfway over the threshold.

I didn't think my heart could beat any faster, but I was pretty sure it was going to break through my ribcage. My vision was getting fuzzy and I tried to blink it away. I lit the newspaper.

The goat raised its head and looked right at me. It seemed more surprised than angry, letting out a loud huff. It went to take a step forward, releasing the door, which was now lacking the hydraulic mechanism. It whipped closed and hit the Leech in the back, sending it stumbling forward with a guttural screech.

It stepped right into the trap.

It snapped shut with a sickening squelch. At the same time, I threw the lit newspaper at the river of paint thinner. It didn't catch.

Shit shit shit!

The Leech screeched and flailed, trying to dislodge the trap. I raised the gun to my shoulder, aimed, and fired. To my immense relief and surprise, it worked. But the sight was way off; I had hit it in the shoulder.

Flesh exploded and the force of the shot caused it to fall backwards, screaming again like nails on a chalkboard. I frantically reloaded and took another shot. Nothing happened. Fumbling and on the verge of full-fledged panic, I took out the dud bullet, threw it aside, and loaded the next one.

I aimed again, trying to compensate for the faulty sight, and pulled the trigger. Its screams cut out abruptly.

Trembling and nearly hyperventilating, I approached the creature. It was most definitely dead. Its head was obliterated. Brain matter and bone fragments splattered the door behind the body, sliding slowly down the glass, leaving trails of gore. Its leg was clamped by the bear trap at the ankle, the metal teeth slick with oily blood.

My vision went spotty and I stifled a sob, trying to take deep breaths to keep from passing out. This was worse than the mantis. Because I did this wholly myself. I killed this creature who was only trying to survive like every other animal. Not only did I kill it, I hunted it. Stalked it for days and came up with a sick plan to murder it.

But I was just surviving too, right? I tried to convince myself. I was on the food chain now. I had no choice, I just needed to use more creative methods to kill my prey.

A dark haze began to rise from the carcass, and with another sob I reached towards it, closing my eyes and trying to steady my breathing. I felt an electric tingle as my hand passed through it.

I was overcome with emotion; despair, fear, elation, tranquility, guilt, everything and more that I had ever felt while I was alive. I fell to my knees and gasped, unprepared for this even though I had experienced it before. This was something I would never get used to. Not even if I was here for eternity.

When it finally faded, I stood slowly, legs wobbling.

It worked.

The hunger, the emptiness inside, was gone again. This was what I had to do to survive, I had confirmation now. The knowledge horrified me.

I had the monster's blood on my knees and fought the urge to frantically scrub it off. Instead, I gathered my wits, trying to avoid looking at the remains of the goat's head, and extracted the bear trap from its ankle, cringing and trying not to gag.

I put my things in my wheelbarrow and headed home, numbness overtaking me. I needed it to; if it hadn't, I would have had a breakdown. I wanted to just give up and let myself waste away, because I definitely didn't want to have to do this every few weeks.

But I'd have to.

CHAPTER 38
ANNA

God, I hated geometry. I sat hunched over my desk, resting my chin on my hand. This was the last final of the year; I just had to get through it. Tapping my pencil on my desk, I read the question for the tenth time.

Explain the isosceles triangle theorem. Give at least two examples to support your answer.

Seriously? I knew the thought was cliché, but when would I *ever* use this knowledge in the real world? I imagined myself on *Who Wants to be a Millionaire?*, the million-dollar question giving me four multiple choice answers for what the isosceles triangle theorem is. I probably still wouldn't remember.

I sighed and moved on to the next question, my optimism about passing the final exam decreasing by the second. It wasn't surprising given that I had been so distracted recently.

I risked a glance across the room at Becca. She was nodding to herself with a small smile on her face, clearly confident in her answers. I should have taken her up on her offer to study together.

My phone vibrated in my pocket. Just one short burst. I had an alert. I was itching to check it but Mrs. Miller's class was definitely not the place to do it; she'd be on that in a heartbeat. I'd have to wait.

The bell rang. I sighed in relief and also disappointment. I'd answered about ninety percent of the questions but was only confident in about three of them. I shuffled out of class and leaned against the lockers. Becca nudged me with her shoulder and scooted up next to me.

"How'd you do?"

"Don't wanna talk about it," I said miserably.

"That bad, huh?" Her face fell.

I grunted in response and pulled my phone out of my pocket. I had an email. Clicking on the envelope icon, I pulled up my inbox.

I had a response from RgulrCat78@gmail.com. My eyes widened and I stood up straighter. Becca was rambling about something but I wasn't paying attention.

"Uh, hello?" she said, noticing I wasn't listening.

"Just…shut up a second."

"Geez. Fine," she said with a huff, noticing that I was reading something.

This is Jackie's mother. She no longer uses this email address. I apologize for the delay in response, I was visiting Jackie. You can write her a letter if you would like. She hasn't gotten any from friends in a while, and I am sure she would appreciate it. Address below.

Patient Jackie Figueroa
Care of: mother, Charlene
Room 204, Psychiatric Ward
Saint Mary's Hospital
Augusta, SC, 30904

I looked up, eyes unfocused, thoughts spinning. Becca ducked her head to catch my gaze.

"What is it?" she asked, concerned.

I handed over my phone without a word. She scanned the email and looked up at me, confusion and surprise written on her face.

"What…what does this mean? *Psychiatric* ward?" she whispered, looking around to make sure no one was listening. Students were rushing around, anxious to start their summer breaks, the last day of school finally over.

"I don't know," I said, finally meeting her gaze, "but I *really* would like to find out." I thought for a moment. "Are you up for a road trip?"

"Seriously? You want to go visit a *stranger*, who is crazy by the way, in case you missed that part of the email, in *South Carolina?* Are you insane?"

"If there's any chance I can get some more info besides what John can tell me, I need to take it. I'll go by myself if I need to."

"Obviously I'm going with you, dumbass," she said,

rolling her eyes, and my heart leapt. "How the hell are we going to convince our parents?"

"Lie, obviously. I've gotten pretty good at it recently," I responded, feeling a little guilty. I was scared but I needed to do this. "We can just tell them we want to go on a celebratory, post-graduation road trip. You're eighteen. I'll be eighteen next week. We're responsible adults, right?"

"I don't know about the 'responsible' part," she said skeptically.

"Graduation is the day after tomorrow, we can leave right after. Get a cheap hotel that night, visit the hospital the next day." I was checking Google Maps. "It's only four and a half hours away. That's not bad; at least it isn't in Oregon or something."

She groaned. "Worst road trip ever."

"Becca," I said. "You don't have to do this. I can go by myself. I really didn't want to drag you into this in the first place." I hadn't told her about my latest session with John. I was trying to figure out if I would tell her at all, and if I did, I was going to leave out some major details. This was already hard enough for me to process, and I had seen it with my own eyes.

"I'm not letting you do this on your own." I saw the sincerity in her eyes and knew there was no way I was going to change her mind. I gave her a hug, trying not to tear up.

"I love you, Bec. You know that, right?" I pulled away and looked at her. She smacked me on the shoulder, giving me a sheepish smile.

"Of course I do. Now let's get out of here and never come back."

~

"Hey, you okay?" Aaron asked in a whisper, nudging me from the next seat over.

"Yeah, just tired," I responded, mustering up a smile. I picked at the sausage on my pizza, trying to summon up an appetite.

The cross country team got together at the end of every year for a celebratory dinner at Sully's, the local pizza joint. I felt awkward and out of place this time, a fraud among my friends. I hadn't run in the last meet and our team had sucked all year.

I tried my best to participate in the conversation and laugh in all the right places, throwing in a comment here and there, trying to hide my preoccupation and anxiety.

I felt a twinge of apprehension when Aaron offered to walk me back to my car parked a few blocks down. Well, my mom's car, the one I had been borrowing since mine got turned into a pancake. I couldn't think of a way to decline without feeling like a bitch, so I agreed.

We walked in awkward silence for the first minute or two. The vibe between us was different, and I didn't like it. I could tell by the easy smile on his face that he didn't reciprocate.

"So, how are you feeling?" he finally asked.

"What do you mean?"

"You know, the car accident? Your arm? The whole reason you abandoned the team in its darkest hour?" He looked at me with a smile and raised an eyebrow.

"Oh." I felt my face flush. "I'm fine. The doctor said everything looks great on x-ray."

"That's good."

More awkward silence. I could see the car and tried not to make it obvious that I wanted to pick up the pace.

"Well, thanks, Aaron," I said, turning my back and reaching for the handle.

"Hey, Anna?" He put his hand over mine to stop me from opening the door. My heart skipped, mostly in anxiety, but with a tiny bit of anticipation as well.

"So." He scratched the back of his neck and looked down. I could see the blush crawling up his neck. "I figured since school is over, we could go out sometime, you know, to like, keep in touch."

"Yeah. Sure. Sounds good." I could feel my skin get hot, my face probably the same shade of red as his. We stood there for a moment, him gripping my hand and me trying not to pull it away.

This felt…weird. But I was also kind of flattered by the attention. I had only been asked out a couple times, and both times the date was a disaster. I usually kept to myself. I had a few select friends I was close to, but was never the type of person to dive into a group and try to get to know everyone. I guess this is why I'd never had an actual boyfriend, I just never wanted one. Maybe I was a late bloomer in that department. Or maybe just an introvert. Probably both.

My heart started racing when I noticed the look on Aaron's face. I was pretty sure he was about to try to kiss me. I turned away and reached for the door with my other hand, the one not caught in his grasp. Out of the corner of my eye, I saw him visibly deflate. I felt awful, but I couldn't add more drama to my life right now.

Once the door was open I turned back to Aaron and gave his hand a squeeze and let a smile warm my eyes, trying to convey that this wasn't total rejection. He stood up a little straighter and grinned half-heartedly at me.

"All right, great. Well, uh, I've got your number. I'll text you," he said, finally releasing my hand.

"Okay. See ya." I got in the car and drove off, giving him a wave in the rearview mirror. He waved back.

I'd text him another time. Maybe soon. I smiled.

CHAPTER 39
JOHN

The goat creature had sustained me for over two weeks, the next Leech over three. It had gotten knocked out of the third story of a parking garage after a fight with another monster. I had hidden nearby and waited for it to die as it writhed and moaned in agony. I cried then. Even though I was terrified of it, it was a living thing that was suffering and I should have put it out of its misery. But I was too much of a coward.

I didn't know why I was getting weaker at different rates each time I killed one. Maybe some were stronger than others.

I sat on the makeshift chair I had built out of crates and plywood and played with the yo-yo I had restrung with fishing line. Up, down, up, down, up, down. The monotony was helping me forget. I wanted the numbness to return.

My life here was miserable, and that was putting it mildly. If I didn't have to devise sick plans to murder monsters and then feast on their souls, it wouldn't have been unbearable. Or even that bad at all. I was an expert with the yo-yo now, teaching myself all sorts of tricks. Throwing a rotting tennis ball against the back wall of my surplus store was another favorite pastime, although it was rapidly losing its ability to bounce.

Exploring people's houses was interesting. Attics, basements, and closets often held the most fascinating artifacts. At first it felt intrusive, but then I began to crave the connection to humanity I felt when I held them, trying to spark a feeling deep inside myself other than crushing loneliness. Sometimes I would bring my deck of cards and play solitaire among the memories that I pretended were my own.

Dodging Leeches wasn't too difficult. They didn't seem very interested in me unless I was close by or startled them. I had been chased once and was certain I was about to meet my end, but I ran through a drainage ditch on the side of the road and it stopped pursuing me, almost as if it didn't want to get wet. To my confusion, exhaustion had washed over me after crossing through the water and I avoided that area ever since.

I would get a distinct feeling if I was about to enter a structure where a monster was, so I was able to avoid them. It felt like the air was thicker, constricting and heavy, sticking my clothes to my skin. There was a dread that would build the closer I got, a survival instinct to stay away. I was grateful for it as it was probably the main reason I was still alive.

I needed to go outside. The walls were suffocating, shutting in the experiences I wanted to forget. There was a small park about a mile away that I kept meaning to check out. It was secluded in a small residential area where I had never seen any Leeches. I stepped outside after scoping out the area, making sure there was nothing around.

After weaving through the three rows of spikes, I crawled on hands and knees underneath the four-layered tin can alarm I had strung across the sidewalk leading up to my store. It was a pathetic measure, but I didn't know what else to do. I wasn't able to dig up the sidewalk, so I had just left it, and dug the ditch on either side. At least the sidewalk was now the only way to safely approach the building, so if a Leech were to try to get close, it would have to trip the alarm. Who knew if I would even hear it, but it made me feel better nonetheless.

I scanned the ditch now, as I did every time I walked across it, to make sure nothing had shifted. Strips of bark and cardboard still littered the bottom, seemingly undisturbed. I gave a quick nod of approval and moved on.

I took a few of my usual routes through areas I had discovered were relatively safe, but still walking through alleyways and sticking close to buildings whenever possible.

When I reached the park, there was a concrete sidewalk that led behind a small, one story building that were probably restrooms. I followed the pavement around the back and saw an old metal jungle gym and the frame of a swing set with no swings.

I leaned against the water fountain that was affixed to the wall and just stared at the playground with a small smile. This place was familiar; I think I used to come here as a little kid. I imagined my dad pushing me on those swings, me yelling for him to push me higher, squealing with delight. My eyes teared up so I tilted my head back and blinked, refusing to acknowledge the despair.

When my vision cleared, I saw an echo sitting on the ground next to the swing set. This one looked a bit different, though, far more solid, maybe because I was so close. It was a woman, sitting cross-legged, back toward me.

I observed her, making sure to keep an eye out for Leeches who might feel her presence. She began to fade after a moment, but not completely. I could still make her out if I squinted. It was very odd; I hadn't seen an echo do this before. She started to move her head back and forth slightly, as though watching someone swinging on swings I couldn't see.

Her image hardened; I could see her clearly again. I stood up straight and cocked my head, confused. She stopped watching the invisible swings and pushed herself up to her feet. I could see the sand was disturbed where she had been sitting. My heart beat faster. Something was very off.

"What the..." I said aloud to myself.

Her head whipped around and I took a step back, eyes widening, startled.

She had heard me.

The woman stared back at me, mouth agape. Clearly she was just as confused as I was. We held eye contact for a few moments, then she darted away, down a sandy path leading into a stand of palm trees.

"Hey, wait!" I yelled, running after her. "Wait! Come back!"

I ran down the path a ways before it forked. I scanned the area, panting, but didn't see any sign of her. I ran my hands through my hair, turning in a circle, trying to process what had just happened.

That wasn't an echo. Echoes didn't leave footprints. They weren't aware that they were in the Void, let alone hear and see what was around them. Even though she had been slightly transparent, she was far more corporeal than any person I had seen thus far.

My mind flooded with questions. What was she? *Who* was she? Was she stuck here like me? Was she dangerous? How was she surviving? Did she know a way to survive that didn't involve slaughtering monsters? How long had she been here? Maybe she knew things I didn't. Maybe I knew things *she* didn't. Maybe if I could find her, I could also find some answers. Maybe I could escape.

Maybe I could go home.

CHAPTER 40
ANNA

After several heated debates with my parents, I finally convinced them to let me go on a road trip to South Carolina to visit "historic Charleston", which was obviously a lie. I was sure they knew I was lying but figured they thought it was because we planned on partying instead. Becca's mom was more laid back and agreed to it pretty easily.

The hardest part was lying to John. I knew he would do everything in his power to not let me go, or at least insist on coming with me, which would mean he would learn that Becca knew almost everything. He would *not* be happy. I had promised him I would never go into the Void by myself, but never said I wouldn't do any other research. I tried to tell myself that made it okay…ish.

We were going to leave literally right after we got our diplomas. I hadn't been excited about the graduation ceremony anyway, and being anxious to leave made it feel twice as long.

I met up with my parents a few minutes after the ceremony finally ended and my dad gave me a rib-crushing hug.

"We're so proud of you, Anna!" my mom said with a giant smile, trying to hold back tears. I chuckled, rolling my eyes.

"Thanks, Mom," I responded, my dad finally releasing me.

I handed my diploma to my mom and started shedding my cap and gown.

"That's it? Just like that and you're off?" my dad said with a smile, shaking his head.

"Yep, my bag is already in Becca's car. Hey, you guys agreed to this."

"I know, I was just really hoping we could have a congratulatory dinner or something," my mom sighed.

"All the parents are probably thinking the same thing. Any restaurant is going to be packed. It's better if we do it when I get back anyway."

"Yeah, you're probably right," she conceded.

After a few more minutes of obligatory conversation, I finally convinced my parents to go home and found Becca.

"That was so freaking boring. You'd think the culmination of our school career would be more… climactic," she said. I laughed.

We wove through the crowd and finally reached Becca's car, our bags in the back seat. It took forever to get out of the parking lot. We expected to reach the motel around 7:00 pm.

We managed to pretend we were on a real road trip for the first three hours or so. Blasting music, laughing, talking about nothing important. The closer we got to our destination, the harder it got. We were somber by the time we saw the motel sign with “vacancy” lit in neon underneath. It was the cheapest room we could find. We promised our parents we would pay them back once we both got summer jobs. I had an interview at a restaurant next week.

We zoned out watching late-night TV, trying to relax. It took me hours to fall asleep; I couldn’t turn off my brain. I heard Becca tossing and turning in the bed next to mine. Clearly neither of us was excited about this plan. I wondered if she was also starting to regret it.

CHAPTER 41
JOHN

I searched for weeks. I went back to the playground every day. I followed those paths to the very end. I wrote messages in the sand for her. I looked for human footprints that weren't mine.

I alternated between excited and vastly disappointed. I had potentially found another person here, but she clearly didn't want anything to do with me and I couldn't figure out why. Did she think I was going to hurt her? I tried to put her out of my mind so I could focus on a new plan. I checked my hash marks. It was my four-month anniversary here, and if my calculations were correct, it was also my nineteenth birthday.

My luck at killing Leeches thus far was making me lazy. It seemed like my go-to plan always worked, so I wasn't trying very hard to come up with a back-up, which I felt would probably come back to bite me in the ass.

I would stalk a Leech that seemed on the weaker side for a couple days. Most of them seemed to have a pretty clear-cut routine. I would dig a pit near the area it usually traversed, or somewhere I could lure it to, and overlaid it with palm branches and cardboard, my bear trap at the bottom. I'd wait for it to fall in and give it a few minutes to weaken, then shoot it. Usually I went through at least three bullets, either because my aim was bad, or they were duds. Most of my exploration was spent looking for guns and ammunition. Guns weren't hard to find; it was ammo that was the issue.

The last time I killed a Leech, I was out of bullets, so I had let it starve to death. It took eight days. I fought down the nausea that came with that memory. The memory of being desperate enough to let a creature die a slow and painful death. I didn't have any ammo; what other choice did I have? I was disgusted with myself, not just because I had committed that act, but also because at the time, it didn't bother me very much. This place was changing me. I didn't like the person I was becoming.

I really just wanted a clean and easy way to do it. I wished for the thousandth time that I had more bullets that worked. Guns were useless without ammo. I had a week or so before I started getting too weak to successfully pull off another hunt.

It was morning and I was planning on leaving for an overnight trip to travel to a Bass Pro Shop that I remembered being about a twenty-minute drive, so maybe ten miles away. I had found a bike trailer, which I considered to be the best thing to have happened to me so far in the last four months. Factoring time to have to hide out from any Leeches, I estimated it might take a whole day to get there. I would have to take the highway and I was not looking forward to being that exposed. I was seriously considering chickening out but I might get a really good haul.

Riding the bike with the trailer attached sucked, but I was still grateful to have it. It took me a half hour just to get up the on-ramp to the highway, since I had to walk the bike. At least it felt like a half hour; I had no way to measure time in this place other than dawn and dusk.

The pavement was punishing. It was cracked and full of potholes. Regret came on quickly. I pulled next to the guardrail to take a break and groaned, stretching my miserable legs. The trailer had already gotten stuck multiple times. It probably would have been faster to walk. I kicked the thing and growled in frustration. I debated just abandoning it, but then I would have no way of getting anything back home other than my backpack. What if I found something big? I'd have to make the trek back with the bike anyway.

Groaning again, I climbed back on the bike and started pedaling, dodging potholes left and right. My mind began to wander. I was thinking about the woman again. I imagined a silly fantasy where we found each other and fell in love. We would destroy monsters with ease and rip a hole in the barrier between the two worlds, strutting back into the human plane, reunited with our shocked loved ones. We would tell them our horror stories with pride and then would stare at us with awe, marveling at our bravery.

My fantasizing was cut tragically short as the front wheel of the bike hit a crack and turned sharply right, stopping abruptly and nearly causing me to fly over the handlebars. The chain had come off.

"Piece of shit! Can't something just be easy for *once?*" I yelled at the bike and kicked the wheel, dislodging the chain further.

I went over to the guardrail, leaning my hands on it and taking a deep breath, trying to calm down. I peered over the edge of the overpass and looked off into the distance. My jaw dropped.

Leeches. Must have been forty or more of them; I could just barely make them out. They circled a hospital whose parking lot was a short ways off the exit.

I wasn't concerned about them seeing me. Even if they could, they wouldn't pursue me. Why were there so many? It made sense that there would be a lot of echoes at a hospital. People in pain, scared family members, high-stress situations. But shouldn't that mean they would be inside? There probably *were* a ton of them inside, preying on the emotions of terrified people.

I shook my head and got back on the bike. This was *not* somewhere I wanted to be for longer than necessary.

It was dusk by the time I reached the parking lot of the Bass Pro Shop, and I was so exhausted I about passed out right there. I'd wanted to stop hours ago but didn't feel safe camping on the side of the road. I left my bike right outside the front doors; it wasn't like someone was going to steal it.

I pulled open the heavy front doors with a giant handle that looked to be made from a board of driftwood. Disappointingly, but not unexpectedly, the store was mostly empty. My best bet would be a storage room. I wasn't going to worry about that right now, though. I moved out of sight of the entrance and lay down, using my backpack as a pillow. Sleep came hard and fast. For the first time in a long time, I had a dreamless night, too exhausted to weave my waking hours into tangled nightmares.

~

The next morning, I found a box with a bunch of random stuff in it, shoved into a corner. I suspected it might have been returned items that were forgotten about and ended up packed behind a bunch of other boxes.

A pair of canvass gloves, snowshoes, an ice-fishing pole, a set of walkie-talkies, a goose decoy for hunting, and a small plate of metal on a chain that I thought might be a fire-starter. Some of that was definitely useless, but I was going to take it anyway.

There was one more box way up on the top shelf. I pushed it off with a ski pole and caught the box before it hit the floor. The cardboard disintegrated beneath my fingers to reveal its contents. Holy Mary, Mother of God.

A crossbow with a quiver of a dozen bolts.

I ran my fingertips over the bow delicately, feeling its

curves and sharp edges. My head was buzzing with excitement and hope, something I hadn't felt in a while. I set it by my backpack. I'd have to wait to figure out how to use it; there was a lot more work to be done.

The store was huge and I scoured it from top to bottom, also finding some netting, a bundle of rope, three pairs of rock-climbing shoes, one of which actually fit, a pair of sunglasses, and a kayak, which was too big to come back with me. There were huge displays of taxidermy animals everywhere—no point in taking any of them. My surplus store was going to start looking like a hoarder's house as it was.

I decided to spend another night so I would have ample time to get back. Leaving early was pivotal since the journey would take even longer than it did to get here. The trailer full of all this stuff was going to be a nightmare to get home.

At sunrise, I started packing up. Carrying the last few items outside, I pushed the door open with my hip and froze. The bike and trailer were tipped over on their sides. I set my armload of stuff down quietly and drew my knife, scanning the area but not seeing anything.

The trailer started wriggling. There was something underneath it. Moving. Heart pounding, knife ready, I crept around to the other side of the bike, giving it a wide berth.

What looked like a fat centipede had gotten trapped under it when it tipped. It was the smallest Leech I had seen, maybe about the size of a bobcat.

An easy kill. Before it could wiggle free, I stabbed it in the side of the head. It gave one final spasm and fell still. I waited a few moments for the death haze to rise, feeling that same electric tingle that I always felt right before the onslaught of emotion. I grabbed my head and waited for it to pass. It wasn't as strong as usual.

Once I had my wits about me, I righted the bike and packed everything back up. It scared me a little how commonplace that had felt. It was just a part of my existence now. I had only taken advantage of a free meal. Every time I did this, the empty hunger would fade, but in its place was a *wrongness*, like I was tainted.

I forced those thoughts to crawl back into the recesses of my brain, and focus on the task at hand. Getting back home without wanting to kill myself.

For the entire journey back, I felt like I was being watched. I kept looking over my shoulder. The feeling didn't go away the whole ride home. By the time I trudged into my surplus store, I was exhausted, miserable, and paranoid.

Even though I was about to pass out after I brought everything inside, I examined the crossbow again. I was too excited about it to be able to go to sleep without checking it out more thoroughly. It looked very straightforward. After about ten minutes of fiddling with it, I was pretty sure I knew how to shoot it. I'd have to make some kind of practice target in the morning. Right now, I needed sleep.

CHAPTER 42
ANNA

"No, no. Left up here."

Becca flipped her turn signal, frustrated. We couldn't find the parking for Saint Mary's hospital.

"There!" I pointed, seeing an entrance to a garage with a sign that read "visitor parking". We found an empty spot on the fourth level near the elevator. I got out of the car, heart racing. I glanced at Becca. Her mouth was set in a hard line, eyebrows drawn together. We got in the elevator and pressed the lobby button, still in silence.

"Bec…" I said turning towards her.

"For the hundredth time, I am going with you," she interrupted, giving me a small smile. I sighed as the elevator doors opened.

We were directed to the third floor by a woman at the help desk. After wandering the hallways for a while, we found a set of double doors with an inconspicuous sign that said "psychiatric". There was a keypad with a call button over it. Obviously only authorized personnel could get in. I pressed the call button.

"How can I help you?" an impatient voice responded through the speaker.

"Uh, we're here to visit a patient?" I said hesitantly.

"Name of patient?"

"Jackie Figueroa."

After a moment the door beeped and swung open. We approached the nurse's desk, where we had to fill out some paperwork and have our IDs scanned, and were given a list of items that we could not take in with us. I took off my belt with shaking fingers and put it in a bin, along with a pen that Becca had in her pocket, and both our purses. This was feeling more surreal by the moment.

We were escorted to room 416 by a very large man who motioned us towards the door.

"We…we just go in?" Becca asked nervously.

"Yep. She's approved to have unsupervised visitors for fifteen minutes at a time. I'll be waiting outside the door."

My heart raced. Becca took my hand and I squeezed back. The orderly looked impatient. I turned the knob, taking a deep breath. We stepped inside and he shut the door behind us, still able to see in through a little window near the top.

The walls were bare but for a small shelf over a comfortable-looking twin sized bed. A few well-worn teddy bears and a picture of an older couple rested there, watching us. A cheery quilt on the bed tried to disguise the fact that the owner was here against her will.

The bright colors and stuffed animals couldn't hide the heaviness in the room. Foreboding seeped from the walls, knotting my insides and prickling my skin. Glancing over at Becca, I could see nervousness painted on her face, and knew she felt it too.

I expected a vibe like this to come from a room plastered with images of insanity scrawled on the walls in black marker, not a space that appeared so harmless.

Where was Jackie? There was another door inside the room, presumably an attached bathroom. Just as I realized this, I heard a click and saw the knob turn. I felt Becca jump.

A woman exited, long brown hair a tangled mess. She looked to be in her early thirties, her young faced permanently etched with the wrinkles of fear and desperation, a tattered T-shirt and sweatpants hanging off her.

What stood out most of all was the black form that overlapped her frail body, fading in and out. One moment I could see her clearly, the next she was blurred behind the shadow of a creature not belonging in this world.

"What do you want?" she said. I froze, heart racing, speechless. Her voice was possessed; underneath her quiet voice was a deeper one, tainted with anger and lacking humanity.

"Um… hi Jackie. I'm Becca, and this is Anna," Becca said, hesitant. She couldn't see it.

"What do you want?" she/it asked again. Her words

were hard to make out, drowned out by a low hiss that faded as her image became clearer, the transparent form of the being within her waning until it was just barely visible.

Her eyes cleared slightly and she looked at me, puzzled. I met her gaze, still in shock, words caught in my throat. She shook her head quickly, as though trying to focus.

"Okay. Do I know you?" the human voice dominated, the deep rasp behind it just a whisper.

She watched us expectantly, and I recognized the expression in her eyes. It was the same I had seen in Brian's, an emptiness tinged with insanity.

"Well, no but…" Becca started the speech we had prepared, but I interrupted.

"How…how…" I didn't even know what question to ask. "…did it…" I trailed off. Our gazes locked, and after a moment, she realized I knew.

Jackie's eyes went wide, desperation breaking through. "It followed me," she whispered quickly, panting. She looked around wildly, as though paranoid someone was listening. "Get it out get it out get it *out!*" She screamed the last words at us, and we both bolted for the door, Becca squeezing my hand so hard I thought it was going to crack.

Jackie's words were drowned out by a low gravelly growl. Right before we rushed out of the room, I caught one last glimpse, Jackie's green eyes almost solid black, her form barely visible behind the creature, an inhuman smile stretching her shadowed lips.

I slammed the door, terrified, and Becca let out a sharp sob, backing toward the far wall, eyes still on the door as if Jackie would break through.

"What…what the *hell* was that?" she said after a moment, taking deep, shaky breaths. I just shook my head, wiping sweat from my forehead.

"She didn't tell us anything! That was pointless!" she continued, voice still trembling.

"No," I said with a mix of confidence and terror, "no, it wasn't."

CHAPTER 43
JOHN

I jolted awake. It was still dark. Something had woken me but I wasn't sure what. I grabbed my knife and the flashlight that were always next to me when I slept. I waited and listened.

Crrrack!

"What in the hell?" I whispered.

Wide awake, I crept out of the storeroom and toward the front door. The glass was covered with plywood so that nothing could see in, but I'd sawed a little slit in the wood to see out when necessary. Putting my eyes against the slit, I peered through.

Snap! Snap!

It took me a few seconds to process what I was seeing. There was a giant centipede snapping my stakes in half like toothpicks. It roared and continued destroying my pathetic fortifications.

I suddenly had the sinking feeling that I had killed its baby.

Shit shit shit!

I raced back to the storeroom, stumbling several times in my panic. Thankfully there was a plan, though not a great or foolproof one, for this situation. I unfolded one of my ladders and set it in the center of the floor, right underneath the grate on the ceiling that led into the attic. Grabbing my backpack, I threw the flashlight, knife, and binoculars I had found a couple weeks ago into it. The lighter went into my pocket.

I grabbed one of the torches I had fashioned and zipped it into the backpack, its end sticking out the top. The layers of cardboard that I had wound tightly around the top of pole would burn as well as kerosene, albeit for a shorter period of time. Thank you, Boy Scouts.

I hauled ass up the ladder and kicked it over once I managed to pull myself through the hatch. Holes in the roof let me see out of the attic in various places, but I had to be careful to not be seen through them. Clicking on my flashlight for just a second, I checked the largest hole in the back, right over the parking lot. I could see the top of the second ladder through it. My only other escape route.

I switched off the flashlight. I had this place memorized so didn't need to see very much. I looked through the peephole overlooking the entrance so I could see the Leech, barely lit by the rising sun. It was *not* happy. It approached the door and leaned its massive head down to ram into the glass. I heard it shatter, then lost sight of the creature. It must be inside.

I listened carefully, heart pounding, breathing

ragged. Quietly pulling the knife out of my backpack, I heard the creature knocking down shelves, my precious scavenged items clattering on the floor. Then silence. I held my breath, afraid of making the slightest noise. It was below me. Waiting.

Wood splintered up ten feet away from me. I clenched my teeth to trap the scream in my throat. Again, five feet away. It was ramming the ceiling. It knew I was up here.

Once more, a few feet to the left, but this time a giant pincer stabbed through and snapped around, searching for flesh. I couldn't help yelping when another deadly spike rammed through not two feet from me. The insect froze. It had heard me.

I screamed as the wood split under me and a searing pain tore through my leg. My blood poured over the pincer still stuck into my thigh. I hacked at it with my knife. The thing hissed below me but didn't seem too affected by my feeble attack. I screamed again as it yanked, trying to rip me through the ceiling by my skewered leg.

It didn't compensate for the pliability of my weak human body and pulled too hard, ripping the pincer out, freeing me with a white-hot pain. I fell backward, my vision going hazy when I looked down and saw exposed muscle. Adrenaline kept me from passing out.

I scooted backward to avoid the crumbling ceiling, trying to make my way to the ladder to the parking lot, the only hope of salvation. My leg was nearly useless, my attempts to walk, hopeless. I remembered the torch and reached over my shoulder to pull it out, using it as a crutch. Leaving a trail of blood in my wake, I desperately hobbled to the hole in roof. Using just my arm strength and left leg, I pulled myself over the ladder, throwing the torch into the parking lot below me.

I glanced back. The Leech was decimating the ceiling, its hissing screams accompanying each blow. I took a moment to mourn the only home I had ever known here, assuming it wouldn't be livable after this, but also realizing I probably wouldn't be alive to go back to it anyway.

I hopped down the ladder. Each time my good foot landed, pain seared up the other leg and I gritted my teeth, trying not to look at the blood that pumped out with each step, illuminated by the muted sickly light of the rising sun.

Picking up my makeshift crutch, I made a beeline for the bookstore next door. I had boarded it up, a heavy bookshelf waiting to blockade the front door. This part of my escape plan seemed moot at this point, considering it was doubtful I would have the strength to tip the shelf over. I headed there anyway, since I didn't have time to come up with an alternate plan. As of now the monster hadn't noticed I was gone, so maybe hiding would be enough to save my life.

The trench ended where the parking lot began, and I spared a moment to stop there and light my torch, beyond grateful that the lighter was still in my pocket. I banged the lit end of the torch on the edge of the trench, dislodging most of the flaming cardboard onto the kindling of stripped bark below. The lack of rain here was a blessing; the wood was dry as a bone and caught quickly.

The original plan was to just throw the torch into the ditch, but I needed it as a crutch. I did my best to put out the flame, grinding the end into the ground. It was still smoldering, but I couldn't waste any more time. Keeping the smoking end on the ground, I used the pole to hobble as quickly as possible, finally making my way through the entrance of the bookstore.

I tripped over the threshold, accidentally flinging my torch to the side. I crawled, dragging my leg behind me. I reached the bookshelf placed strategically next to the door, and hoisted myself up. I glanced outside in time to see that the Leech was exiting my store through the giant hole where it had busted through the front door.

With a sinking feeling, I saw that the giant fire caused by the flaming kindling hadn't jumped the sidewalk to the other side of the trench. How did I not think of that? All this planning and I missed that one huge, possibly life-ending detail. At least the fire was causing a distraction; the Leech was hesitating and hadn't spotted me yet.

I tried to push the bookshelf, grunting with effort, but it was no use. I couldn't get enough leverage with just one foot on the floor. This was the end for me, I could feel it.

Powerful heat on my back cut through my resignation, and I turned around. My torch was resting on pile of books I had knocked off the shelf, and its smoldering end had caused it to catch flame.

I panicked. There were two choices. Stay in this building and most likely burn to death, or leave and probably get killed by a giant insect. There was a back entrance to the bookstore, but I didn't know if I could get there in time by just crawling. I paused, looking outside one final time. The Leech had spotted me. I couldn't just go back outside and let it slaughter me. So I started crawling.

The bookstore was catching fire rapidly. There weren't many books on the cases, but most of them were on the highest shelves, creating a giant match, waiting patiently for the ceiling to go up in flames.

I regretted my decision. The monster would probably catch me anyway, and if it didn't, I was pretty positive burning alive would be worse. I crawled behind a large bookcase just as the Leech entered. I lay on my belly and peered around the corner to watch my demise unfold.

It made it several yards inside before it realized it was surrounded by fire, its hissing screeches growing frenzied. The front wall of the building began to crumble, blocking its path back outside.

I took advantage of its panic and army-crawled toward the back of the store, arms burning with the effort of dragging my useless leg, blood leaving a smeared trail behind me. I could feel the heat intensifying, growing almost unbearable. Terror fueled me, dulling the pain. Just fifteen more feet to the open door leading to the alleyway.

A burning book fell in front of me and I cried out as embers scorched my face. I pushed it aside with my hand, hearing my skin sizzle, but I continued. I had no choice. Agony tore through me each time I placed my hand on the floor to drag myself another foot, the friction of my raw, blistered skin against the cracked linoleum like nothing I had ever felt, worse even than the creature slicing open my leg. Something heavy and flaming dropped onto my shoulder and I screamed. The ceiling was collapsing.

I didn't look back; there was no point. I was dead whether the monster was pursuing me or not. Its frantic, inhuman screams bounced on my eardrums, percussion to the chorus of crackling fire. With one last burst of strength, I pushed myself through the door, the force of which caused me to tumble down a small ramp and come to rest on my back on the pavement.

Tasting blood and smelling my own burnt flesh, I blessedly lost consciousness. Hopefully I would die before I woke and this nightmare would be over.

CHAPTER 44
ANNA

It was a tense drive back from South Carolina. I didn't explain what I had seen to Becca and she was too shaken to ask me anything.

"What's going on?" Becca said, parking on the curb about a block away from my house. An ambulance blocked my driveway.

I shook my head, a terrible dread settling in the in the pit of my stomach.

"I…I gotta go, I'll call you." I rushed out of the car and slammed the door, not even waiting for a response. The ambulance pulled away just as I reached the sidewalk. I sprinted up my front steps, throwing the door open.

"Mom! Dad!"

"In here, sweetie!" I heard my mom's voice call from the living room. Both my parents' faces were lined with worry.

"You're back early," my dad said.

"What happened?" I asked, relieved that they were okay, but the dread was still there.

"We found Mr. Marshall lying on his front lawn so we called 911. The paramedics think he had a stroke. I'm so sorry, honey, I know how much you care about him." My mom stood up and put a hand on my shoulder. I felt the blood drain from my face.

"He seems to be in okay condition as of now, we—" my dad started.

"You couldn't have led with that! Jesus, Mom!" I threw my hands up and glared at her.

"Oh, sweetie! I'm sorry, I didn't mean to scare—"

"Whatever," I interrupted, impatient for answers. "Is he gonna be okay?"

"We saw him get wheeled out a few minutes before you got here and he looked alert, so that's good," my dad said, trying to sound optimistic. I flopped on the couch, putting my head in my hands.

"Can I go visit him?" I asked, looking up. "I mean, there's no reason I can't, right?"

"I suppose, but he has to be admitted and stabilized first," my mom answered. "You should at least wait until morning. You'd probably just have to hang out in the waiting room for hours anyway."

"Okay, I'll do that then," I grabbed the backpack I had thrown on the floor and hefted it onto my shoulder.

"You'll do what? Sit in the waiting room for hours?" my dad asked, confused.

"Yeah. Can I borrow your car, Mom?" I scanned the

end table, looking for her keys.

"Anna," my dad said. I ignored him. "Anna, come on. Get some sleep. At least a few hours. He won't benefit from an exhausted visitor." He hugged me, but I pushed him away, tears in my eyes.

"Fine!" I stomped up the stairs. I was being irrational, but I couldn't do this alone. I needed John. I knew the thought was selfish; obviously I wanted him to be okay. He was my friend, my mentor.

I threw my backpack on the floor and flopped down on my bed, taking out my phone and calling Becca. She answered on the first ring.

"Is everything okay?" she asked immediately, concern in her voice.

"It's John." I broke down, recounting what my parents told me, trying not to sound like a complete mess. She said she would go with me tomorrow to see him, and I hesitantly agreed. If he was gone, Becca was all I had left.

CHAPTER 45
JOHN

Pain. Pain everywhere. The sound of tormented screeching woke me, born from the throat of a species other than my own. My clothes were nearly gone, my exposed skin black and blistered. I lay in a pool of my own blood. Agony overwhelmed me, nearly blocking out the eerie screams.

I turned my head toward the sound and white hot burst of pain shot down my spine. The monster was about five yards from me, half trapped under rubble. It pincers feebly snapped in my direction, but its life was draining, just as mine was. I imagined it was looking back at me, but its bulging insect eyes made it impossible to tell.

Seconds, minutes, maybe hours went by, and it finally surrendered, giving a final shudder and breathing its last breath. Mine would follow soon.

With this realization came peace. This nightmare would be over. I would be dead soon and it was all right. I had done my best to survive; there was no need to feel guilty for finally giving up. Humans weren't meant to exist here.

But as the death haze rose from the Leech's body, I felt the need deep within me. The hunger that accompanied it was enough to jumpstart my survival instinct. I tried to fight it. A part of me, a *big* part, wanted to die. This felt like the right time. But my mind had cleared just enough to realize that I had a chance and I needed to take it. Otherwise I was nothing but a coward. Dying was the easy way out.

I rolled over and began to pull myself along, each movement a new level of suffering. Blackened flesh grated off my abdomen. I screamed but kept moving. Three more feet. Two. One. I reached my hand out when I thought I could take it no longer, my vision about to go dark, my body about to fail. My fingertips made contact.

The emotional rush blocked out the pain and exhaustion with a disorienting contrast, causing me to collapse onto the rubble, trying to hold onto something real.

I opened my eyes as the pain dulled and sat up slowly. I ran my fingertips over where the gash in my leg had been. It was covered by a delicate grey scar that looked like it might rip at any moment, but I was no longer bleeding. The haze lifted from my mind, the exhaustion at bay.

I did it. I was alive. It was pure luck that I came through this. I had been positive that today was the day I was going to die, but I hadn't.

The ruins smoldered around me. I had to get out of here. Something else was going to catch fire and I *really* did not want to be around when that happened, but I was so caught up in my relief and shock that all I could do was lie there.

I stood up, still weak and shaking, and took in my surroundings. The bookstore was burned to the ground, embers glowing like an old campfire. My surplus store was as good as destroyed, but maybe some of the items inside were salvageable.

I stepped out of the rubble, my eyes catching on the dead creature. For a moment, I was jealous. I shook the thought from my head and grimaced. I was still in pain but not even close to the magnitude I had felt before I fed off the Leech. But I was alive, and tomorrow was another day.

CHAPTER 46
JOHN

I peered down the sight, eyes focused on my target. I pulled the trigger of the crossbow with a practiced exhale as I had done many times before. The bolt hit its mark, piercing the Leech's eye from thirty yards away. Not surprising.

I lowered the bow carefully and jogged towards the dead Leech. I had under two minutes to make it there. In the last seven months I had had a lot of practice. I was a skilled hunter. My dad would be proud, although instead of deer, I hunted monsters.

Waiting a moment to steady myself after the emotion subsided, I ripped the bolt from the Leech's skull with a grunt, wiping the oily blood on my shorts. I left the body where it was, starting the hike back home.

I walked unafraid. Purposefully. Confidently. They were afraid of *me* now.

I was something the denizens of the Void had had no experience with before I arrived, and all they knew now was that I was a creature who brought them death. So they stayed away.

I had hardened, become a cruel and ruthless thing that I didn't know was possible to turn into. I no longer slaughtered just for sustenance, but I usually took advantage of the meal regardless, for the more often I ate, the stronger I became. If a creature got too close to me, I killed it. If something was an annoyance or I felt it could become a danger, an arrow would pierce its skull before it even realized it had been seen.

Only one thing mattered to me right now besides survival. Finding the girl.

I'd spotted her again a few months ago. I was a skilled enough hunter now to stalk her without her knowledge. She split her time between a few different places. A small gift shop on the boardwalk next to the beach was a favorite. She would sit on the sand, staring at the ocean as if she saw the crystal clear waves of the human world, rather than the murky, thick water that lapped at the gray grit, a poor imitation of the hot white sand that I remembered warming my feet as a child.

She would fade in and out, something I still couldn't understand, but made me recognize that she was different from me, that she didn't exist here under the same circumstances as I did.

The girl didn't seem too concerned about Leeches. If one got too close, she would fade, her image like the first few seconds of a Polaroid coming into focus. It seemed they couldn't sense her then, and the monsters moved on, perpetually searching for another meal.

She had control over her corporeality and I didn't know how.

The biggest conundrum was why she often visited the hospital. I wanted to follow her inside, but the place was swarming with Leeches. While they were hesitant of me, I still didn't like being so outnumbered. But, being bored, I decided I would find a way to get inside. Unfortunately, I couldn't fade away into almost nothing in order to enter unnoticed.

There were few nocturnal Leeches, and none seemed to actually spend the night near the hospital, so I figured that would be the best time to enter. That posed a problem. They couldn't see me, but that also meant I couldn't see the girl.

She always went in the main entrance. So my plan was to enter the building at night and wait in the lobby. She had been going back to the hospital every day for the last four days so I thought I could time it out reasonably well to catch her coming in. Today was the day.

Once I got back home, I gathered the essentials in my backpack and started the walk to the hospital. I wasn't looking forward to it. It was long and tedious, but I had killed two Leeches in the last three days so I would have ample strength to make the journey easily.

I took the highway, hopping over potholes and seeing how far I could kick chunks of pavement. Little things to pass the time. I wore combat boots now, so it wasn't difficult. I had shed my sandals long ago. For some reason I still didn't understand, they no longer reappeared as my clothes did every day. Maybe because I didn't want them anymore.

It was the very beginning of dusk by the time I reached the hospital. I had timed it perfectly. I hiked down the off-ramp that led almost directly to the parking lot and hid behind a concrete divider, watching the Leeches with my binoculars until I was sure there was a clear path to the entrance. They would start to leave soon.

It was a while before the area was clear enough for me to creep slowly across the lot, keeping low, not wanting to use an arrow and risk not being able to collect it. I stood up straight and scanned the area once I reached the sliding glass door. I had to pry it open and could see the glass was scratched and foggy exactly where I needed to place my fingertips. This had been done many times before by a different set of hands.

Inside was a large reception area with a desk in the center that would probably hold at least four computer stations. I ran my hand over the top. It was a dingy brown vinyl, peeling in places. It was probably made to look like wood in the human world. I absently pulled a few strips off and dropped them on the floor, trying to figure out my next move.

There were wide, low windowsills underneath the large picture windows that doubled as benches. Enough light was streaming so I could make out the reception area well, but to my dismay, there wasn't much else in it. There was some artwork and a bank of elevators on the far wall.

I sighed and ran my fingers through my hair, taking in my surroundings. Where there were elevators, there was usually a stairwell.

I saw the door. It looked heavy, a small window set into it inlaid with metal mesh, the kind that prevents someone from punching through the glass.

I approached the door and cocked my head, just staring at it, thinking that maybe I should look around the first floor for a better option. The decision was made for me when a shadow passed over the door, as if something had walked in front of the large windows in the lobby. I ducked inside the stairwell, the heavy door squeaking as I closed it, making me cringe.

Loading my crossbow, I held it ready and peered out the small pane of glass. A Leech walked across the lobby and down a hallway. It was in shadow so I couldn't make it out clearly, other than that it was about average sized, walked on two legs and looked vaguely humanoid. Its shadow didn't disappear. It paused, then turned around, entering my line of vision again. It swept its head back and forth. I thought it might have sensed me.

I shifted my bow into position, waiting, seeing if I might need to kill it. After a moment, it continued on its way, and I lowered my weapon and put the bolt back in the quiver.

What now? There was a good chance the girl would enter this stairwell, but I didn't have anywhere else I could hide. I guess I could duck down a hallway, but…

My options disappeared when I heard the squeal of the front doors being pried apart by something very corporeal.

"Shit," I whispered, and ran down a flight of stairs. I reached the bottom and sank to the floor, back against a door that had a faded "B" painted on it. I only had to wait a minute.

I heard the squeak of the door being shut and then the soft sound of human footsteps moving upward, away from me. I counted the steps until I heard another door open with a metallic squeal and then shut gently.

I dashed up the stairs as quietly as I could, counting my own steps until I stood in front of the fourth floor, where she must have gone. I pushed open the door with the faded number four painted on it. The hallway was pitch black. There was no choice but to turn on my flashlight. I didn't hear any more footsteps so I figured she was far enough away that she might not see it. Even if she did and started running, I could chase her, yelling all the way that I just wanted to talk, that I didn't mean her any harm.

I panned my flashlight up and down the hallway, seeing a sign that said "imaging" on one end and one that said "ICU" on the other. I'd start with imaging.

I kept alert for any sound or movement, human or otherwise, but hadn't seen or heard anything so far. This place felt weird. I couldn't place it. It sparked an odd feeling in my chest. I heard a door creak and switched off my crank flashlight, trying to determine where it came from. It was behind me. Back toward the ICU. I turned around and headed back the way I had come, trying to soften my footsteps to glide across the floor, as I did when I was hunting. Killing.

I ran my fingertips over the walls, trying to get my bearings since I could see almost nothing without the flashlight. As I turned the corner, however, the crack under the door to the ICU was visible, as though there were windows on the other side, letting the dusky sunlight in.

I pushed the doors open just a crack and peered through. I clutched my chest as the odd feeling grew stronger, and saw the girl. She was sitting on a desk, kicking her legs, staring at the door of a patient room, seemingly deep in thought. Not only was the girl there, but echoes of people were fading in and out constantly. Every once in a while she would study one for a moment, then go back to staring vacantly through the window of the door.

It was getting darker and I was losing sight of her. But I didn't know what to do. I was distracted by the pulling in my chest. I wanted to follow it. It felt familiar. Good.

I could see her well enough to notice her turn her head to the side, away from me, and focus on something, then hop off the desk and walk in that direction. She seemed to be looking at the echo of a man, hunched over and hobbling with the slow movements of old age. She *hugged* him.

It was another person. Like her. My jaw dropped.

"Where's Jayden?" she asked.

The old man shook his head and her shoulders dropped, disappointment clear in her body language.

"He couldn't…" the old man started, but they turned a corner and I didn't hear the rest of his words. I opened the door just enough to sneak in but stepped in a puddle of water. It startled me, and I looked down at my boot. I didn't often see water in this place, and when I did, I avoided it when possible. As soon as I took a step forward and crossed the water, exhaustion hit me like a ton of bricks, and I almost fell to my knees. This had happened to me once before when I ran through a drainage ditch. Just one more thing I didn't understand.

I shook my head, trying to fight the urge to sleep. It helped that my heart was still racing, not just with the realization that there were others like her, maybe even others like *me* here, but because I was drawn to something. The pulling was stronger, it was becoming a *need*, not unlike when I was starting to weaken and knew I had to kill something soon. But it was different too, not as tainted. More like a longing than a hunger.

I followed the two of them around the corner, staying in the shadows.

"When did it happen?" the girl asked.

"This morning," the old man replied, sadness in his voice.

"Was it a Stalker?" she asked.

"No," he said, "his parents made the decision."

I saw her shake her head and look down at the floor. “I’m so close, Albert, I know it,” she said desperately.

I heard him sigh and he took her hand. “Liz, I don’t have much time, I’m going to let go. If I can.”

“No, I just need a little more time!” she implored. The emotion hurt my heart. I hadn’t heard a human voice other than my own in almost a year. I had forgotten how powerful words could be. I gripped my chest again, compelled to move towards them.

He took her hand in his. “I’m an old man. Even if you found a way back, how long would I live? It’s my time to go, it has been since before I arrived here. Keep trying if that’s what you need to do, stay strong. I can’t help you in this. None of us have been able to do the things you can, and I’m sorry, but maybe you will find someone soon who can help. I wish I could be here for you, I truly do, but my heart isn’t in it. I’m sorry, Liz.” He hugged her and walked a few rooms down, back in my direction. Leaving her where she stood.

“Albert, wait!”

“I love you, honey, I really do, but you’ve got to let me go.” He pushed open the door to one of the patient rooms, still facing out toward her. I gasped when the feeling hit me, stronger than ever. I knew what it was now, the familiarity. The time in my parents’ basement. The moment before the demise of my body, right before I touched it, right before it was hit by a car. That feeling of connection. The pull of the physical world. It was there, in that room.

I jumped up and took a few steps forward, unable to stop myself. I heard the girl yelp in surprise and the old man stumbled back a few steps.

"Who are you?" he said with a shaking voice.

"I… I…" I couldn't answer. I was focused on the room. The closer I got, the more intense the feeling became. The need drew me in, overwhelming my exhaustion. I approached the man. He took a few steps back. The girl came forward and got between us defensively.

"Do you know where you are? My name is Liz, I can help you," she said, her voice trying to be reassuring. I kept coming closer, not answering. I took at glance at her face and saw a change in her expression, flashing from comforting to suspicious to afraid.

"It's you! Stop! Don't come any closer!" She tried to get between me and the door, but I pushed her out of the way and darted inside.

Barely visible in the center of the room was a body, seemingly floating in midair. The old man's body. Its transparency waxing and waning ever so slightly.

The feeling I had was such a contrast to this world that I let out a sharp sob. I felt the connection to humanity just out of reach.

Hands shaking, breathing ragged, I forgot about the people on the other side of the door, unable to focus on anything other than the pulling in my chest. There was a welcoming emptiness waiting for me, a different kind of Void, one that would bring warmth and joy and *life.*

“Wait! Stop!” a woman’s voice cried as the door slammed open.

I reached out. I just needed to touch it…

CHAPTER 47
ANNA

"Perfect timing. He's being discharged," a cheerful nurse said to me.

"What? Really? So he's fine?" I said, relieved and confused.

"He's in room 116 if you'd like to go see for yourself."

I jogged down the hall, following the room numbers, Becca at my heels. The door was open and John was sitting on the bed, putting his shoes on. He looked up as we entered and smiled.

"Anna! It's great you're here, you can give me a ride home," he said casually. "And you must be Becca?" He stood and shook her hand.

"Uh, yeah, hi, nice to meet you," she said, smiling.

"What happened? Did you have a stroke like they said?" I asked, concerned and baffled by his nonchalance.

"No," he chuckled, "I guess I just passed out. The heat, I suppose." I wasn't convinced.

He filled out some paperwork while a doctor spoke to him. I saw John shake his head and sigh after the doctor walked away.

"What's that about?"

"Oh, nothing. Just treating me like an old man. Talking loud and slow like they assume I'm deaf and senile. Telling me to drink enough water."

"Yeah, I mean you're obviously only like, thirty," I laughed. He chuckled, Becca laughed along, obviously not in on the joke.

We reached her car and she held the back door open for John. It was cute. I rode shotgun.

We had been driving for several minutes and Becca was making small talk. I had been silent.

"Everything okay, Anna?" John asked.

"Becca knows almost everything," I blurted the out the words before I had the sense to change my mind.

"What?" John asked slowly, his voice tinged with confusion.

"I was doing research, like you said I could, and then I found someone online who seemed like she might have some information about the Void, so we went to go see her and it sucked and I think she has a Leech attached to her and I think some serious shit is happening to Brian," I rushed, just a little too loud, ringing my hands and waiting for his response. I heard Becca facepalm and groan.

Silence.

"The only thing you specifically told me not to do

was go into the Void on my own."

"You've involved her in a dangerous situation and that's on you. I hope you realize that."

I nodded. I *did* realize that and felt guilty about it every time I saw her. Becca pulled into John's driveway.

"Come over later so we can talk more about this," John said as we got out of the car.

"Can I come?" Becca asked.

"No!" John and I both responded.

"Fine, geez. See you later, Anna." She gave me a reassuring nod and drove off.

"What were you thinking?" John asked, clearly annoyed.

"She already knew a *few* things and she could tell something was going on with me so… okay, I screwed up. It's done, can we move on now?" I crossed my arms over my chest.

"Yeah, nothing we can do now except keep her as far away from all of this as possible," he responded, his lips pressed in a hard line.

"Oh, John! You're okay!" my mom said loudly from across the yard, walking toward us. He let her know that he only fainted and thanked her for her concern, asking if I could come over and help make him something to eat since he was still feeling a little weak. She of course agreed.

Making him something to eat equated to me ordering pizza. John grilled me on what I had told Becca. I told him I hadn't said anything about our trip to the Void together and everything I had learned that day, like that he was actually a thirty-year-old man who looked like a nineteen-year-old kid who was living in an almost ninety-year-old body he had stolen from a dying man. Just saying it out loud was ridiculous in itself. She didn't know that there was a way to intentionally enter the Void, and that it required leaving your physical body. I didn't tell her we were making headway on the plan to banish or kill the Leech that had attached itself to Brian.

"Okay, so she actually knows a lot less than I assumed," John said, nodding. "That's good. So what about you guys going to see someone who had information about the Void?"

"Well, we didn't really go to Charleston..." I told him about Jackie and what I had seen. He listened with a grim expression until I was finished. "So we have to kill the Leech that has latched onto Brian, right? Because it seems pretty likely that this will happen to him, otherwise."

"Yeah, seems that way," John said, shaking his head. "This makes things more difficult. If Brian is in the same boat as Jackie, which seems likely, the Leech probably won't want to return to its body in the Void."

"So what's the plan now, then?" I asked, unable to hide the distress in my voice.

"I don't know. I'm going to have to start over."

I groaned. Every day that went by was one day closer to that happening to Brian.

"But we have another problem," John said, closing

his eyes and leaning back on the couch.

"Great. What now?"

"I didn't pass out. I slipped into the Void accidently and couldn't get back right away. I'm losing my connection to this body. Even if I come up with a plan, if we don't act soon, I might not be around to help carry it out. You'll be on your own."

CHAPTER 48
JOHN

Light blinded me, even behind closed eyelids. I squeezed my eyes shut tighter and tried to bring my arm across them to block the brightness. I couldn't. My arm barely moved; I had never experienced weakness like this. My muscles were nonexistent, pulling at my bones without success.

There was a beeping like a hot poker piercing my eardrums. Too much light and sound and feeling. I felt cloth on my skin like sandpaper, a hard pillow under my head, a stinging draft on my face.

After the burning in my eyes subsided enough, I opened them to slits. The ceiling tiles above my head were painfully white and clean. The walls were sky-blue, crystal clear and blinding. Too much sensation. I wanted to scream.

I coughed and it hurt. There was something in my throat. It was hard to breathe around it, I choked and sputtered, the sound ringing inside my skull.

The beeping grew faster and I heard footsteps. Gasping for breath, I looked towards the sound, a woman ran in and stopped dead in front of me, mouth agape.

"Oh my god," she whispered. A man followed a moment later, his expression mirroring hers.

"Code…code…I don't know! Just get a doctor in here now!" he yelled to someone behind him. The red of his uniform was too bright, his voice too loud. I shut my eyes again. Everything hurt.

I heard a third set of running footsteps and a moment later felt the tube being pulled from my throat. I gagged and coughed.

"Albert? Can you hear me?" I heard the man say, his voice calm but with a slight quiver. I flinched away from a soft touch on my arm, the sensation so foreign that it was frightening.

I opened my eyes, the colors bombarding me. A man looked down at me questioningly. It was then that I realized his words were directed at me.

"Yes," I croaked.

"How are you feeling, Albert?"

How was I feeling? Well, my name wasn't Albert. All of my senses felt heightened to the point of pain, and I was clearly in a hospital. The room was familiar.

I had no answer for him.

"Can you stay with him, Shannon?" the man said, turning towards the woman. She nodded. "I have to make a few calls."

Shannon. My sister's name. Of course this wasn't

my sister. I hadn't thought about her in so long. She was two lifetimes ago.

She waited with me. Held my hand. I tried to pull away at first, her skin hot, the touch rough. Had human contact always felt this way? I couldn't remember.

Remember...

Memories. A daughter. She was a blurry image in my mind. Dusky blonde hair and a crooked grin. She had a daughter, too. Her first birthday cake was in the shape of a whale. A wife. Dead many years ago from a stroke. A small dog, maybe a Jack Russell terrier.

Facts and images peppered my brain. Hazy and barely within reach. I knew my name was John. But I also felt it in this other life that was materializing in my head. It was dimmer though, insignificant. A middle name. Yes, that was it.

The beeping slowed as the sounds grew less painful. The colors began to look familiar again, like I had been seeing them in a haze all this time.

The memories grew clearer in my head, but I was remembering them from a distance, like recalling a bedtime story read to me a thousand times. They always remained just out of reach. Never really mine, just plagiarized. All of it was, I realized. I wasn't me and I wasn't him. The memories, the feelings, the humanity. A borrowed life. A stolen life. A life I could never return. But I knew that even if I could, I wouldn't. I didn't want to. It was mine now, and I was going to live it.

CHAPTER 49
ELIZABETH

The thought had been hitting me more often lately despite my efforts to shove it back into the little box in my mind. I wished my parents would give up. Curse my dad and his PhD in Computer Engineering with his three-hundred-thousand-dollar annual salary. I never thought that being able to afford to keep your child on life support would be a bad thing. I should have written a will. I didn't want this; no one would.

But if they had faith that one day I would come back, I owed it to them to at least try. I was out of ideas, though, and with no one around long enough to help. I was on my own. I tried to deny it, but I wanted to make it back because of Jordan, too. Not because I still loved him, though I did, but because he had moved on, and I wanted to make him feel guilty about it.

This was terrible and irrational and I knew it. Did I really want him to live the rest of his life alone just because he couldn't spend it with me? Of course not, and yet the feeling tickled the back of my brain.

Mindful Meditation and Yoga, LLC had been dissolved. Nobody wanted to run the business and no wonder; after two years I had only had eight regular clients and was tens of thousands of dollars in the hole. I looked back on it with embarrassment. The skills I taught my clients weren't very useful in everyday life, although they might be if any of them ever ended up here.

I had stopped going to the boardwalk years ago; it was too painful a reminder of the life I no longer led. I spent most of the time at the hospital, trying to pick up the vibrations of a new vacancy. It was the only place that one would be around for long, and I only had the time and energy to keep one location protected from Stalkers, anyway.

I had felt something odd a week or so ago. It felt similar to a vacancy, but not quite as open, as if the soul was still hanging on. It was strange; I hadn't felt anything like it the thirteen years I had spent so far in this purgatory. I let my mind flow out again, searching for the feeling once more. I would get a hint of it now and again.

There it was. Somewhere north of me. I sighed, kicking my heels against the front of the nurses' desk, swinging my legs as I sat atop it, as I had done countless times over the years. Should I try to find it? It was something new, which could be bad. Or it could be a chance I had yet to pursue. I decided to go for it.

I took a moment to feel for my parents. They didn't visit me often anymore. Maybe twice a month. Breathing deep, I focused my mind and shifted myself closer to the physical. Medical staff swarmed around like a busy hive of bees, their drone audible over the silence of the Echo. They couldn't see me and it made my heart ache, how I longed to just be noticed. And while they weren't solid to me either, just a projection over the empty landscape where I spent most of my time, I liked to pretend I was there.

I didn't feel the presence of my parents. Disappointment resonated through me, just like it did every time. I didn't bother taking my usual stroll through the hospital corridors, watching the people walk through me. Instead, I let myself fade back out, once again alone in the emptiness, only experiencing the physical world as a movie in the background.

I pushed open the hospital doors, then faded out quickly to make sure I remained unseen. I hated walking. I had yet to figure out how to travel without walking. I could skip a short distance but was still working on it; it was difficult and unsuccessful most of the time. I could project my mind far distances and yet still had to walk my only partially physical form from point A to point B. And having to fade in and out repeatedly to avoid Stalkers was draining.

I walked for a long time. When I finally stopped, I found myself in front of an ordinary-looking house, but it felt ominous. The vacancy was in there somewhere but I again felt that it was only…partial. Something was wrong. I peered through the hazy window, unwilling to open the front door. I was too nervous. I debated leaving, but again thought of my family and how desperately they wanted me back, and how badly I needed to escape.

I saw nothing through the front window, so I circled the house, looking for others. Coming around to the side of the house, I spotted another window. Standing on my toes, I gazed in. A boy sat on a bed. I could see the overlay of sheet and blankets covering a mattress, where in the Echo, it was nothing but an empty bedframe. The boy was neither here nor there, which was what I would have expected in regular circumstances, except he wasn't right in the middle, either; he was much further toward the physical.

I furrowed my eyebrows, confused, and leaned to the side, trying to get a better view of the rest of the room.

There, in the corner. A Stalker.

I ducked quickly, heart pounding. Normally I wouldn't be too concerned, I would just press myself closer to the physical and it would leave me alone, but this one was different. It was here with me, in the Barrier.

How? *How?* It was far more solid than the boy, but still not completely in the Barrier. I had never come across this before. It felt…dangerous.

I slowly peeked inside again, rising on my toes. The boy's soul was still inside his body, but it felt slightly off. Almost like it was out of sync with his physical form. It only took me a second to realize why.

The Stalker was no longer in the corner, instead, I could see the two forms overlapping, moving as one. I

back again, she was still staring at me.

"What…" she trailed off, our eyes locking once more. I inhaled sharply. She *was* looking at me! Then I saw the Stalker behind her, its red eyes peering out from the bedroom, giant claws gripping the doorframe, and I yelped, losing my shift toward the physical and coming to rest back at the center of the Barrier, opaque in neither world.

I ran, I even managed to skip a few short distances, putting more space between me and the Stalker with each passing moment. I risked a glance back and didn't see it. I wasn't going to pursue this. Not a chance. But that girl. I needed to find that girl.

CHAPTER 50
ELIZABETH

I spent an absurd amount of time trying to locate her. I stopped searching for other vacancies. I neglected my weekly task of lugging water up to the ICU to keep the Stalkers away, and would lose the safe place I had created if I didn't do it again soon. But I didn't care. I found a possible connection to the physical world. A way to talk to my parents and tell them what I truly wanted. *Or maybe the girl would do it.*

I couldn't stay at the boy's house for long because he and the Stalker were almost always there, so I followed his mother to work instead. I was getting better at skipping, so I was able to keep up with her car. Keeping myself next to the physical for such long periods of time was incredibly draining, but I had an opportunity that I wasn't about to let slip away.

His mom, Sue, was a receptionist at a dental office. She had pictures of her son playing football and talked of him often. His name was Brian.

The other employees talked in hushed tones about Sue's son. Wasn't it just so sad what happened to Sue's son? Did you hear he might not ever recover? She needs some time off, others would say, feigning genuine concern. Mental health issues run in the family, you know.

Backstabbers, all of them.

I waited for her to make some mention of the girl, but she never did. I thought she was a girlfriend, maybe, but no. I did find out that Brian went to Cypress High, so I searched there often, but there were hundreds of kids. I knew I could pick her out easily if I just saw her face. It was burned into my memory.

I stood in the middle of the girls' bathroom next to the cafeteria, listening to them talk shit about each other while they walked through me. I ran my hands through my dark brown hair and pretended to examine the status of my makeup in the mirror. I was wearing no makeup, nor did I have a reflection. All I knew was that I was wearing the same faded blue jeans with a hole in the knee and light blue turtleneck sweater that I was wearing on January fourteenth, thirteen years ago, the day I died. Every once and a while if I focused hard enough I could change the color of my shirt a few shades or fix the hole in the knee. I had even tried making my pixie-cut hair longer a few times, but it didn't work.

"Oh come on Becca, you're serious?" I heard a familiar voice say.

"I swear to *God*, Anna!" Another girl laughed.

"You're full of shit." More laughter.

I looked towards the swinging bathroom door and saw the girl. Anna, I assumed, based on the overheard conversation. My heart leapt and I faded out enough where if I didn't move, she probably couldn't see me. Well, that was a big probably considering she shouldn't be able to see me in the first place.

I crouched in the corner of the bathroom by the handicapped stall, observing. They were much harder to see now, just ghostly traces and whispered words, but I didn't want to scare her.

I almost lost track of her when I was forced to avoid a Stalker that was a little too close for comfort, praying on the troubles of stressed out students. I needed to find out where she lived. I followed her all the way home, since her friend drove her to school.

Her parents were home so I didn't bother going inside. I needed to get her alone so I wouldn't terrify her when she saw me, and also so that she wouldn't look crazy when she began talking to thin air, assuming she could still see me and was willing to talk.

I had been close to the physical for too long and was getting exhausted. I wanted to talk to her today, but it wasn't going to happen. But I knew where she lived now, so I could come back another day.

When I finally made it back to the hospital, I noticed that the water surrounding the ICU was almost completely gone. If I didn't take care of it, it would soon be overwhelmed by Stalkers.

I wasted two days doing that. It was always an exhausting task. Then I went back to the school to see if I could get more information on Brian before I gathered the courage to talk to Anna. It was empty. School had let out for the summer.

I kept going to her house to try to talk to her, but she was never alone. I was beginning to get really frustrated. Finally, the fifth time I visited, her parents weren't home and she was getting out of her car. Perfect timing. This was it.

Only it wasn't. Her friend was with her. I groaned. Whatever, I was going to do it anyway.

I went inside to wait for them and double-checked that no one was home. The house was empty. I waited in the living room, close to the Echo, so that she wouldn't see me as soon as she walked in. I didn't want to scare her.

I was exhausted. Fading in and out like this all day for close to two weeks was draining me. I let myself rest for a moment; the furnishings of the living room faded almost completely as I settled back in between the two worlds, the purgatory where I existed as my whole self. Neither here nor there.

My rest was cut short when I spotted a Stalker outside. I pressed up close to the physical, protecting myself from the creature who couldn't follow me there. The couch came into focus and I ducked behind it out of habit, even though it didn't exist where the Stalker was anyway.

I heard the startled squeal of a young girl and stood to face her.

"Oh my god, I'm so sorry!" I said, I held up my hands and backed away, trying to look non-threatening. Her wide eyes examined my face; she was clearly confused and nervous.

"Anna? Are you okay?" the redhead asked. I recognized her as the one from the bathroom conversation. Becca.

"Yeah…" she said, still looking at me, expression unchanged.

"What…what are you doing?" Becca said, noticing her staring at nothing, and waved her hand in front of Anna's face.

"Just…" Anna said to her. "Can you go get us some sodas?"

"Oh, nuh-uh. You're looking at something, aren't you!" Becca tried to follow her gaze but obviously couldn't see me.

"Anna, you're scaring me!" she pulled on her arm, trying to get her attention.

"It's that woman I told you about," Anna half-whispered to Becca. I was surprised.

"Wait…the ghost lady?" Becca said, glancing in my direction nervously. I laughed out loud, her dramatic whisper made me sound like I floated around in a long white nightgown and howled in the shadows.

"What is she doing?" Becca whispered again, grabbing Anna's arm with both hands and pulling her close. I chuckled.

"Nothing. She's—" Anna grinned "—laughing at you."

"What? Seriously?" Becca scoffed, standing up straight, "Why?"

"Who…what are you?" Anna asked, ignoring Becca and addressing me.

"I'm Liz. I…I need your help. Please. I don't know why you can see me but I've never come across anyone else here who can so…please just hear me out."

"Okay, but like, what…" she started, trailing off. "What are you? Are you dead? A ghost? What's going on? This is just too much." Anna said, scrubbing her hands over her eyes. "It's just one more thing, every day, there's just something else."

"What'd she say?" Becca asked, wide-eyed.

"She wants…just give me a sec, okay?" Becca sat down on the couch with a huff, crossing her arms impatiently. She kept glancing over to Anna and then back in my general direction, hoping to see something.

"So… it's complicated. I guess you could say I'm dead…"

"So you *are* a ghost!" Anna interrupted, and I heard Becca inhale sharply.

"Well…sort of?" I said, impatient to get on with the important part of the conversation.

"How can you be *sort of* a ghost?" Anna asked, confused.

"Well, my body is…alive…sort of," I continued,

exasperated, not knowing how to explain. How could she possibly understand without me retelling my entire life story? Or death story, I guess.

"But…"

"My body is on life support in the hospital. But *me*, I'm… in a different place. There's this place that people go when they are in my situation. It's really complicated to explain and I don't want to scare you…" I began.

"Wait, are you in the Void?" Anna asked, looking like she had some kind of epiphany.

"The what?"

"The Void—well, that's what John calls it. He's…gah, doesn't matter. Is it sort of empty but full of monsters?"

I was shocked. "How…how do you know about that?"

"I've been there. It was by accident at first…but why were you at Brian's house? Do you know what's happening to him?" She sounded so desperate, it struck a chord with me. I felt the same for different reasons.

"I'm not *entirely* sure. I've never come across something like his situation. I think the Stalker is somehow where I am."

"Stalker? Oh, a Leech. *Somehow* where you are? I thought you were in the Void, where all of them are."

I let out a deep breath. It was getting hard to keep myself pressed up against the physical for this long so I needed to get this conversation going. It took another ten minutes to give a rough explanation of neither existing in the world she did, nor the world that the Stalkers did, but somewhere in between. I told her that I believed it had something to do with still being connected to the physical plane. She was rapt the whole time. She interjected that she thought she could see me because she had a connection to what she called "the Void".

"So what do you want from me?" Anna asked.

I steeled myself for my next explanation and attempted to tell it as calmly as possible. I needed her to sympathize. "My time on this earth was supposed to end thirteen years ago. My parents have kept my dead body alive for too long. I need them to let go. I need to move on." I tried to not let my doubt show. I had spent so long trying to figure out how to get back into my body, but ten years ago, I had finally begun to come to terms with the fact that it was impossible. But then I saw Albert's body get stolen. And though I was furious and upset that someone would violate him like that, it also renewed my hope that I could do the same to my own body.

I couldn't, though. There was something different about the boy who had soaked into Albert like water into a dry sponge. Now, instead of hoping to accomplish the same as the boy, I longed for Albert's demise, who had faded very soon after his connection to his body was severed. He was peaceful when he went, and I was envious of the look of serenity that had come over him. I was torn between fury, jealously, and grief for a long time, even though I had known Albert such a short while. The boy killed Albert's soul. It wasn't his intent, but that was the truth of it. But it had been the old man's time for over a week already and he wanted to move on. I just wished it hadn't been forced upon him so unexpectedly.

"You mean you want them to…pull the plug?" Anna whispered the last part, trying not to sound insensitive.

"Well…yes. Although it's a bit more complicated than that," I responded matter-of-factly.

"How I am supposed to convince them to do that? They don't know me. It's not like I can tell them you told me that that's what you want."

I took a deep breath. I knew this. My parents were skeptical atheists. I didn't think there was any way she could convince them.

"I was hoping that…you would do it." I didn't know how to say it delicately. So I just said it.

"*Me?*" she asked incredulously. "You've *got* to be kidding. You just want me to walk into a hospital and pull the plug on someone like it's no big deal? How would I even get into your room? How would I do it without it being *murder*? Have you even thought this through?"

"I have no other solution. You could disable the alarms on the machines—I know how to do it—and I am pretty sure I know how to turn off the equipment. I could be on the lookout, tell you if someone was coming. Hopefully no one would notice until I was…well, dead."

"There is no *way* I wouldn't be caught! This is insane. There have to be so many things in place to prevent people from doing that in the first place!"

Meanwhile, Becca sat up straight on the couch, mouth agape, staring at Anna. Chances were she was putting two and two together on at least a few things we were discussing.

"What if I help you?" The thought struck me. I might have a bargaining chip. The life raft she was hoping for. "With Brian." I didn't even know if I could. Or how. But I would try if it meant I could finally rest in peace.

She paused. A good minute went by, her eyes unfocused. They blurred with tears.

"How?" she asked, finally looking up at me.

"I…I don't know exactly. But I'm on the same plane with the Stalker who's draining him. You don't have that advantage."

I was terrified that she would accept my terms. But I also prayed she would. I was done with this life, had been for a long time. Souls didn't belong where I was. There was an afterlife beyond this. I could feel it at my fingertips. It was warm and welcoming, like sitting in front of a fireplace on a perfect Christmas day. Pure serenity.

I deserved it. I had waited long enough. I was willing to do anything, I decided. Absolutely anything. My potential savior came in the form of a naïve high school girl. My fate was in her unfortunate hands.

CHAPTER 51
ANNA

"Okay," I said.

"Okay?" Liz responded, surprised. Becca cut off my response when she stood up suddenly and gripped my arm.

"Anna. I'm not totally sure what you just agreed to, but I think I got the gist of it. Think about this. Please. You could be getting yourself tangled up in some serious shit right now."

"*I* am responsible for fixing this, Becca! *I* messed up Brian. *I* did! I can't let him end up like Jackie!"

"It was an accident! This might have happened anyway, regardless of if you were involved or not. You don't know for sure it was all you," she pleaded.

"Yes. I do. You don't understand how it works."

"Then explain it to me! I want to be here for you Anna, I'm worried about you."

"I can't! I don't want you mixed up in this any more than you already are." She threw up her hands in defeat, tears in her eyes. I shifted my focus to Liz. If I kept looking at Becca the guilt was going to overwhelm me. I should have never told her anything.

"We should all go talk to John," I said. "He definitely needs to be in on this."

"Who's John?" Liz asked.

"He's my neighbor. He can travel to the Void too. He knows way more than I do; he was stuck there for a while."

She cocked her head and narrowed her eyes, looking suspicious. Did she think I was lying? "You're going to have to do that on your own for now. I can't hold myself here any longer. I have to go. Can we meet again soon?"

"Uh, yeah. How about day after tomorrow? Around this time. My mom won't be home and I will have had time to talk to John."

"Okay. Can we…" She faded out of existence before she could finish the sentence. I shrugged. We managed to come up with a meeting place so she could finish her sentence then.

"So?" Becca asked, arms crossed, looking pissed.

I filled her in on what she hadn't deduced already. She was looking more and more worried by the moment. I could tell how badly she wanted to argue but she knew I had made up my mind.

She had to go home and I had to go see John. I promised I would fill her in, but I wasn't sure I wouldn't leave out some details.

I headed over to John's after shoving some food in

my face and waking myself up with a soda. I took another can with me. I had a feeling this was going to be a lengthy conversation.

~

"No," he said.

"Wait, what?" I was confused. "What do you mean 'no'? She can totally help us! And you're not the only one who gets to weigh in here. I think we should take advantage of her offer."

"It's too risky. You could get caught."

"So, what? We just let Brian go nuts? I *can't* do that."

"Anna…"

"This is bullshit! This isn't like you! What the hell, John?" Ever since I'd told him about Liz, he had been acting weird. I thought he would at least consider it.

"You know if they catch you, you'll be charged with murder!"

"She's already dead. She can't go back."

"Not in the eyes of her parents. Or the law."

"I'm not letting this go. I'll do it without you if I have to."

John lowered his head and rested the bridge of his nose on his fist. He was clenching his teeth, the muscles in his jaw taut. He met my eyes after a long moment, then looked away.

"I'll do it," he said.

"You'll do what?"

"I'll pull the plug. She doesn't have to help us. I'll just do it."

"What? You're confusing the hell out of me. You just said that was the risky part. Why would you want to do that and not let her help us?"

"I just…I don't want her help."

"Why? You're not making any sense."

"I don't want anyone else involved. You've already involved Becca."

"This is different and you know it! Can't you just talk to her?"

"Just leave it alone, Anna," John said. He wouldn't make eye contact.

"Whatever. You're being so freaking ridiculous right now, you know that?!" I grabbed my soda and stormed out. This did not go as planned.

I thought I had finally gotten one step closer to saving Brian. I guess I was wrong.

~

"Then make him talk to me!" Liz pleaded. This was such a disaster.

"Maybe we can come up with a plan and then it will convince him," I offered.

"It would be better to have three minds working on this. And no offense, but you don't seem to know much about Stalkers."

I scoffed. "Maybe not, but I'm here in the human plane and I'm the only one we've got right now, so maybe you can just fill me in."

It was taking me a while to get used to talking to Liz. Her image was wobbly and transparent, her voice sounded far away and echoed slightly. Sometimes she would be more opaque than at other times. It looked like it took a great effort to stay visible to me.

"I have thirteen years' worth of knowledge. I don't even know where to start."

"Well, you said the Leech is attached to Brian, right? Is there a way to…unattach them?"

"Probably."

"How?"

"In normal circumstances, and let me stress that this is *not* a situation I have ever encountered, so I don't know if the same rules apply, Stalkers have to be close to the person they are feeding off. Just getting it away from him might be enough, but I don't know what would happen after that. It doesn't have a physical body in the…what did you call it? Void? It doesn't have a body there. There's a chance it might die if it doesn't have a host to feed off."

"So can't we just lure it away?"

"And then what? And how?" Liz asked with a raised eyebrow.

"Well…okay, I don't know." My shoulders slumped. She was right, I didn't know enough. We needed John.

"It might just be able to latch onto another person. I

feel like that's probably not the case, though. I've observed them a few more times and it seems like they have some kind of co-dependent, parasitic relationship."

"This is stupid," I said after a moment, standing up from the couch. "I'm gonna go talk to him again. Can we meet up again tomorrow?"

She sighed. "Sure. You're going now?" she asked, frustration clear in her voice.

"Might as well. I have nothing better to do." I did have a job interview coming up. Was that tomorrow? I couldn't keep the days straight. Maybe a job would stop me from feeling so useless. And broke.

She faded out without a word.

CHAPTER 52
ELIZABETH

I watched through the window. I could only see Anna. I shifted from side to side, trying to get a look at the man. Maybe I could read their lips if I could just get in a position where I could see them both. They turned a corner and I could no longer see Anna either.

"Crap," I whispered.

Now was my chance. I faded out as much as I could, watching the world break down in front of me. The door knocker rusted, the wood around it rotting and moldy. The siding on the house was cracked and gray. The furniture I had been able to see in the living room just moments before was gone.

I opened the door slowly and crept inside. My fingertips sank into the rotting wood and some of the door crumbled as I began to shut it. I could see the vague overlap of the door on the physical side, out of sync with the decrepit one in the Echo. One closing slowly behind me, the other still shut, unmoved from Anna's perspective.

I crouched behind the wall next to the entrance to the kitchen, where I had seen the two of them go a few minutes ago, and faded back toward the physical. Anna, and maybe John too, would be able to see me now, so I waited a moment before peering around the corner. I could hear Anna telling him what I had told her about how luring the Stalker away from Brian might break the bond. I listened for his response.

"And how would we even do that? There's nothing that I can think of that it would be interested enough in to detach itself from Brian except maybe one of us, and I'm not willing to risk that."

My mouth dropped open. I knew that voice.

"Albert?" I whispered in disbelief, standing up and turning the corner to face them.

They both whipped around toward me. He met my gaze and I saw a flood of emotion in his eyes once recognition hit. Surprise, resignation, shame. But most prominently, guilt.

"I knew it would be you," he said, dropping his eyes.

"What's going on?" Anna asked, looking back and forth between us.

"You…you're the boy. Ten years ago. How…" I didn't know what to say.

"Yes," he said, eyes still lowered, shame in his voice.

Anger hit me. Fresh anger, the same as when I felt the connection between Albert and his body break. I couldn't speak. There was no question I could think to ask that I didn't already know the answer to. Why did he do it? Because he wanted to escape, same as the rest of us. How did he do it? Neither of us knew.

"You killed him," I said, voice dangerously calm, holding the rage back.

"I didn't! I heard your conversation with him. It might have been ten years ago, but it's still there. He was almost gone, he said so himself. He couldn't use his body anymore!"

He pleaded for my understanding but it was tinged with guilt. He doubted his own words.

"Oh my God," Anna said, understanding washing over her. "This is why you didn't want her to help us! It had nothing to do with being worried about me!"

"I admit that this was a part of it, but I still think the plan is dangerous," John said, a different shade of guilt this time. The one that came with being caught in a lie.

"I can't *believe* you! You're so selfish! You would sacrifice Brian's sanity so you didn't have to face your past? Maybe it's about time! I *knew* you'd done something horrible to get that body!"

"Anna, please, you have to understand…" He took a step towards her, reaching out, but she turned away, tears in her eyes.

"No. I trusted you. You promised to help me because you think it's partly your fault. You could have at least atoned for *one* mistake you made."

What did *that* mean? My anger ebbed a bit.

"What mistake?" I asked.

"I accidentally let the Leech out because I crossed into the Void without meaning to. John thinks the reason I started being able to do that in the first place was because he made the barrier thinner. By going in and out so much," she answered, sniffling.

"Why would you do that?" I asked John, my voice still quivering with rage and suspicion.

"Go back all the time?" He sighed. "It's how I keep my astral alive. I need to kill Leeches." His lip curled up at the end of his sentence. He was disgusted with himself. I saw the same disgust mirrored on Anna's face. Clearly she hadn't known this either.

"How are *you* still alive? After more than ten years?" he asked.

"I just am. I don't know. I think it's because I'm still connected to my body. I certainly don't have to *kill* anything."

"Don't they try to kill you?" Anna asked, still refusing to look at John.

"They would, but I can protect myself from them. I can fade next to the physical like I am now. They can't touch me here. And I use the water to keep them away from the ICU."

"The water?"

"Yes," I answered her. "The water drains them, I don't know why, but they avoid it. I saw a Stalker fall in once. It didn't have the energy to get out and drowned."

I spared a look at John. Realization passed over his face.

"So have you..." John began to ask me another question but I cut him off.

"I can't just stand here and have a casual conversation with you. When I look at you, I still see him. And what you did."

"I need to go too," Anna said. "I can't..." She just shook her head and left, slamming the front door behind her.

John looked devastated. So much regret in his eyes. I almost felt sorry for him. Almost.

"I didn't mean to do what I did ten years ago. I felt...life...within my reach when I stepped into that hospital, and I was so drawn to it that I didn't even know what was happening. Or the consequences of what I was doing. I didn't even *realize* what was going to happen when I touched him. I had lived in hell for a year. I was losing my humanity. I hadn't touched or spoken to another human being in so long. You had other people. *Friends.* You can obviously see this world. Could you do that then? I had none of that. I was alone. Miserable. Killing monsters to survive. I am so sorry. So, so sorry." He looked away, trying to hide the tears in his eyes. As much as I wanted to hate him, I pitied him. I tried to shake the feeling away but I couldn't.

"I need to go," I said. I didn't want him to see the emotion.

"But..."

I faded out. I couldn't be here anymore. The mixed feelings were killing me. I left him with his remorse.

How could I forgive him if he didn't even forgive himself?

~

I sat cross-legged next to the slide on my favorite playground, leaning back against the rusted metal. I had been going over what John had said over and over in my mind for the last two hours. I didn't want to but I couldn't help it.

How would I have felt if I was alone? I had discovered other people pretty shortly after I had arrived in the Barrier. My ability to fade had come pretty quickly as well, the years of intense meditative control over my mind and spirt in the physical world becoming invaluable.

By myself for a *year*? I would have gone crazy. And he had to kill Stalkers to stay alive? How did he even figure that out? What happened after he killed them that kept him alive? I shuddered. I imagined him eating their flesh. No. *No.* I would die before I resorted to that. But would I? Self-preservation is so ingrained in humanity, in *all* creatures. If I figured out that would keep me alive, maybe I *would* do it. There were stories about people cutting off their own limbs to save themselves. I'd hear that and think, *I could never do that*. But I could if I had to.

He felt a way back, a connection to humanity, and was so desperate for it that he seemed to be in a trance, unable to stop what he was doing. He didn't know the consequences of his actions. And Albert was happy to go. He was done with this place. I was mad because I missed him and didn't get to say goodbye. I hated to admit it, but my anger was selfish.

I sighed and rested my head back, staring up at the dirty yellow sky. The withered trees. I felt brittle, dead grass tickling my skin, growing in sand that felt thick and dirty. I wasn't stuck here. Well, I was, but not the way John had been. I could fade to watch people in the physical world whenever I wanted. I didn't have to fear Stalkers most of the time. He must have had to be on constant alert, never knowing when violence and death would come for him. It was no wonder that he did what he had. He hadn't stolen a body; he had found a door out of hell.

I understood.

I groaned, realizing I was beginning to forgive him. I needed to help him and Anna. Like she'd said, he could at least atone for one of the mistakes he had made. I wasn't going to let the second chance at life that Albert had given him go to waste. He was *going* to help Brian. And maybe once he had, he would help me, too.

CHAPTER 53
ANNA

"Anna."

I squealed and jumped up from my bed, my moping cut short. I wiped the tears from my eyes and saw the fluctuating form of Liz standing in my bedroom door.

"You okay, honey?" I heard my mom yell from downstairs.

"I'm fine!"

I heard her footsteps coming up the stairs. She knocked on the door.

"Are you sure? Do you need some help? I can get Dad to help you with some potential questions. He'd be good at that."

"No thanks, Mom. I got it." I had told her I was prepping for my interview scheduled for tomorrow.

"Okay. Well, let me know if you change your mind," she said, and walked away.

"What are you doing here?" I whispered. "My parents are home."

"Sorry," she said. "I wanted to talk to you." Her demeanor was different than the last time I had seen her.

"What is it?"

"I want to help you."

"Really?" I was surprised.

"Yes, I think we can do this. I think Brian still has a chance."

"Oh, thank God!" Hope spread through me. But also doubt. "I don't know much about the Void. I haven't tried traveling there by myself yet. I don't know how much I can help without John."

"We need him, too."

"What?" I was shocked. "Don't you hate him? Why would you be willing to work with him after what he did?"

"We both need to forgive him. I think I already have," she stated with a shrug.

"Are you serious? Just like that?"

"No, not just like that. After you left, we talked some more. I understand what he did and why he did it. I hate myself a little for accepting it, but I've harbored this anger for ten years and it's time to let it go and realize that he deserves some understanding."

"Seriously? Okay, well he totally lied to me. Why should *I* forgive him?" I didn't think I could get over it as easily as she appeared to have.

"He was scared. I don't agree with how he handled that, but you should at least try to put it aside for now if you—if *we* have any chance of saving Brian."

She sounded determined. It was hard not to let it resonate.

"Okay. I'll try. I still need some time," I said, resigned to the fact that this was going to happen.

"I completely understand. Took me ten years. Can we meet up tomorrow morning? Will your parents let you go over John's house again?"

"Yeah," I said, "they think he's getting too old to take care of himself so they think I'm, like, his helper or whatever. They encourage it."

"Okay, that works out then. Go over there around…ten o'clock? I'll meet you inside, presuming he's home and lets you in."

"Yeah, sure," I said.

I was still angry but trying to not let it leak into my voice. She was right. If we had any chance of saving Brian, I had to let the feeling of betrayal go for now, although I didn't know if John deserved it.

CHAPTER 54
ELIZABETH

We stood in John's kitchen. He looked at us with nervous expectation. I glanced at Anna, who was still avoiding looking at him, arms crossed, mouth set in a thin line, looking pissed.

"I'll still help you," I stated.

"You will?" John asked, shocked.

"I refuse to let you cut another life short. One time is more than enough," I said. Although I forgave him, I didn't want him to know it yet. My words sounded cruel and he flinched, but I wanted his guilt to spur him into action.

"Besides, I have an idea," I continued.

They listened intensely, absorbing every word. Nodding along in the right places, asking questions and throwing in their own suggestions. When we finally came to a conclusion, it was quiet for a while, each of us pondering our own role in the plan. John broke the silence.

"You really think you can do that?" John asked.

"Yes. It'll take a lot of effort, but I think I can. I've taken things deeper into the Barrier with me before. I've never tried doing it with water, though. Hopefully it works the same way and will have the same effect on the Stalker."

"What if it, like, eats you or something? I mean, that's what they do, right?" Anna interjected.

"Well, not exactly, but I guess you could say that. Maybe it would be the end of me, but that's what I want anyway. It's not the way I would *prefer* to go, obviously, and I need to finish my part first. Albert seemed so peaceful when he faded. I'd rather have that experience than be terrified."

"We will do everything in our power to not let that happen," John said. I couldn't trust him, though. Not quite yet. "If we can get you away from it in time, you should be fine."

"That's a big if. This whole plan is built on assumptions. One is bound not to be correct," I said.

"That's not true. We know a few things for sure." He began ticking off on his fingers. "A. An astral, or soul as you call it, can only be in the Barrier if it is connected to a body. Therefore, if we cut its connection to Brian's body, it shouldn't be able to survive, same as what happened to Albert." John's cheeks flushed in shame as he said this.

"Again, that's an assumption. We don't know that the same rules apply to the Stalker."

"Okay, so for the sake of optimism, let's pretend it's true," John said. I rolled my eyes.

"B. Water weakens the Leeches." I opened my mouth to propose the same argument. He cut me off.

"We *know* that's true. There is no reason it wouldn't be the case in this situation. C. Distance should break the bond between it and Brian, as it does between a person's echo and a Leech in the Void. The water should make it easier. And D, I will admit is an assumption. It will *probably* be too weak to latch onto one of us."

Anna raised her hand. "So how I am supposed to kidnap Brian?"

John groaned. "For the sixteenth time, you are not *kidnapping* him."

Anna shrugged. "He *hates* me. How else am I supposed to do it?"

"She's right. Maybe we should just knock him out or something," I interjected.

"Oh my God, you guys. There has to be a way to do this without committing a felony," John said, exasperated, pacing the kitchen.

Anna sat up straighter. "He had a drinking problem for a while. Or that's what the rumor going around was."

"Okay, we might be able to use…" he started, then fell to a heap on the tile.

Anna gasped and jumped up.

"What the…" I began, then I saw him. The boy. A weak image of him. He was on the other side. He was looking around, confused. He squinted at me. He must have been able to see a faint outline of me. I was pressed up against the physical, far away from where he was.

"Oh my God, John!" Anna rushed over, kneeling next to him.

"It's okay. I see him," I said, trying to be reassuring. She just looked at me, not understanding. "Just wait here, I'll be right back." I faded out, back toward the Echo. We could now see each other clearly.

"Welp," he said, shrugging.

"What happened?" I asked.

"I'm beginning to lose connection to this body…Albert. This has been happening a lot. I was hoping Anna wouldn't be around to see it. I should be able to get back in it in a sec."

"How often does this happen?" His soul looked worn and battered. Much different than the first time I had seen him.

"At least three times a day. It's getting more frequent. I think it's because I need so much energy to keep the body alive. As you know, it was effectively dead when I took it, and it's only continuing to age. It's *way* past its expiration date…sorry, not trying to be insensitive."

I could see the reflection of Albert's body, waning in and out, and conflicting emotions rose in me again. I kept telling myself that I had forgiven John… mostly. I summoned up the calming meditative state that I spent years teaching my former clients.

He waited until the image of the body solidified and

stopped flickering, then reached toward it, as I had seen him do once before. I faded back to Anna before I could witness it again.

She came into focus, sniffling and terrified. John stood up, wobbling a bit. She jumped up and helped him to his feet.

"Are you okay?" she asked.

"I'm fine. Just lost the connection for a moment. No big deal." He tried on a reassuring smile. Anna looked skeptical.

After John took a moment to rest, we talked a bit more, changing a few details.

"I don't want to involve Becca," John said.

"Well, neither do I, but she actually has an excuse to visit him, being his cousin, so I think it'll work. Besides, all she needs to do is get him to the car," I said.

"Okay, fine," John said, scrubbing his hands over his eyes. "So when do we do this?"

"Tomorrow? I don't need more than a day to rest." I answered.

"I can't, I have a job interview," Anna said. We both looked at her, eyebrows raised.

"What?" she continued, putting her hands on her hips. "I have a life, you know."

"Okay, fine. What works for you then?"

"My mom works Saturday and my dad will be out of town on a business trip. Liz knows Mrs. Wilkes works Thursday through Sunday since she was stalking her," Anna said.

"I was trying to find you!" I scoffed.

We all agreed that Saturday was ideal and went our separate ways. I was exhausted and Anna had to go home to eat dinner with her parents. So much rode on the success of this plan. Anna and John had an obligation to save Brian's life. And end mine.

CHAPTER 55
ANNA

I wore black dress pants, a dark blue blouse, and fake enthusiasm on my face. I floated through the interview, distracted and nervous. I should have postponed.

The years of practiced bullshitting fined-tuned from hundreds of high school essays paid off, though. I answered their questions pretty easily, laughed in all the right places, nodded along when appropriate. It went surprisingly well. Even though I had never waited tables before, I felt I had a chance.

The interviewer told me to expect a call back and looked forward to talking to me again soon. Sounded like good news.

When I got home, I called Becca. I hadn't talked to her in a few days and I was dreading the conversation we needed to have.

"Hey, what's up?" She sounded excited to hear from me and it made me feel guilty.

"Well, we need your help," I said bluntly.

"Okay? Who's 'we', and with what?"

"John and Liz. To help Brian."

"Really? I thought you were insisting on not involving me in this stuff." I could hear her close her laptop. She was ready for a serious conversation.

"Yeah. I really didn't want to, but Brian isn't going to be willing to talk to me. I think he might talk to you, though, since you're related, even though you aren't really close." I heard a skeptical grunt on her end. "Your part in this is pretty basic. I just need you to find out where Brian's going to be tomorrow. If he won't be at home, convince him to be home, that you want to come over to visit and take him out to lunch or the mall or whatever. And make sure his mom will be at work."

"Okay, that shouldn't be too hard. Why though?"

"I just need you to get him out of the house at a very specific time. Do you think you could just wait in his driveway until I call you and tell you to go in?" The timing had to be spot-on or this would all fall apart.

"Okay. You're kind of scaring me, though. This sounds very…heist-y? Is that a word?"

"No, it's not. This isn't *Ocean's Eleven*. It should all go down fine." I was incredibly doubtful, though. Scared too. I tried not to let her hear it. "So? Think you can do it? Can you go over there today to make the plans to see him tomorrow?"

"Uh, yeah, I think so. I'll try. I actually won't have to lie to my mom, she's been encouraging me to go see him since my brother already did."

"Okay. Call me after?"

"Definitely." Becca's voice was shaky. She knew there was much more that was going to happen that she wouldn't be a part of. She was worried about me. She had been since the day of my car accident. She was such a huge part of my life. The sister I never had. I was terrified something would happen to her.

I *needed* her help. I had no choice. I just hoped neither of us would regret it.

~

I was watching TV with my dad and anxiously chain-drinking soda when my phone finally rang. I jumped up a little too suddenly and tried not to run out of the room.

"I'll be back down soon, Dad. Don't wait for me."

"Okay," he said, giving me an odd look. "Can we make that your last soda, please? You're looking a little too…caffeinated."

"Yep." He was right, but most of my restlessness was from nervous anticipation. I ran upstairs, answering the phone midstride.

"Hey, how'd it go?" I asked, shutting my door.

"Not good," Becca said. My heart sank.

"What do you mean 'not good'? What happened?" I paced the carpet.

"He's been committed, Anna."

My mouth dropped. "Committed? You mean…like

Jackie?"

"Yeah," she said, a small hiccup escaping her. "His mom was such a wreck. She said I can go visit him tomorrow if I want. He's allowed to hang out in the hospital courtyard for an hour a day as long as there is a staff member supervising nearby. His mom put me on an approved list."

Oh my god. It had gotten to this point already? He spiraled down so much faster than I expected. We had to move fast but the plan had just been tanked.

Or maybe not.

"Do you think she would put me on the list too?" I asked hopefully.

"After what you told me happened the last time you went to see him? I seriously doubt it."

"Dammit." She was right. I guess she was going to have to play a bigger role in this than I thought.

~

John and I waited. Liz said she would be at John's at nine in the morning so we could start the plan, although she wasn't yet aware that it wasn't going to happen. She was late. I was worried.

She finally faded in around 9:30. I let out a breath I didn't know I had been holding.

"Oh, thank God! I thought something had happened to you!" I said, clutching my chest in relief.

"Sorry about that. I had to dodge a few Stalkers on

the way over." She scanned our faces, picking up the vibe. "What's wrong? What's going on?"

"We have to postpone," John said with a sigh. "Brian's in the hospital."

Liz groaned. It echoed like she was at the bottom of a well. Still creeped me out. "So what are we supposed to do now?" she asked.

"Becca got visitation rights. I think it can be a huge advantage," I said.

"Unfortunately it means the timing needs to be even more spot-on than before," John continued. "We have to act fast, though. He's going downhill pretty quickly."

"So when? Can we still do it today?"

"No," I said. "Visiting hours are at eleven. You won't be able to walk to the hospital in time once we get all the details figured out."

"Is he at Saint Mary's?" Liz asked.

"Yeah," I answered.

"That's where my body is. I can get there in fifteen minutes," she said confidently.

"How?" John asked skeptically.

"I figured out how to skip—never mind. Just trust me. Can you get Becca to make it?"

"I think so," I said.

"Okay, get on it. I already left the water at Brian's house and I won't be able to take it with me that far, but there's a pond by the hospital. I'll get more there."

I was trembling but tried to keep it out of my voice. "So we're really doing this?"

"Looks like," said John with a shrug.

I called Becca, and she said she could do it. Brian's mom had told Becca where his room was, so luckily we had that information.

We all knew where we needed to be. John would be outside the doors of the mental health unit, waiting for Becca. I would be in the lobby, watching for when Becca and Brian came out. I had a clear view of the courtyard from there. I felt bad that I was playing such a small role in this, but there really wasn't much I could contribute. I was the one who caused this mess; I should be the one fixing it.

I hated that Liz was carrying out the most dangerous part. She didn't even need to be involved in this. She volunteered. I think she was okay with it because if something happened to her, if she died, it was what she wanted anyway. But I had a terrible feeling that if the Leech *did* kill her, her soul would be gone. Rather than dying and moving on to a better place, she would be gone.

I didn't bring this up. I didn't think it was my place, and I didn't want to scare her. But now I wish I had. She shouldn't have to risk that. It wasn't fair. We could have found another way. I pushed the thought out of my mind and tried to focus on the task at hand.

It was go time.

CHAPTER 55
ELIZABETH

I located the room Becca had told us Brian would be in and peered in the window. There he was, sitting on the bed, mumbling to himself. Or maybe to the Stalker sitting next to him.

I ducked with a gasp. I had expected this, but a fresh wave of dread washed over me anyway. The sounds and people dissolved into almost nothing as I faded back into the Echo. Thankfully I could get close enough to interact with my surroundings there. I picked up my gas canister full of water. It was heavy. I grunted with the effort.

Now was the tough part. I took a calming, meditative breath and focused on the gas canister, feeding some of my energy into it, connecting it to me so I could draw it into the Barrier. I began to fade back toward Brian.

It took so much effort and focus to take the water with me, but I felt it break through and then I was able to relax. For a moment anyway.

I waited, ducking down in front of the door so the

Stalker couldn't see me. I had a feeling Brian would be able to see me too. I kept glancing over to the entrance of the ward, which I could barely see from my position; it was mostly blocked by the reception desk. I heard her voice and my heart skipped. It was go time.

"Yeah, it should be there. Becca Marsters?"

"Yes, I see you here. And your name, sir?" the male nurse asked impatiently.

Becca answered for him, "Oh, this is my grandpa. They told me I needed an adult to accompany me because I'm a minor." She wasn't a minor, but they didn't bother checking her ID. The phone rang at that moment and the nurse picked it up, waving John and Becca through distractedly.

Wow, that was easier than expected. I knew that visitor protocol was pretty lax in this hospital but I had thought there would be *some* convincing necessary.

I watched the two of them walk towards me accompanied by an orderly. My heart raced; I was on the verge of backing out. Why the hell did I suggest this plan?

John glanced at me and gave a slight nod as the orderly opened Brian's door. John would be able to see the Stalker once he went in. It was going to be hard for him to pretend he didn't.

I heard muffled voices and tried to make out conversation. It was almost completely one-sided. I only heard a few mumbled words from Brian.

Waiting was killing me. I couldn't make my move

until Becca and Brian were about to leave. The door opened and I jumped up. Becca was delicately holding Brian's hand with twitchy fingers. I swore I could almost hear her heart pounding. I wished she could see me and I could at least give an encouraging nod. All she had to do was get him away from the room. It would be easy. In theory.

As soon as the two kids had exited the room, I poured a puddle of water in the doorway then jumped over it, crossing the threshold.

John was standing in front of the Stalker, trying to distract it. They couldn't interact, but the Stalker was confused. It was standing upright, making twitchy movements with its giant claws, its elongated head cocked to the side, unsure.

The Stalker was definitely on the same plane as me. It wasn't often that I saw something completely corporeal. Everything in the physical was always slightly translucent, the Echo always just a little blurry. This creature was solid. It was here. With me. And I was terrified.

With a yell, I splashed the Stalker with the water from my canister. It shrank away from me and gave a startled hiss, wobbling slightly. Becca knew once they were out of the ward, she had to get them outside as fast as possible, running if she could get Brian to follow. I hoped it would be enough.

John ran out of the room and I followed close behind. Startled staff members yelled at the old man to slow down, but John ignored them. I risked a glance over my shoulder and to my dismay, the Stalker was following.

When it stepped in the puddle, it almost lost its footing, but it kept coming.

"Shit shit shit!" I yelled, "Hurry up John!"

John burst through the exit doors, still running, almost head on into a stretcher. He was going back the way he had come.

"No, no, not that way! You're going closer to Brian! We've got to go the other way!"

He shuffled, not knowing which way to go. I didn't know either. The Stalker was gaining on us. I saw the remnants of the door in the Echo, overlapping the world that John occupied. It was in splinters. The Stalker had busted through it. It seemed to follow the same laws of physics I did. It could interact with the Echo but not with the physical. Which most likely meant it could interact with me.

"This way!" I shouted. I only knew of one other place that might be safe. The ICU. Where my body was. The whole unit was protected with water. Obviously the water didn't affect Brian's Stalker nearly as much as one that existed completely in the Echo, but it was worth a shot.

I turn a corner and risked a glance over my shoulder. It was going to catch up. I tipped the canister as I ran, leaving a stream behind me. It lunged forward right before its foot splashed into it.

I arched my back and screamed, feeling a claw rake through my flesh. I stumbled but caught my footing at the last second, trying to block out the white-hot pain that throbbed down my spine. I hadn't felt real pain in thirteen years, didn't even know I could. I had forgotten how to cope.

"Liz!" John yelled from in front of me.

"Just…" I sobbed out. "Go up the stairs. I… ICU. Go!"

I knew it couldn't hurt John. Or at least, I was pretty sure. But I needed him to be with me in case something went wrong. Which was clearly already happening.

The Stalker had fallen back a little. The water was working.

John was sprinting up the stairs as fast as Albert's body could take him. I was close behind, gritting my teeth and trying to block out the searing pain in my back. The Stalker was a flight of stairs behind us.

Fourth floor. One step closer. The creature hadn't caught up. I ran through the puddle of water in the doorway.

I was fading further and further away from the physical. The wound in my back and the sheer amount of time I had spent keeping myself so close were wearing me down fast. Unfortunately, no matter what level I was at in the Barrier, the Stalker was always just as solid as I was.

This is it. I thought. *This is probably the end.*

I wouldn't get the peaceful exit I hoped for. Instead,

I would be mauled to death by a monster.

This thought was cut short as I heard and actually *felt* a snap, physically making me stumble. John slowed for a second; he had obviously felt it too.

"Keep going!" I yelled, ignoring it and regaining my footing. "It's slowing down!"

I thought if I could just get it to run through water one more time, it would be too exhausted to continue. There was a puddle in front of the ICU doors.

The scratching of its claws on the cracked tile of the Echo were slowing and its low hiss was fading.

I slowed and looked behind me. The solid red orbs of its eyes met mine. It had no pupils but I could tell it was looking right at me. It dropped to one knee and opened its huge jaws one more time. I could almost feel its hiss like a physical force, the sound jarring my ears and shaking my bones.

I heard John's phone ring. He came to a stop in front of the ICU doors. He looked at the screen.

"It's Anna," he said, lungs heaving, bending over with his hands on her knees, glancing nervously at the fallen Stalker.

"Get inside first. That thing is still alive. There's water behind that door," I pointed to the entrance to the ICU, "and more in front of my room. That's got to be enough." I cringed in pain. Just talking hurt. I felt hot liquid run down the back of my leg and finally noticed the bloody footsteps I was leaving behind me. I hadn't even realized I *could* bleed.

John answered the phone as he asked me frantically how he was supposed to get in. The door was locked but had a keypad next to it.

"The code is 55362," I said. "I'll meet you in there."

"What? Where are they taking him?" I heard John say into the phone. His voice was getting warbled as I lost my hold to the physical.

"Follow them up if you can," he continued, typing the code as he was speaking. "If they don't, the code to the entrance is 55362."

I didn't know what was going on but ducked into the ICU before I heard the rest of it, waiting for the door to open for John. It finally swung open. Painfully slowly. The Stalker hadn't moved more than a couple feet. I watched as it slowly faded and sobbed in relief.

"Yeah, we're…" John started as he began to walk in, and then I heard a crack as his skull hit the floor.

"Damn it!" I pressed myself back against the physical with the last strength I had and went to examine his body. I saw some blood on the floor. I assumed it was trickling from his head. This wasn't good.

"Hello? Hello!" I heard Anna yell from the phone that had skid across the floor when John fell.

"Fu—" I heard her begin, then she hung up.

I faded back out toward the Echo to see if I could find John. He wasn't in the hallway. I heard a hiss and swung around. John was in the ICU.

So was the Stalker.

I thought it would be gone. I hadn't anticipated it

appearing back in the Echo. It didn't have a physical body. How was it there?

But it wasn't completely. It was sort of…wispy. Like a strong gust of wind might dissipate it.

The monster's back was toward me. It was facing John, who was backing away slowly. John looked unsure. He met my gaze and gave the smallest shake of his head.

I couldn't focus. I could see the faint overlap of the physical. Medical staff were lifting John's empty body onto a stretcher and wheeling him into the ICU. I guess this would be the best place to crack your head open. Silver lining?

I tried to block out the chaos and focus back on John's predicament. We locked eyes again.

"Run?" I mouthed.

He shrugged. It shocked me how nonchalant he seemed. But I guess he had had far more run-ins with Stalkers than I had.

I watched the faint image of Albert being wheeled down the hall, just to the left of the Stalker. It froze and raised its head as if sniffing. Then it stalked off in the same direction.

"What?" I said, confused. It just left? Did it really just lose interest in him that quickly? I pointed down the hallway where they had just wheeled the body, trying to communicate to John that if he wanted to get back into his body, he needed to go that way.

John's eyebrows were furrowed as he tried to understand what I was signaling. Then he nodded. He paused for a moment, thinking. Then his eyes turned to saucers and he gasped, running down the hallway after the Stalker.

CHAPTER 55
ANNA

I sat on the wide window ledge facing the courtyard, tapping my foot impatiently. What was taking so long?

Finally I saw Becca and Brian walk into the center of the courtyard. I hadn't been in view of whatever door they had come out of. I breathed a sigh of relief. She was holding his elbow and leading him to a bench in the center of the lawn. An orderly followed about ten yards behind.

Now I just had to wait for John's call. I glanced around the lobby. There were people coming and going in every direction. Doctors, nurses, family, patients. Just going about their lives with no idea about the world full of monsters that lay just out of sight. I envied them.

I turned my attention back to the bench outside, wishing I could hear their conversation. Brian was twitchy and nervous. The Leech wasn't with him. Thank God. The plan had worked. Relief washed over me.

I debated going outside and trying to talk to them but

I didn't want to risk Brian losing his shit, especially with Becca there. So I just had to sit there in the lobby like a useless bump on a log.

Becca was ringing her hands, trying to keep the awkward conversation going. If you could even call it that. Brian seemed to rarely actually notice her.

Suddenly Brian's body went slack, head slumped against his chest. He slid off the bench, crumpling to the ground. Becca leapt up and took a few steps backwards, hands over her mouth. The orderly ran over and kneeled next to Brian, pulling out a hand radio and speaking into it.

I ran outside and sprinted over to Becca.

"What happened?" I asked, catching my breath.

"I…I don't know," she said, finally taking her hands away from her mouth. I wrapped her in a hug, feeling awful for dragging her into this. Again.

The orderly was still kneeling next to Brian's body. He had two fingers pressed into Brian's neck, checking for pulse. Still talking into the radio.

"The ER is *full?* Yes, I *know* it's being renovated, but there should still be…okay, so where do you want me to bring him, then?"

I heard the static of his radio clicking on and someone on the other side saying that they were on their way with a stretcher to bring him to ICU.

Becca and I stepped back to watch the scene unfold. As four people loaded him onto a stretcher, I called John. I couldn't wait any longer. If he was busy, he just wouldn't answer.

It rang three times. "Damn it, pick up the…John!" I gripped the phone hard and heard it squeak. I tried to relax my grip but I was too nervous. "Brian passed out in the courtyard. They just loaded him onto a stretcher and are wheeling him inside."

"What? Where are they taking him?" John said, sounding out of breath and distracted.

"I think I heard them say the ICU."

"Follow them up if you can," he said quickly.

"What if they don't let us in?" I asked, switching the phone to the other ear.

"If they don't, the code to the entrance is 55362."

"How do you know that? Wait, is that where you are?" I asked. That didn't seem right.

"Yeah, we're…" John started, then cut off. I heard the crackling noise that signified him dropping the phone. Great.

"Hello? Hello!" I swore under my breath and pressed the end button.

"What's going on?" Becca asked nervously, chewing on her nails.

"I'm not sure," I said, frustrated. "Sounds like John, maybe Liz too, are also in the ICU. But I don't know. He dropped the phone mid-sentence."

"Well, let's go then," she said, starting to walk back. I grabbed her sleeve to stop her.

"What?" she asked, annoyed.

"You should just go home. I doubt there's anything

more you can do," I said.

She looked hurt. "You brought me here to help. I'm gonna help. He's my cousin. Come on, let's *go*."

I groaned. I wasn't going to win this one. "Fine," I conceded, and let her drag me toward the building.

We took the elevator to the fourth floor in silence, each ding getting us one floor closer. The doors opened and I released a breath. We turned the corner into absolute chaos.

Brian's stretcher was parked not too far ahead of us, waiting for a different group of medical staff to get out of the way. There was a lot of shouting. I tried to see around Brian and his entourage, but there were too many people. It looked like there was another stretcher blocking the entrance to the ICU.

Once the traffic jam cleared up, we followed Brian inside. No one stopped us; there was too much going on. There was a streak of red where the first stretcher had wheeled through some blood. I twisted my mouth and shuddered. The sight of blood had always made me queasy.

I saw no sign of Liz or John.

"Are we in the wrong place?" Becca asked impatiently, looking around.

"He specifically said ICU. He even gave me the code for the door." I sank down onto small bench against a far wall, set in a little alcove clearly meant for visitors. She sat next to me.

"Call him again?" she suggested.

"Yeah, I guess." I took out my phone and hit John's contact. I held the phone to my ear and waited. One ring. Two. Three. Voicemail. I shook my head and hung up.

"He knew we were coming here. Should we just wait?" she asked.

"I guess. I don't know what else to do. I'm freaking out a little," I confessed.

"Yeah. Me too."

CHAPTER 56
ELIZABETH

I rushed after John. He wouldn't be able to see what was going on in the physical world so I needed to help.

"Which way is my body!" he shouted at me.

"That way," I said, pointing down the hall.

He was running, getting closer to the Stalker.

"Slow down! You're getting too close!"

"Doesn't matter, I have to get in front of it!" he yelled.

"What? Why? Just wait, I don't think it's gonna survive here! We can just hide until it's dead." I stopped.

"What are you doing? Come on!" John said, hearing my footsteps cease. He motioned me along frantically.

"John, just…" I began, trying to calm him down. If we just kept away from it a while longer, we would be in the clear.

"No, no! You don't understand. I can't see my body unless I get close to it; you have to tell me where it went!" He darted his eyes around, turning in a circle and scanning the area. He ran over to me and grabbed me by the shoulders. I was close enough to the Echo for him to be able to interact with me.

"Liz, listen to me. I think the Leech is able to get into my body."

"Why?" I asked, my pulse quickening. I was starting to understand why he was acting the way he was.

"Anna came across a girl who had a Leech get into her body when she got stuck in the Void. It's…it's not exactly the same situation, but I think it's possible. Help me!" he pleaded, taking my hands in both of his. "I can't get stuck here again, I can't!"

I couldn't let Albert be violated by a Stalker. I knew it wasn't Albert anymore, but knowing his body would be used by one of those things made me sick.

"Okay, yeah. But I don't know what to do!" I thought for a moment and an obvious fact struck me. I protected bodies from Stalkers all the time. I was doing it with my own right now. Granted, his didn't still have a soul attached it so it might be a little different, but it probably worked the same way. Water should affect it way more when it existed completely in the Echo like it did now, rather than when it was in the Barrier with me. Although it had been able to get into the ICU after it faded from the Barrier, but it looked significantly weaker now that it had moments ago.

"What? Do you know—"

I cut John off. "Just give me a second."

But John's body was probably still moving. There

was no way I could surround it with water. Plus I didn't have any.

"Hold on, I'll be right back," I said, fading back towards the physical.

"But…" His voice faded until I could barely still hear him.

I ran in the direction that the Stalker had gone. I was safe from it here. Sure enough, it *was* following the body.

I whipped around when I heard Anna's voice. I saw Brian on a stretcher coming toward me. He was unconscious and Anna and Becca were following close behind.

"Anna!" I yelled.

"Oh, thank God!" she said, relieved. "What's going on?"

"Who are you talking to?" Becca asked. "Is it Liz? You look like a crazy person right now, talking to thin air."

"Yeah it's her. Just nod along like I'm talking to you."

"I need you to do something for me, and fast. But you're not gonna like it."

"Uh oh. What?"

"There was a stretcher that came through right before Brian." She nodded. Her reaction told me she didn't know it was John. "It's John—" I started, and she cut me off.

"Oh my God, is he okay?"

"It's complicated. Just listen. Do you see that room

up there? 202? That's my room."

She looked the way I was pointing, standing on her tiptoes and trying to see over the four people surrounding Brian. They wheeled his body around a corner and then we saw John. She gasped when she saw it was indeed him. He was parked against the far wall, two doors down from 202. A woman was checking his vitals. I saw her mouth something to someone and then jog away, leaving the stretcher unattended for a moment.

It was now or never.

"Push him into 202!" I said quickly.

She looked at me confused. "But…"

"Just do it! If you don't, he's never coming back! Go! Now!"

She looked at me wide-eyed, mouth parted, then finally darted in his direction.

"Wait!" Becca called after her. She took a couple steps forward, not knowing if she should follow.

I tried running after Anna but I was getting too weak. I was bleeding and in pain. I tried to stay close to the physical but at the same time, needed to make out what was happening on the other side. I couldn't. There were too many people running around. It was hard to make out the faint overlap of the Echo with so much movement on this side. I stumbled forward a few steps.

I saw Anna reach in front of the stretcher to turn the knob of the door to my room and push it inside. I stumbled along, slowly making it a few more feet in her direction, thinking we were in the clear, regardless of the fact that staff were banging on the door. Anna had managed to secure the door somehow, buying herself precious time. I was flooded with relief. We had done it.

Then I heard her scream.

CHAPTER 57
JOHN

"I can't get stuck here again, I can't!" I said to Liz, grabbing her hands in mine. I was terrified.

"Okay, yeah. But I don't know what to do!" Liz said. Her pause felt like an eternity. Every fraction of a second that went by I lost more and more hope that I would be able to return to my old life. Then a look of realization passed over her and she hit herself in the forehead. She had an idea, I could see it.

"What?" She didn't answer. "What? Do you know—"

She cut me off. "Just give me a second." She squeezed her eyes shut and held up a finger. I stared at her, growing more and more impatient.

"Hold on, I'll be right back," she said, and faded.

"Wait!" I yelled after her. I squinted to try to see her outline and was able to follow for short distance before I lost sight of her. I had lost track of the Leech too, but could still feel it nearby. Damn it.

I crept in the direction she had gone, staying close to the wall. I crouched down behind the nurses' desk and waited a couple minutes, trying to sense the connection to my body and not scream in frustration. Every moment that went by was a moment closer to losing my entire life.

Yes! There, I could feel it. The pull toward my body. I knew if I got close enough, I would be able to see it. I followed the direction of the sensation and turned a corner. I almost walked right into the back of the Leech, catching myself a moment before. It was standing at the entrance of a patient room, looking inside, not attempting to step over the puddle of water on the floor.

The creature lifted its arm. I was so close that I could see its muscles contracting, its claws twitching.

And my body. Directly in front of it, on the other side of the threshold. It extended one claw delicately…

"*No*!" I screamed, and the reflection of my body disappeared.

The creature was gone.

CHAPTER 58
ANNA

She wanted me to basically go steal an unconscious patient. Yes, it was John, but wouldn't they stop me? There was no one around him now but…

"Just do it! If you don't, he's never coming back! Go! Now!"

I heard the truth in her words and I was terrified. I froze for a moment but then took off. I couldn't lose him.

"Wait!" I heard Becca call after me. I didn't.

I reached him and grabbed the handle, trying to push it towards the room. It was heavy but I managed. I looked down at his face as I wheeled it, my arms straining. He was unconscious, his chest barely moving up and down. It kind of looked like when he had passed out in his kitchen except his head was bleeding and his skin was pale.

"Hey! What are you doing? Stop!" I heard footsteps running toward me from the opposite hallway where Liz and Becca were. I ignored them and quickened my pace.

I managed to get the door to 202 open, get John inside and slam the door before anyone reached me. I parked the stretcher directly in front of the door and searched frantically for something to lock the wheels. There was no lock on the actual door so I had to block it. I found a foot pedal with a picture of a lock on it and stepped down. It worked. Thank God.

Steady beeping echoed around me, and I gasped when I saw Liz's body was in the room with us. I barely recognized her. Tubes and wires came out of everywhere. She was pale and thin. I could tell it wasn't Liz. Now I understood why John and Liz considered themselves completely different from their physical body. That wasn't a person. It was an empty shell. Barely more than a corpse. I shuddered.

I didn't know the purpose of what I had just done, but I had succeeded. I knew it was important. I leaned against the wall and closed my eyes, trying to catch my breath, and ignored the banging and yelling on the other side of the door.

I heard the sheets rustle. I snapped my eyes open and stood up straight.

"John!" I said as he began to sit up. "Thank God you're—" I froze midstep. He looked at me and an inhuman growl fell from his lips. That wasn't John.

He jumped off the stretcher and began stalking towards me, taking odd jerky steps. My heart was racing and I looked around for an exit. There wasn't one. There was a bathroom door.

He—*it*—lunged at me. I screamed and dodged out of the way just in time, making it to the bathroom. I slammed the door behind me and locked it. I walked backward and let out a sob. My heels hit the toilet and I almost fell, stumbling and grabbing onto the sink.

I looked around, panting and desperate. There was nowhere to go. I had barricaded the door to the hallway, and who knew how long it would take before anyone was able to get in?

I heard growling and banging from outside the bathroom door. The beeping of the machines grew irregular and alarms blared. I sank to the tile, hands clasped over my mouth, tears streaming down my face.

The steady trill of a flat-line hit my ears.

I closed my eyes and sobbed.

CHAPTER 59
ELIZABETH

Her scream willed me to move faster, but it was difficult. I feared the worst had happened. I saw medical personnel bust open the door to my room. As I got closer, I heard yelling and…growling.

Something else was wrong too, though. It took me a moment to put my finger on it. I didn't hear the familiar harmony of the machines keeping me alive. I heard alarms and chaos.

I let out a sharp sob when I finally reached the entrance to my room. Chaos was putting it lightly. Four men attempted to restrain the body that once belonged to Albert. It was growling and spitting at them, an inhuman strength keeping them at bay.

But my body. The huge bypass machine had been knocked over, tubes and wires disconnected. I watched in shock as the heart monitor beeped sporadically, and then flat-lined.

I almost fell over when I felt a weight immediately

lift from my chest. Despite the commotion in front of me, it brought an immediate sense of peace. I hadn't felt this since January fourteenth, thirteen years ago, in the short span of time between when I died, and when I had been put on life support, my body kept alive by the drugs and plastic tubing of Western medicine.

I dropped to my knees and cried tears of joy despite the fact that I knew our plan had gone horribly awry. The Stalker wasn't dead—in fact we had inadvertently given it a vessel to enter the physical world. John had failed to get back into Albert's body and was therefore stuck in the Echo. Brian might be dead or worse. Anna was somewhere in the confusion in front of me, she could be dead for all I knew. I should be terrified and trying to figure out how to put the pieces back together. But I couldn't. Relief overwhelmed every other emotion.

I was free.

CHAPTER 60
JOHN

I sank to my knees. Disbelief and denial paralyzed me. No.

No.

This couldn't be happening. Silent tears rolled down my cheeks. I couldn't be stuck here again. Alone.

I couldn't do it again. I refused. I wasn't going to murder Leeches or find a new home to fortify or pick up a crossbow ever again. I would rather let myself waste away. I couldn't bear the thought of even being trapped here for one more day, let alone forever.

I refused to lose my humanity again, refused to succumb to the despair of loneliness. *I refuse.*

Everything had gone to hell. The situation was exponentially worse. Not one thing had gone as planned.

I sat on the floor, hugging my knees and crying, the hopelessness dragging out every passing moment. I barely felt the gentle touch on my shoulder.

I looked up, my vision blurry with tears, and blinked

them away. It was Liz. The look on her face was the polar opposite of what I was feeling. A delicate, effortless smile shined down on me, the epitome of tranquility. There was pure happiness radiating from her eyes, almost tangible, a warmth sending shivers across my skin.

The emotion seeped into me, slowing the tears and calming my heart just enough to keep the despair from drowning me.

She crouched down so we were face to face, and gave me a hug. I closed my eyes and breathed it in, trying to imprint it in my soul, knowing I wouldn't feel human contact beyond this moment ever again.

"I forgive you John, and it's going to be okay," she said, pulling away and stroking my cheek. I leaned in to her touch.

"How? How is it going to be okay?"

"There's a way back for you. I can feel it. I can always feel it," she said, standing and turning away from me.

I stood up and grabbed for her arm, but my fingers passed through it. She was fading away, different from how she usually did. She was glowing with an internal light. Each second her image faded more, the light overtaking it.

"What do you mean? Liz!" I called after her as she walked away. She turned to face me once more and I was touched with another wave of warmth, bringing with it a peace that conflicted so strongly with every other emotion running through me.

"I have to go now, John. You can do it. Survive…"

Then she was gone. And with her she took my last connection to humanity.

I got to my feet, breath ragged and shaking, and walked in a trance, turning in to a stairwell. Every step downward felt like I was going deeper and deeper.

Into the Void.

I stopped and looked back upward, seeing the spiral of the staircase leading back to the blue number four, the doorway that would take me back to the ICU.

"Survive…" I whispered.

CHAPTER 61
ANNA

The growling and hissing was cut short after I heard the electric buzz of a taser. I flinched and backed against the wall. The handle of the bathroom door rattled, someone trying to open it. I heard a woman's voice asking me to open the door, telling me I was safe now.

I emerged in time to see John's body on the ground, a woman with her fingers on his neck, checking his pulse. She shook her head and yelled, "Crash cart!"

A black form was drifting up from John's body. I just watched, numb. It threw its head back and howled, the sound slowly dissipating to nothing, along with its image.

I was pushed aside as a machine was wheeled into the room. A woman in pale green scrubs kneeled down to rip open John's shirt, placing paddles on his bare chest.

"Clear!" she yelled, and his body jerked. Nothing happened.

"Clear!" she yelled again.

I closed my eyes, blocking out the nightmare in front of me. The sounds faded as I went into shock. I felt someone grab me by the arm and lead me out of the room.

The person left me in the hallway and went back in, leaving me without a word. I stood there, staring at nothing, uncomprehending.

"Anna!"

I heard my name being called by a familiar voice.

"Anna!" There were hands on my shoulders, shaking me. It was Becca.

"It's Brian! Come on!" She dragged me down the hall. I ran after her on autopilot. "Code blue ICU" was echoing from the loud speaker. People were everywhere, many of them looking confused. I heard some saying "202" and some saying "214".

I watched the room numbers go by. 211, 212, 213. We stopped, stuck behind people running in and out of 214. My trance was fading, I was trying to focus. What was going on?

It took a long while for people to clear out so we could get close enough to see into the room. To see Brian.

A nurse was standing next to him, hanging an IV bag on a pole. There was a tube down his throat, his chest rising and falling mechanically. There were pads on his chest, hooked up to wires that led up to a machine, steadily beeping away. His heartbeat. His heart was beating. For now.

"You girls need to leave," a female voice said. I looked up. I thought it might be the same person who led me out of Liz's room. Away from John.

John.

Becca put her arm over my shoulders and led me down to the lobby to sit on the wide window sill overlooking the courtyard. My spirit was broken.

She held me as I cried.

EPILOGUE
3 MONTHS LATER

John's funeral had been small. He hadn't had many friends or family. Albert had had a daughter, but John hadn't spoken to her in many, many years. The relationship had been deteriorating even before he had woken up from a coma an entirely different person. My parents and Becca came to the funeral with me to be supportive but I still hadn't made it through the whole ceremony.

I never saw or heard from Liz again, but I hoped she had gotten her wish and been able to move on. I was pretty sure she had. That was the only silver lining to the ordeal.

I had gotten the job at the restaurant and they let me start three weeks later than I said I was able to, trying to be understanding that I had had a loss in my family. I was reclusive for quite a while. I couldn't cope, didn't know how.

I walked into the house and hung my purse next to

the front door, anxious to change out of the uniform that reeked of fried food. I kicked off my shoes and went to the fridge, grabbed a soda, and popped the tab. I sipped the fizz off the top and sat down on the couch.

"Sweetie, you home?" I heard my mom call.

"Yep," I responded, taking another sip. She came down the stairs holding a basket of dirty laundry and set it on the coffee table, coming to sit next to me on the couch.

"Brian Wilkes's mom called me today. I am not sure how she got my number but they're back in town."

"Huh?" I said, taking another sip. I hadn't thought about him in a while. I tried not to. Too many emotions accompanied the thought of him.

Brian had woken up less than an hour after we left the hospital but Becca and I hadn't heard anything other than that. His parents had taken him "on vacation" for the summer shortly after he was released, but I was pretty sure they left to avoid the rumors that would start shortly after. Three months is an awfully long vacation. I didn't think anyone believed it.

"He wants to know if you would come over to see him. I guess he got a new phone and doesn't have your number."

"What? Why?" I was the cause of everything that had happened to him. I didn't know if he knew that, but he undoubtedly sensed I was involved in some way.

"She said he wants to say thank you."

"Thank you? For what?" I certainly hadn't done

anything that deserved thanks. I put my soda down next to the laundry basket and faced my mom for the first time since she sat down. She didn't know.

"She said you can stop over anytime this weekend. They're getting settled back into the house so they'll be there."

I took a deep breath. "I guess," I said hesitantly. I didn't want to see Brian. Everything that happened during those few months revolved around him. I hated thinking about it. It was too traumatic. And I didn't want to think about John.

My eyes filled with tears, but I blinked them away before they could fall. I didn't want my mom to see. She assured me I didn't have to go if it was too hard on me, but I decided I would. After all I put Brian through, I could at least see him if that was what he wanted.

~

I knocked on the front door, tapping my foot nervously. The door opened just as I was about to leave.

I was face to face with Brian. He looked a *lot* better than the last time I had seen him. His eyes lit up when he saw me, and his mouth spread in a huge smile. I tried not to let my confusion show.

"Come on in!" he said cheerfully, and motioned me inside.

"Um, okay," I said, following him hesitantly. He led me into the kitchen and I stood there awkwardly.

"You can sit," he said pointing to the kitchen table. I sat.

"Uh, thanks. So your mom said you wanted me to come over…"

"Yeah! We have a *lot* to catch up on," he said smiling.

"We do?"

"Of course. We haven't seen each other in months," he said, grabbing two glasses out of the cabinet. He turned to face me and grinned. His smile was so familiar, even though we had rarely hung out, even at school. Just the few times I had been to one of Becca's family functions.

He bent down and grabbed a pitcher out of the fridge. He turned around and raised it questioningly.

"Lemonade? Oh, no thanks," I said, pulling my hair into a ponytail.

"Are you sure? It's just lemonade this time. I promise." I paused, letting my hair fall. I met his gaze, the green eyes above that familiar lopsided grin staring back at me.

I stood up abruptly, knocking the chair over, mouth parted. His smile wavered.

We stared at each other until I could no longer meet his gaze.

I left without a word.

Made in the USA
Columbia, SC
18 September 2019